D0788241

DEATH WILL EXTEND YOUR VACATION

Death Will Extend Your Vacation

Elizabeth Zelvin

FIVE STAR
A part of Gale, Cengage Learning

Detroit • New York • San Francisco • New Haven, Conn • Waterville, Maine • London

Set in 11 pt. Plantin.

LIBRARY OF CONGRESS CATALOGING-IN-PUBLICATION DATA

Zelvin, Elizabeth.
Death will extend your vacation / Elizabeth Zelvin. — 1st ed.
p. cm.
ISBN 978-1-4328-2577-5 (hardcover) — ISBN 1-4328-2577-1
(hardcover) 1. Alcoholics—Fiction. 2. Murder—Investigation—
Fiction. I. Title.
PS3576.E48D38 2012
813′.54—dc23 2011047034

Published in 2012 in conjunction with Tekno Books and Ed Gorman.

Printed in Mexico
1 2 3 4 5 6 7 16 15 14 13 12

To Brian, always

ACKNOWLEDGMENTS

First, my deepest gratitude to all the readers who told me that they loved Bruce, Barbara, and Jimmy and wanted to hear more about them. As always, I am grateful for the unfailing support of my friends and colleagues in Mystery Writers of America and Sisters in Crime. Without them, I doubt I could have persevered through the long period it took to get this book into readers' hands. Heartfelt thanks to Avery Aames, Persia Walker, and Sharon Wildwind for keen critique and many constructive suggestions. Their help was crucial in turning a flawed first draft into a book I can be proud of. Thanks, too, to Kathleen A. Ryan, Suffolk County Police Department (retired), who answered questions about police procedure. Kathy exemplifies the humanity and integrity of real-life law enforcement.

Special thanks, with affection and regret that the book took so long, to the late Bob Liptrot for a glorious afternoon on Gardiner's Bay. He taught me how to cast for blues, cleaned the ones I caught, demonstrated the nautical use of GPS and cell phone, and told fascinating stories of the area whenever the fish weren't biting. He was a kind and patient teacher and a wonderful friend and neighbor.

Please note that Dedhampton (or Deadhampton) is an imaginary Hampton. It lies in a never-never land on the East End of Long Island and is not a part of any existing town, county, state, or federal jurisdiction.

Chapter One

"I'll fry!" My best friend, Jimmy, cast an apprehensive glance at the cloudless sky.

"You couldn't fry an egg on the beach at this hour." His girlfriend, Barbara, went on slathering sun block across his broad, freckled back.

"It's the crack of dawn," Jimmy said. "I want to be asleep. I want to be back in Manhattan in my air-conditioned apartment."

"You know, most people consider a summer share in the Hamptons a treat," Barbara said, "not an ordeal. If we don't get a move on, half the day will be gone." She wiped goo off her hands along the sides of his arms and stepped back to contemplate her work.

"Very artistic," I said.

Mistake. She turned on me.

"Bruce, put the rest of that coffee in the thermos, don't tank up on it."

"You wanted me awake, didn't you?" I chugged the last half inch of java. The cup had a ceramic frog in the bottom. Group house decorating. "Okay, okay, I'll make more. One picnic breakfast on the beach, coming up."

"Want me to do your back too?" Barbara waggled the big tube of sun block.

"Save it for Jimmy." I skipped away from her. Jimmy can turn as red as a lobster in a pot of boiling water in about the same time as it takes the lobster.

Twenty minutes later, Barbara had us loaded up like Sherpas. You'd think we were about to scale K2. Bounding out onto the deck like a mountain goat, she raised both arms to the sun. She took a deep lungful of air, then exhaled with a loud "Ahhhhh!" in case we missed the point. The house smelled of mildew to me. Outside, I admit the mix of salt and flowers beat the stink of the city back home. We trailed her down the winding path, crunching gravel and broken shells underfoot.

Barbara reached the car and started it up so she could roll all the windows down. She popped the trunk as we arrived. Jimmy and I began to divest. Beach chairs, umbrella, tatty old bedspread for a blanket. Towels. Bulging insulated food carrier the size of a duffel bag.

"Sand castle molds?" Jimmy held up a net bag filled with crenellated towers and sections of defensive wall in neon plastic.

"They were in the house," Barbara said. "I thought you'd like them, Jimmy. You love medieval military stuff."

"Did you also think we'd like these?" I held up a couple of industrial-strength buckets and hummed a bar or two of *The Sorcerer's Apprentice.* "Which one of us is Mickey Mouse?"

"Throw them in the trunk," Barbara ordered. "I'll drive. I got directions from Clea."

I slid into the rear of the Toyota. I tried to avoid the death seat when Barbara drove. It wasn't her driving so much as the way she used both hands in conversation.

"I haven't sorted all our housemates out yet." We'd only arrived in Dedhampton the day before. "Which one is Clea?"

"Have a bagel," Barbara said. "Very tall and thin. Streaky blonde, not quite kinky long hair and gorgeous skin the color of a ginger snap. I figure either interesting ethnic genes or a world class tan and a great hairdresser."

"Oh, yeah," I said, "the Botticelli Venus." The one I had

watched more closely the night before at dinner than I was ready to admit to Barbara or Jimmy.

"Thank her for the bagels," Barbara mumbled through a full mouth. "She runs. She said she'd pick them up early, drop them off, and head for the beach."

I looked out the window. We emerged into farmland from the scrub oak and pine that surrounded the group house. Mist rose gently in the nippy air from fields of corn and potatoes. A couple of teenagers on horses ambled along the grassy side of the road. In the yards of weathered gray cedar houses, a few straw-hatted gardeners crouched among the flowers, weeding in the cool of the day. Now and then I caught a sparkling glimpse of the bay. As we neared the ocean, the landscape changed to wetlands, then to dunes.

"Jimmy, look for a sandy road to the right," Barbara said. "That'll be Dedhampton Beach. There's no sign. I heard somebody changed it to Deadhampton, D-E-A-D, and the sign got stolen in less than a week."

The dunes didn't leave much of a road. Jimmy gave a yelp as we passed it. Barbara made a wide U-turn and aimed the car between stands of tall grasses and reeds so close their fuzzy heads thrust through the window. A fat tuft tickled my nose. I sneezed.

"Gesundheit," Barbara said. "And here we are." She swung the wheel with a flourish. The car stopped with its nose in a dune.

"Where's the ocean?" I said.

"No boardwalk?" Jimmy said.

"We're in the country." Barbara flung up the lid of the trunk and loaded us up again.

"Why do Irish mothers pray for sons, Mr. Jones?" Jimmy asked.

"Because we make such good pack animals, Mr. Bones."

"Here, give me that." Barbara snatched up the only thing I really wanted, the thermos of coffee, from the top of Jimmy's pile. "Come on!" She danced away, slipping a little on the hill of sand.

"No cars in the parking lot," Jimmy observed as we trudged after her. "We're the only fools not still asleep at this hour."

"What about the ginger snap?" I asked.

"Surely she wouldn't come all this way on foot," he said. Jimmy emerges from behind his computer only after prolonged prodding. He says walking is for Luddites.

"I told you," Barbara said, "she's a runner. It's only about four miles." She crested the dune and stood backlit with the edges of her frizzy dark hair glowing like a halo. "Oh, wow, look—it's so beautiful!"

We reached the top right behind her, Jimmy breathing heavily and me pretending not to. I looked where she was looking.

Okay, it was beautiful. The deserted beach stretched right and left, with the jade Atlantic beyond it. The sun, still low over the water, turned the sand to a warm pink. A ruffle of dark seaweed and scattered shells marked the high tide line. Below it, the beach looked perfect for running if you liked strenuous. I wouldn't mind a stroll on it myself. The flat, wet surface picked up the robin's egg blue of the sky. The surf was no big deal, baby swells that pushed a swathe of creamy bubbles up onto the beach and then ran out again with a whisper.

Barbara clutched at Jimmy's arm for balance as she shook her sandals off her feet. She wiggled her toes in the sand.

"Ooooh, that feels good. Let's go." She frisked around us like a puppy as we made our way toward the water. "Here, this is good—a front row view of the ocean, but the sand is still soft. No, don't park the stuff near the seaweed—that's where the flies will be."

Jimmy threw his head up like a shying horse. She hadn't

mentioned flies when she talked us into this beach house share.

Jimmy and I set up the chairs, dug in the pole of the umbrella, and flapped the blanket. Barbara went and paddled in the water. Little screams announced the temperature: too cold for me. She splashed around till we'd done all the work. Then she trotted back to us.

"It's not cold once you get used to it. Come and wade. It's great!"

"You're out of your mind," Jimmy said. "I'm not so much as rolling up my pants."

"Then come for a walk. It's really hard packed, practically like a sidewalk."

"Have a heart, pumpkin," Jimmy said. "I need to catch my breath."

"Let's have breakfast first," I said.

I located the coffee and the Styrofoam cups, poured out two shots, and handed one to Jimmy.

"Give me another bagel," Barbara said. "I can't sit still. I'm going to take a little jog. See way down the beach? There." She pointed to the left. "About halfway to where it gets misty, above the waterline. It looks like a driftwood log. It won't take long to run up to it and back."

Holding the bagel in her teeth, she stripped off her shorts and T-shirt. She wore a bathing suit underneath, a serviceable black tank. Jimmy and I hadn't even taken off our sweatshirts, much less our long pants.

"Where do you plan to put the bagel?" I inquired. "You're not going to run the whole way with it in your mouth, are you?"

Barbara shook her head. She plucked the bagel from her mouth and tucked it into her cleavage. "Back in twenty minutes or so."

"Have fun."

We drank our coffee and watched her skim along the hard

sand with an occasional leap like an exuberant gazelle.

We had just about finished our coffee when we heard Barbara yell. She came racing toward us like a steam engine. We heard the urgency in her cries before we could make out words. We ran down the beach to meet her.

"It wasn't a log," she panted. She bent over from the waist, trembling on stiff legs and trying to catch her breath. "It's Clea, and she's dead."

Chapter Two

"She had seaweed in her hair," Barbara said. Her teeth clattered like castanets.

"Hang on, peanut." Jimmy enveloped her in his arms. "You're in shock."

Barbara burrowed into his chest.

"I think you're right. Look." She stuck an arm out of the meld. We could see her fingers tremble. "You know how a dead fish looks, with the gray belly and the glassy eyes? I'll never think of mermaids as romantic again."

"Shh, it's all right. It's going to be all right," Jimmy crooned as he rocked her. The only other sounds were the waves breaking on the beach. I turned away.

"Her mouth was filled with sand," Barbara said. "I threw up."

"Jim, we'd better go," I said. "The tide is coming in."

Barbara shook herself out of Jimmy's embrace and stepped back.

"I'm okay." She shook out her shoulders, sniffed, and dragged her arm across her nostrils. "Let's go."

We jogged back along the beach, Barbara in the lead. The shallow waves crept up the beach, spent their foam, and retreated, washing away Barbara's footprints as she ran. As we approached the crumpled body, I scanned the immediate area for any clue to what had happened. Unidentified footprints around the high tide line. A weapon. A suicide note. I also checked underfoot for vomit, but Barbara had made it to the water to upchuck.

Clea didn't look so much like the Botticelli Venus anymore. Her green eyes were open, opaque as jade. Her jaw hung slack. It didn't stir when I looked away and back again. I saw what Barbara meant about the mermaid. The detritus in Clea's tangled hair and the careless position of her tumbled body made her look like garbage.

"Maybe we should drag her higher up the beach," Barbara suggested. "When the tide turns, it could pull her out to sea."

"Better not touch her," Jimmy said. "The cops won't be pleased with us if we mess with a crime scene."

"You don't think she drowned?" It hadn't been my first thought either, but I couldn't say why. I couldn't see any marks of violence on her body beyond what washing up on shore might have done. Scratches. Bits of shell sticking to her skin.

"She was an athlete," Jimmy said. "I'd guess she was a strong swimmer, or she wouldn't have gone in alone."

"She talked about that four-mile run like it was nothing," Barbara said.

"Cramp?" I suggested.

"I can't believe she wouldn't have managed to swim to shore," Barbara said, "even if the cramp felt agonizing. People do amazing things when they're desperate."

"That's why I'm wondering if someone stopped her," Jimmy said. "Pushed her in and under. Or wouldn't let her come ashore."

"To me she looks drowned," I said. "No blood, no obvious wound, no dark marks on her neck. I've been looking around for any sign of a weapon. A rock, a metal object, a piece of driftwood. I don't see a thing."

"I'd like to see the back of her head," Jimmy said.

"Don't touch her!" Barbara said. "We need to call the cops. I still can't believe it. An hour or two ago she was buying bagels, and now she's gone."

Jimmy took out his cell phone.

"No signal."

I scanned the beach. It was still early. Not a soul within earshot, though a few specks far off in either direction had to be people and dogs.

"Look, there's her stuff." I ran up to the little pile of belongings. Running shoes with athletic socks stuffed into them, a plain gray sweatshirt, and a towel lay heaped in the soft sand.

Jimmy followed me, frowning at his cell phone and hitting redial every few steps.

"Better not touch that either," Jimmy said. "Finally! It's ringing. It's staticky. I need to get higher up the beach. Get Barbara to come away from there, will you? If I try, she'll say I'm overprotecting her."

"Sure, man." I marched back toward Barbara and the dead girl. "Hey, c'mon, Barb, let's get a little distance."

Barbara clutched at my arm with an icy hand.

"I don't want to look at her anymore," she said.

"Me neither," I confessed. I cupped her elbow very lightly and took a few steps up the beach. As I'd hoped, she moved with me. "It's hard to be objective when you keep remembering her laughing."

"And grabbing the last brownie," Barbara said.

At dinner last night, Clea's eyes had twinkled as she'd given her fingers a long, sensuous lick, curling her tongue around the last bits of gooey brownie. Now death had drained that sparkle out of her.

"Did you notice how she flirted with all the guys?" Barbara asked.

"Yeah, I guess I'd call it flirting. Challenging. An edge to everything she said."

"And now she's meat and, oh, I don't know—compost. It's horrible."

"I know," I said. "Hey, you're still shivering. Want my shirt?"

Jimmy came toward us, tucking the cell phone into his pants pocket.

"I told them there's been an accident. They told me to meet them back in the parking lot," Jimmy said. "And they said at least one of us should stay with her."

"You two go," I said. "I don't mind."

"Thanks." He put his arm around Barbara.

"I don't need protecting!" Barbara snapped. "Oh, hell. Sorry. I could use my sweatshirt, anyway."

I plowed through the soft sand back toward Clea as they trudged off. As the tide advanced, it ate away at the hard walking surface along the edge of the water. Would it reach Clea or the scalloped rim of seaweed and broken shells that marked last night's high tide before Jimmy and Barbara came back with the cops? I hoped they'd get here fast.

I looked out toward where Spain would be if you swam three thousand miles. Or would it? Didn't the Long Island ocean beach face south? A flock of black birds passed from left to right, skimming low over the water. A few gulls bobbed closer to shore. I heard a dog bark in the distance. I hoped it wouldn't come any closer and get curious about the body. I watched the breakers break. They never got tired of it. First a crash as the green water curled up and over into surf. Then shallow fingers grasped at the shore. The foam hissed on its way in and giggled as the water ran out, tumbling little shells and pebbles on the way.

Accident? Maybe. But if Clea had got in trouble out beyond the breakers all by herself, wouldn't she have drifted more? We'd found her stuff pretty close to where she'd washed up. I pictured a hand pressing hard on the top of her head, pushing her under and not letting up. I didn't think those Botticelli curls would have held fingerprints.

What about the tide? The body had ended up pretty close to the high tide line. The tide was coming in. If it had been going out, she might not have been found at all. Or not in such good condition. I squinted at the sparkling water and lazy rollers. They looked inviting, but the ocean was still icy, even with the sun high in the sky. Had Clea gone in for a swim? She might have been *macha* enough. In or out of the water, by chance or design, she could have met someone who wanted her dead.

I wished I had a cigarette. Better, the whole pack. I'd left them in Barbara's backpack down the beach. Maybe they'd think to bring them. And coffee. I needed an antidote to sudden death. Booze had always topped my list. Did I want it now? Probably. Too bad, buddy, I told myself. As they said in AA, I didn't need that one more problem. I had a feeling life was about to get complicated. Welcome to Deadhampton.

I heard a shout and looked up to see Jimmy and Barbara plodding toward me. With them were a couple of guys in uniforms. I waved, then shivered as a gust of wind swept across the beach, stirring the tangle of curls and seaweed in Clea's hair. I closed my eyes against the sting of sand. She didn't.

Chapter Three

"Full name, sir," the younger of the two cops said, "and spell it, please."

He looked no more than thirty, with bright blue eyes and very rosy cheeks. His thumbs flew over the touch screen of his mobile device. When I thought how hard I'd struggled to learn touch typing so I could temp, I felt old.

"Bruce Kohler," I said. "K-O-H-L-E-R."

"Local address."

"We *told* you—" Barbara burst out. She seemed to have recovered her moxie.

"It's okay, Barbara," Jimmy and I said simultaneously.

"We have our procedures, ma'am. Mike, why don't you escort Ms. Rose and Mr. Cullen over there." He jerked his head at the stump of a log half buried in sand, about fifty feet away.

Jimmy shushed Barbara's protest at being called "ma'am." He and the other cop, whose steel blue five-o'clock shadow made him look older, herded her toward the log.

My cop's cell phone rang.

"Yes, sir. Arrived on scene. Yes, sir. No, sir. We're about to secure the scene. Uh, extended."

He tucked the cell phone between his shoulder and his ear and gestured toward Mike. If I read the two-handed signals correctly, he was telling him to go get the car and start circling the wagons. I wondered how they planned to secure a beach.

"Ten-sixty-one," the officer said. I could hear an exasperated quacking on the other end of the line. "Sorry, sir. Witnesses present—I'm just getting their information. Ten-four—uh, affirmative. Yes. No. Understood, sir." He thumbed the phone to end the call and slid it back onto his belt. "Bring it up behind the dunes, Mike," he called.

He cast a stern glance at Jimmy and Barbara, who sat obediently on their log.

"Now, Mr. Kohler."

I arranged my face to look sincere and cooperative. I had to remind myself that I was just a witness. To tell the truth, cops made me nervous. I'd spent too much of my life out of control or unable to remember. Feeling threatened was one of those things I'd always done drunk and now had to learn to do sober. God grant me the serenity.

He didn't ask me anything I didn't know. I kept my answers as straight as I could. To my relief, he stayed at the shallow end. He had just walked me over to the log to sit with the rest of the class when Mike came back, sliding over the dunes with his arms full. I guess they didn't want to add police car tire tracks to a scene that even I could see would be hard to read. Mike started sticking stakes in the ground and stringing yellow crime scene tape between them.

"Tide's coming in," he said as he rounded the seaward end of Clea's body.

"Do the best you can. Detectives are on their way, and we've got at least an hour."

"Okay, Frank." Mike shoved a stake in the spongy surface that would be completely covered when the tide came all the way in. Little bubbles formed around the area and spread outward, as if tiny sea animals were running for their lives.

"How far do I take it?"

"Back to where these folks came on the scene," Frank said. "You can secure their car separately."

"Our car?" I blurted. "Sorry, but—how do we get back to our house? It's at least four miles."

"The whole area has to be secured," Frank said. "It will be a while before you can leave."

"How long is a while?" Barbara demanded. "Who are we waiting for?"

"Detectives."

"Will there be an autopsy?" Jimmy asked.

The word added more grim images to my inner gallery of portraits of Clea.

"It's Sergeant Wiznewski's call," the cop said.

"How long does that take?" Barbara asked.

The cop shrugged.

"It's a holiday weekend."

"So after the detectives interview us," Barbara said, "will you let us go home, I mean to the house?"

"Sorry, miss, no can do."

Barbara scowled. She didn't like being called "miss" either.

"Since you've all informed us that the deceased is a resident of your house, that will be secured as well. You won't be able to enter until we're through there too."

"The whole house? But—but we hardly know her. We just arrived yesterday. We hardly know any of them. It's a group house."

"Group houses are illegal throughout the Town. But that's between the Town and your landlord."

That was news. I'd never paid any attention to the Hamptons, but Jimmy and Barbara knew dozens of people who'd had shares. I guess renting to a group was one of those crimes that homeowners committed without a second thought, like what Arlo Guthrie called "litterin'." Could we get kicked out? One problem at a time. First, we needed to find out whether we were knee, thigh, or waist deep in a murder.

We watched as Mike, still staking and taping, made his way

back toward where we'd left our things.

"If you're through with us for now," Jimmy said, "can't we wait back at our blanket? We'd be out of the way and much more comfortable."

Frank thought about it.

"You can accompany the officer," he conceded. "But your effects are also part of the scene. Mike, you make sure it's not contaminated before the team gets here."

"We can't even put on a pair of socks?" Barbara asked as Mike herded us back toward our blanket, stopping every twenty-five feet, maybe, to stake and tape. "Or drink our coffee if there's any left?"

"Once the CS guys are done," Mike said. He added, "You knew the deceased. You found the body. We have to check everything in the largest possible area that could give us information."

"What if we'd found her floating?" Barbara asked. "You can't put yellow tape around the ocean."

"That would be an entirely different set of procedures." His face cracked in about a quarter of a grin. "This is a lot easier on the Town budget."

That was the last explanation we got for a while. The detectives who arrived shortly questioned us a lot more thoroughly than Frank had. Wiznewski was the sergeant, a guy in his forties with the long face of a basset hound, sleepy eyes with droopy pouches under them. He wore a hairpiece as brassy as his gold shield, but I bet nobody teased him about it. The regular detective was Butler, a stocky woman, maybe ten years younger than Wiznewski, with raw umber skin, a very firm jaw, and close-cropped hair so nappy it made a political statement. She nipped in the bud my attempt to charm her without wasting a word.

They didn't let us touch anything, not so much as a Styrofoam cup we'd already used for coffee. The whole beach between our car and blanket and the place where we'd found Clea was part of the secured area. The cops kept not calling it a crime scene, but it was hard to remember there was a difference.

Officer Mike escorted each of us in turn up over the dune to the parking lot. They made us sit in a police car. Another cop car, lights flashing, blocked access to the lot and to the beach beyond it. Since this was the nearest beach access to the spot where we'd found Clea, the road from this point was hardly more than a sandy track running parallel to the dunes. That was taped off. They used a ton of yellow tape. The only part they left alone was the piping plover nesting area, which was already taped off, though not with crime scene tape.

The CS folks literally sifted sand. Detective Butler did the verbal equivalent when she questioned me. She wasn't hostile, but she was thorough. Clea probably hadn't even handled the two bagels I'd eaten, but Butler sure was interested in the fact she'd bought them. I didn't much like admitting that I couldn't have afforded a share in the Hamptons if Jimmy hadn't paid for it. But I couldn't think of any reason not to tell her. The point was that I hadn't picked the house or known who'd be there before the season started.

I hated to do it, but I broke the house's anonymity. Butler had trouble understanding how people could share a house without knowing each other's last names. I could only repeat, "It didn't come up," so many times before I broke down and mentioned AA and other twelve-step programs. They interviewed me first, since I'd been alone with Clea's body the longest—if they believed what all three of us said about how long it had taken Barbara to walk down there, see she was dead, and run back. I didn't know what Jimmy and Barbara would say. Jimmy holds the program sacred, and he has a lot of self-control. Barbara has the discretion of a mouse, but she loves the program too. I didn't know how they'd feel when the detective said, "Mr. Kohler told us it's a clean and sober house." I've tried not to disappoint Jimmy since I got sober. I've got a lot of bad years to make up for.

Once they'd finished with the three of us, we still had to hang around while they looked for evidence of any connection with Clea and what had happened to her. Checking all our belongings, including the car, took ages. They let us sit on the beach. The sun beat down on us. People started walking by and had to be stopped from continuing on toward what I thought of as the real scene. A few turned and walked the other way. Most of them stayed and gawked.

"This is embarrassing," Barbara said. "They'll think we're criminals."

I opened my mouth and shut it again. Why bother asking a chronic codependent why she cares what other people think?

"Speaking of turning red," Jimmy said, "if I don't get out of this sun soon, we are all going to regret it by this evening."

"Oh, baby, no!" Barbara exclaimed. "Let me tell them. They've got to give you the sun block or let you sit under the umbrella." They'd both be up all night if Jimmy got a bad sunburn.

She started to jump up, but Jimmy pulled her back down.

"I can do it myself, petunia."

He used his grip on her arm to lever himself from the sand where we were sitting to a standing position.

"Officer!" he called. The uniformed guy was still there, keeping an eye on us and acting as a gofer for the detectives. "Is it okay if we move into the shade?"

"Sure, go ahead."

The shadow the umbrella cast had moved off the blanket. We moved it and plunked ourselves down again. Officer Mike even got a tube of sun block from the patrol car and handed it to Jimmy.

"I'm starving," Barbara announced.

"Sorry, ma'am. Can't help you there. Please be patient. It won't be much longer."

He lied. There was a mild commotion when another police car squealed into the lot and headed down the track. I would have thought they'd use four-wheel drive vehicles, which could go on the beach. But tire tracks would stir up the sand, maybe contaminate the crime scene. Worse, they might damage a baby piping plover. Lewis, the guy who'd organized our house, had already told us that not just Dedhampton, but the whole East End, got passionate about environmental issues. Actually, the word he used was "nuts."

"Look, it's Lewis," Barbara said, "in the back of that police car."

"You're right," Jimmy said. "He's so tall that that firecracker hair of his is practically hitting the roof of the cop car."

"I bet they asked him to identify the body," Barbara said. "Wouldn't he know her full name?"

"He's the guy I wrote the check to," Jimmy said. "Probably the others did too."

A few minutes later, the cop came over to us.

"I just talked to Sergeant Wiznewski at the scene. The body's been identified. We're taking the witness back to your house, so you might as well ride along."

"I would kill for lunch," Barbara said, and then clapped her hand to her mouth. "Anyhow, why can't we take our car?"

"Part of the scene, miss."

"They've got our keys, Barb," Jimmy said.

"So you drive us back, I mean the officers do, and then what?"

"The officers will find a place for you to wait." Officer Mike's face twitched.

"You mean in the house?"

"That's part of the scene, too, miss. Maybe the deck. Someone will brief you." He took in Barbara's dismayed expression and got human again. "I'll tell the officer driving you to stop at the deli on the way."

Chapter Four

"I can't believe you told them we're a clean and sober house," Lewis said. He stabbed his fork into a mound of spaghetti and twirled it. He was such a big guy that he got a lot of torque.

He scowled at Jimmy as he spoke.

"Don't look at him, dude," I said. "It was me. Rigorous honesty, right? They were gonna find out, anyhow."

I helped myself to a freshly made biscuit, dancing my fingers over it till I decided it wasn't too hot to hold. Sudden death seemed to have made all of us hungry. There'd been a cooking frenzy in the kitchen once the cops had left. And now the whole gang of us sat around the table shoveling in the results.

The house had an upside-down design. The entrance was on the ground floor with the four bedrooms. Upstairs was a big living room open to the beams of the roof, a loft where three of the women bunked, and the kitchen. We ate in the living room, laid out to catch as much light and air as possible. Right now, twilight deepening outside the windows leached color from the treetops.

"I can't believe you told them we're a group house, Lewis." Karen picked olives out of her salad, her big-boned frame hunched over the plate as if she were a giant who had trouble perceiving objects on that scale. Or maybe she needed glasses. She and Lewis were married. "We could get thrown out. We could lose our deposit."

"Clea's dead, and you're worried about our *deposit?*" Lewis turned brick red.

"Guys, hey, easy does it." Jeannette, large and pink like the overblown roses on her muumuu, mopped her damp forehead, plastered with tendrils of dark curly hair, with a napkin as she tried to make peace. "We're all upset."

A second team of detectives had been there all afternoon, taking depositions and searching not just Clea's room, but everyone's. Waiting out on the deck until they said we could go in had gotten very, very boring. It had been hardest on Jimmy, because he'd left his laptop in the house. Jimmy unplugged is a shadow of himself.

In a different kind of group, it would have seemed callous how, right after that, we calmly sat down to a good dinner. But for alcoholics, booze is the hard shell that armors that vulnerable inner child we're supposed to have. We don't know how to deal with feelings, and we're good at finding ways to avoid them. Me, I get flippant. I'm working on it. Clea's staring face and sprawled limbs on the beach hadn't evoked a single wisecrack.

"Who wouldn't be upset with the Gestapo pounding at the door?" Lewis reached out and snagged the last biscuit. "I hadn't even had a cup of coffee."

"Oh, come on, Lewis," Cindy said. I liked the look of her. Compact, like me, with a forthright way of talking. Her sweatshirt said "Beach Blanket Babe," but the way she wore it, it was clothing, not a come-on. "They didn't have their weapons out. They were perfectly courteous. And they didn't drag anyone away."

"They did drag me away," Lewis said.

"Only because you could identify her. They brought you right back."

"Clea's dead!" Barbara burst out. "Doesn't anybody care?"

"Thank you, Barbara!" Stewie, my roommate for the summer, folded his arms across his chest and glared around the table. He had the muscle definition of a body builder. Oiled tan skin and a tank top made the most of it. "We should be celebrating her beautiful spirit, not wallowing in self-centered fear."

"Self-centered fear" was an AA tag line. I thought it hit the nail on the head. I had at least one secret I wanted to keep from the cops, and I'd only arrived yesterday. Some of these folks had done shares with Clea before. Did they all agree she had a beautiful spirit? She had been working the room last night. It was possible not everybody read her vibe the same.

"I was scared." Skinny little Stephanie ran the tip of her tongue over the braces on her slightly protruding teeth. "They asked a million questions, and they didn't really say what happened."

"Thank you," Karen said. "I'm tired of pretending I'm not scared."

"Asking questions is their job," Cindy said. "And they don't know what happened yet. They will, though."

"I'm grieving for Clea," Jeannette said. Her face flushed an even hotter pink. "So much beauty. So much potential for happiness. I'm sad for her and I'm sad for me—for all of us."

" 'Ask not for whom the bell tolls,' " Jimmy quoted.

"That's what I meant," Jeannette said. She blotted her face with a fresh napkin, hiding either tears or rivulets of sweat. Maybe both. She hadn't mentioned Clea's spirit or claimed that Clea had been happy.

"If we were a bunch of civilians," I said. "we'd probably be getting drunk right now and congratulating ourselves on holding a damn fine wake."

"You've got a point," Karen said. "When I was drinking, I had one all-purpose response that worked for everything, even death."

Same here.

" 'Fuck it, let's have a drink,' " I said. "Was that your mantra too?"

"Right before 'Let's have another,' " Karen said.

"Yea and amen," Lewis said.

Cindy raised her water glass in a mock toast and tossed it back. I looked around the table. For a split second, I felt as if I knew all of them very, very well. The moment passed when I remembered the murder. If it was a murder. Sure, she could have drowned by accident. But something told me different. Maybe all that yellow crime scene tape. Or the hairs on the back of my neck.

"Anyhow, don't worry about the group house," Lewis said. "We've never had a problem, and neither has Oscar."

"Oscar?" Barbara asked.

"The nearest other clean and sober house, down by Dedhampton Beach," Jeannette explained across the table. "Some of us had shares there last year."

"And the year before," Stephanie said.

"Oscar owns the house," Karen said. "They can't stop him from having guests."

"Town ordinance puts a limit on how many unrelated people he can have," Cindy said. Maybe she was a lawyer. "If it's a clean and sober house, I guess his parties aren't wild enough to draw police attention. Anyhow, all that happens is the landlord gets a ticket. A big ticket, like mid-five figures."

"Oscar has plenty of money," Karen said. "And his parties were mega wild until he got clean."

"So all the program people in the neighborhood knew Clea?" Barbara asked.

"Oh, yes. Especially anyone who's stayed at Oscar's."

Silence fell. I could hear a heavy branch that grew too close to the house scrape against a window. The big battery-operated clock over the kitchen sink tocked. The birds outside got ready for bed.

"Talk about an elephant in the living room," Lewis said finally.

" 'Don't drink and go to meetings' won't make a murder go away," Karen said.

"Maybe she just drowned," Stephanie said.

"We'll know when they do the autopsy," Cindy said.

Stewie shuddered.

"I don't like to think about that."

"Still, we'll probably feel a lot better once we know one way or the other."

"The cops aren't interested in our feelings," Jeannette said. "And why should they tell us anything?"

"Do you think they'll keep coming back?" Stephanie hunched her shoulders and shivered like a pixie in a snowstorm.

"If they find evidence of a homicide, they will," Cindy said. "If they determined she drowned by accident, they'll drop the investigation, and we won't see much more of them."

"So what was Clea like?" Barbara asked. "Can you imagine anyone having a reason to kill her?"

"She was a free spirit," Stewie said. "I knew her in the city—she's the one who told me about this house. Actually I met her a few summers ago when she came out to visit my old group house in the Pines. We used to go shopping together, and we both loved to cook." He lifted a few curly strands of pasta with his fork and let them slide slowly back down onto his plate. "I used her special sun-dried tomato and fresh basil sauce recipe tonight. And we always used fusilli for the pasta. We used to joke that it was like her hair."

I got the feeling this guy wasn't going to be my rival for Cindy's affections.

"The Pines is in Fire Island, right?" Barbara said. "So you switched to be with Clea."

"Not exactly," Stewie said. "When I got into SCA, my sponsor thought I'd better stay away from people, places, and things, you know?"

Everybody else seemed to know what SCA was. I didn't want to ask, so I puzzled it out. Sexual Compulsives Anonymous. Don't drink, go to meetings, and, in Stewie's case, sleep with me on his vacation. I wondered what straight sexual compulsives did to avoid people, places, and things that triggered their addiction. Hang out in gay bars? Spend the summer in the Pines?

"So Clea never threatened anyone," Jimmy said.

Stephanie looked at Karen. Karen and Lewis looked away from each other. Jeannette looked down at her plate.

"She was a doll," Stewie said. No one chimed in.

"She was a very determined person," Karen said. "She wanted what she wanted, and she liked to get her way."

"She was a journalist," Lewis said. "Did you know?"

Barbara, Jimmy, Cindy, and I shook our heads.

"She could have ticked someone off," Stephanie said, "in an article or something. She liked to nose around. She was always writing things down in one of her notebooks."

"She was a bit of a crusader," Karen said.

"She drowned!" Jeannette pushed back her chair. It clattered and almost fell as she blundered into the kitchen. Did this conversation upset her more than the rest of us? Or did she simply want her dessert? She came back to the table in a minute, a pie in either hand.

"Strawberry rhubarb and lemon tart," she announced. "Mrs. Dowling made them, the farmer's wife down the road."

"She's kind of a lemon tart herself," Karen said.

"A tart?" I asked, intrigued in spite of myself.

"More of a lemon. American Gothic. But she makes a great pie."

Barbara wasn't ready to let it go.

"Is there any chance Clea could have killed herself?" she asked. "People do swim out to sea sometimes."

"No way."

"Absolutely not."

"Clea? Never in a million years."

Besides, I thought, if she'd swum out far enough to have no choice about getting back, she wouldn't have been washed back to shore right where she'd left her clothes and gone in. We'd been only an hour or two behind her. If she'd drowned well out to sea, would she have washed ashore at all by the time we'd found her?

"So everybody here knew her," Cindy said, "except me?"

"I knew her from meetings," Karen said, "and she was in Oscar's house before."

"We didn't," Barbara said. "Jimmy and Bruce and me. It's our first time in Dedhampton."

"Mine too," Stewie said. "I've always gone to the Pines."

"So Oscar and maybe his housemates all knew Clea," Cindy said. "Did anybody mention that to the police?"

Karen and Lewis looked at each other. So did Stephanie and Jeannette.

"It didn't come up," Jeannette said.

Stephanie nodded. Karen shook her head. Lewis shrugged.

"Who's Clea's roommate this summer?" Barbara asked.

"She was supposed to bring a friend," Lewis said. "This part I did tell the cops. When she sent the check in, she said she wasn't sure who she'd be inviting to share the room with her. She paid for both shares."

"She didn't bring someone with her?" Barbara asked. "Or tell you who her roommate would be?"

"She only got here yesterday," Lewis said. "We didn't see her till dinner."

We had arrived the day before too. Everybody around the dinner table now, plus Clea, had gathered for last night's dinner. There'd been a lot of talk and laughter. We'd had lobster and strawberry shortcake to kick off what was evidently going to be a season of serious eating.

"I never got a chance to ask her," Lewis said. "And no one showed up."

Right on cue, a car pulled up on the gravel. The engine choked and died. A trunk slammed. A door banged. Something crashed, maybe gear being dumped on the floor.

"Yo! Ahoy! Anybody home?" a male voice called.

We heard tromping on the stairs. The guy's head appeared in the stairwell by installments. First the bald part in front. Then the slicked back brown hair and the broad forehead. Mirrored shades, though it was getting dark outside by now. Beaky nose. Droopy graying mustache. Not much of a chin. When we could see his Izod shirt down to the waist and the big brass buckle on his belt, he spoke again.

"Hi, I'm Phil."

We all stared.

"Am I in time for dinner?" he asked. "The traffic sucked. Where's Clea? I'm her boyfriend."

Chapter Five

"You paid for the shares," Oscar said. "You might as well enjoy the summer."

A big group of us lay sprawled on the beach, making the most of a hot Memorial Day. You'd think it was August, unless you happened to dip your toes in the frigid ocean. Everyone from our house was there except Phil, who'd gone to talk to the police. Following Lewis and Karen's lead, we'd all plunked down our blankets, towels, and gear next to the gang of clean and sober folks from Oscar's house. Oscar himself was a genial mine-host kind of guy. I'd have bet money he'd had a world class beer gut before he got sober. Piercing blue eyes and a rich, warm voice made him attractive. A luxuriant mustache lent him *gravitas.* All the women from his house clustered around him, putting me in mind of a walrus with his harem. One of them, little Corky, followed him around like a pilot fish cozying up to a shark. She'd trotted behind him out to the beach carrying two folding chaise longues and an umbrella. He'd carried a beach towel and a Panama hat.

The sun beat down on us. All but Jimmy. He huddled under the sole umbrella wearing a long-sleeved shirt, long pants, and a ridiculous big hat. His iPad perched on his knees. His pink face wore as sour an expression as the sweetest tempered guy I knew ever got. Jimmy's problem was not getting online, but keeping sand off of his iPad.

Oscar's house rode a dune right off the beach, so close his

wireless worked down here near the water. That made him Big Daddy to any clean and sober computer nut in the vicinity.

"It doesn't seem right," Barbara said, "but it doesn't make sense not to, either."

"I know what you mean," Corky said. Punk to the ring threaded over her left eyebrow and the stand-up spikes of her inky hair, she wore the briefest of bikinis over a tan that stopped for nothing. "You'll feel guilty either way."

"It's spooky at the house," Jeannette said. "I keep thinking she's in the next room."

"It could be worse," Karen said. "She could have died there."

"She wouldn't have drowned in the house," Stephanie said.

"Did she drown?" Oscar asked. "Did you hear anything from the police?"

"They're treating it as a suspicious death so far," Cindy said. "That means the detectives can act as if it's a homicide until evidence tells them any different."

"Maybe I can find out more," Oscar said.

"Oscar knows everyone in this town," Corky said with pride.

"They searched through all our stuff," Stephanie said. "Every room."

"They didn't put everything back, either," Barbara said "They left things heaped on the bed and hanging out of drawers."

"They're allowed to look for evidence," Cindy said. She wore an NYPD sweatshirt today. She chose that moment to take it off. I couldn't help looking, but I tried to think post-feminist thoughts.

"I hate it." Jeannette pulled off her splashy red and purple muumuu, revealing a matching bathing suit and a quantity of opulent flesh. "Why do they have to keep coming back?"

"One of the cops told me it's against the law to die in the State of New York," Karen said.

"What does that mean?" I asked.

"It means there has to be a reason," Karen said, "and they won't stop looking until they find one." She rose to her knees to fish a tube of sun block out of a big straw carryall, then stood up to smooth it onto her long limbs. Her shadow fell on the patch of sun I'd been basking in.

"The reason was that she drowned," Stewie said. "Nobody would have killed Clea."

The remark dropped into a well of silence. Or it might have been my imagination. Lewis climbed to his feet, increasing the shade. He dusted sand off his hands and took the tube of sun block from Karen. She turned her back. He slathered it on, making circles on her back and pushing the straps of her suit out of the way without ceremony. They didn't seem mad at each other today. A guy named Shep from Oscar's house started doing pushups on a towel. Jimmy raised the hand that wasn't scurrying around the touch pad to slap at no-see-ums on his neck.

"People had strong feelings about Clea," Oscar said finally. "Did anybody see her on the beach?"

"We did," Barbara said, "Jimmy and Bruce and I, and I wish we hadn't."

"Sorry," Corky said. Apologizing for Oscar's insensitivity? I bet she went to Al-Anon. She'd now used both the passwords. Guilty and sorry, guilty and sorry all day long.

"I meant before you found her dead," Oscar said.

"The last place she was seen," Jimmy said, "must have been the deli. She got bagels for the house and dropped them off. None of us at the house saw her then, as far as I know."

"Nobody was up when I found the bag on the kitchen counter," Barbara said.

"The police didn't know she'd gone to the deli until you told them," Cindy said.

"Someone might have seen her on the beach," Barbara said.

"They're knocking on doors near where they found her," Shep said. "Including ours. I talked to them yesterday afternoon."

"What?" Oscar sat up so abruptly that his chaise longue almost snapped shut on him.

"You were in the shower. Everybody else was out."

"What did you tell them?"

"Nothing. I hadn't seen her. They showed me a picture, but I didn't know her."

"I did," Corky said, "and so did Oscar and the others who were in the house last year."

"We didn't say anything about you guys," Karen said.

"They dropped a stitch, not thinking of past summers and asking where she'd stayed," Lewis said.

Oscar closed his eyes. His lips moved. Silent prayer. Or silent cursing.

"They will. I guess I'd better expect them back."

"What about the day before?" Cindy asked. "I saw Clea when I arrived, mid-afternoon, and she said she'd taken an early train out. Did anybody spend much time with her?"

"We didn't," Barbara said. "We got there in the afternoon too."

"We weren't there," Lewis said. "We drove out to Montauk for the day. We didn't get back till dinnertime."

"Did the cops ask why everybody's last name was Alcoholic?" Oscar asked.

"It came up," I admitted.

"That's bad." Oscar shook his head.

"Not telling them would have been worse," Jimmy said.

I was relieved to hear he thought so.

"Would you rather they thought we were a bunch of drunken assholes," Jimmy asked, "who kept a stash of dope in every room and might have drowned poor Clea horsing around?"

That was more or less what I'd figured when I blew the gaffe.

"They probably wouldn't have been surprised to find a stash of dope," Jimmy said. "I bet nine times out of ten when they get called, it's a party house."

"I could tell you stories," Oscar said. He sounded awfully cheerful for a guy who'd fielded so many questions and expected the police to come back asking more. I wondered what the strong feelings about Clea that he'd mentioned had been.

"Well, we're all clean and sober now," Corky said. "Barbara found her, right? You couldn't tell if she drowned?"

"I tried not to look," Barbara admitted, "even though I had to."

"Bruce and I saw her too," Jimmy said. "We didn't see a gunshot wound or a rope around her neck."

He shut down his iPad carefully, stood up, shook out his pants, and picked his way around the blanket to where Barbara sat. He lowered himself to a seated position behind her. She leaned back against his legs.

"So how did you know she was dead? Did you try CPR?"

"We saw her already lying there before I started down the beach," Barbara explained. "I thought she was a log."

"She had to come back to tell us," Jimmy added.

"Didn't you have a cell phone?"

"All I was wearing was a bathing suit and a bagel," Barbara said.

"Oh! I'm sick of this!" Karen said. She stamped her foot, spraying sand in all directions. "Let's not talk about Clea anymore." Lewis reached out to her. She shook his hand off her arm. "I'm going up to the house." She stalked away toward the dunes, where a flight of wooden steps led up to Oscar's deck.

The steady growl of a motor overhead distracted us all. We watched as a small plane, the kind with the wings on top, flew by, low and parallel to the beach. It trailed a banner exhorting us to drink a well-known beer.

"I knew it well," I said.

"Nevermore," Jimmy said.

"Oy, have you got the wrong beach," Barbara said.

As the plane puttered out of sight, I realized that half the group had left. The rest shook the sand out of towels, applied more sun block, and drank from their water bottles.

Someone took out a set of beach paddles and the bounceless ball that went with them. The *thock thock thock* of the game provided rhythm beneath the swish of the surf and the cries of gulls. A shadow swept down the beach as a black sheep amid the fleecy clouds blew briefly across the sun. I shivered.

"Catch." Barbara flung a T-shirt in my general direction. I made an awkward left-handed catch. "Jimmy and I are going for a walk. Want to come?"

"No, that's okay."

I wanted a cigarette. Recovering alcoholics used to smoke like chimneys. But like chimneys, most of them no longer smoked. Our house had "Smoke Free Zone" signs posted everywhere, even on the deck. Having a cigarette, like shooting up or jerking off, had become something you snuck away to take care of privately.

When I stood up, I could feel the kiss of the ocean in the breeze. My lips tasted of salt. I palmed the pack of cigarettes I'd rolled in a towel and added a matchbook. I pulled the T-shirt over my head. Barbara and Jimmy, hand in hand like kids, receded in the distance. I turned the other way. The hard-packed sand close to the water still made the easiest walking. But in this direction and on this tide, it slanted, so I had to gimp along. The soft sand farther back toward the dunes was level, except where the fat tires of off-road four-by-fours and pickup trucks had carved their tracks in the sand. It gave my arches a workout. I sat down near the dunes with my back against a log. Then it took me a dozen tries to strike a match. Next time, I'd bring my lighter.

As I dragged deep, I decided lolling on the beach was idyllic only in the eye of the beholder. First I sat on a clam shell. Then two big green glistening flies decided my legs made a tasty snack. When I stood up, the hot sand burned the soles of my feet. Then I had to pee. I thought better of relieving myself on the beach or into the water. No pissing on the Hamptons. As my sponsor kept telling me, it was better not to do anything I'd have to make amends for later. Besides, the beach was anything but deserted. People kept walking by. Families with kids and dogs. I didn't want to get arrested. Using the dunes as an outhouse was not an option either. Eastern Long Island was a hotbed of environmental activism. I didn't feel inclined to clamber up past the sign that said that walking on the dunes was *verboten.*

I smoked my cigarette down to the filter, tossed it into the sand, and kicked some more sand over it. Then I trudged back toward Oscar's house. He'd invited us to use the facilities and help ourselves to soda from the refrigerator. The big weathered cedar ark had decks fore and aft and plate glass windows on the ocean side. Peering in, I saw no sign of life apart from brightly colored tropical fish swimming in a wall-mounted aquarium.

The door gave when I pushed it. People left their doors unlocked out here. Amazing. I found myself in a kind of mud room, or rather, sand room, with terra cotta tiles cool beneath my feet. A wall of hooks and cubbies. Washing machine and dryer. Towels, flip-flops, a broom, a couple of clamming rakes. The living room lay beyond it. Nobody there. The faint scent of tobacco hung in the air. Oscar's house was not a no-smoking zone. I thought of calling out. Instead, I crossed to the kitchen. It was vast, with marble counters, pristine steel appliances, and a forest of gleaming copper-bottomed pots hanging from the ceiling. The whole kitchen could have been photographed for a gourmet or design magazine.

The light from the big picture window provided a transition from the dazzle outside. I heard what sounded like a moan from the other end of the house. A dark corridor led toward other rooms, probably bedrooms. Again, I thought of calling out, decided not to. My bare feet made no sound on the hardwood floor. I followed the moaning, which got louder and more unmistakable as I got closer. It was none of my business who was having a quickie in the middle of the afternoon. But I was curious. I suppose spying was one of those things I would be expected to make amends for. But I rationalized it. I couldn't embarrass them by saying I'd seen them screwing, could I? If I knew who it was, I'd know who not to embarrass, right? It didn't convince me either. But snooping was better than sneaking a drink. I wondered if Oscar had a cold frosty in his refrigerator.

That's why they call it a slip. It can sneak right up on you when you're thinking of something else. But hey, I didn't do it. I felt downright virtuous as I tiptoed closer to the duet of moans and panting and the thump of a rocking bed. They hadn't shut the door all the way. I applied my eye to the crack.

It seemed to be the master bedroom, a corner room with plate glass on two sides. The light flooding in was amplified by a mirror over the bed. I caught a glimpse of my startled face in the reflected shadows around the door. I jerked my head back. Luckily the couple now reaching paradise and making a joyful noise were too focused to look up. The guy was Oscar. The woman was Karen.

Chapter Six

"So Karen is cheating on Lewis," Barbara said.

We sat squinched together on a lifeguard chair, watching the sunset over the bay. The glowing red ball had just sunk below the horizon. Now layers of gold and rose and violet bounced back and folded in on themselves in the banks of low-lying clouds around the rim of the darkening sky.

"They've organized group houses out here for years," Barbara said. "Lewis showed us scrapbooks full of photos before Jimmy gave him a check. And Oscar owns that house. He must be rich as a quart of Häagen-Dazs."

"You've got food on the brain, my pet," Jimmy said.

"I love summer food," Barbara said. "Strawberries and ice cream and corn and tomatoes and ice cream and hey, did you see the fancy gas grill out back? Mmm, steak and grilled jumbo shrimp and ice cream. The whole point of cheating is to keep things steamy—speaking as a professional. I mean a professional *counselor.*"

"They didn't have a whole lot of time for foreplay," I said. "Someone else could have walked in any minute."

"Do you think what you saw was an episode of an ongoing drama," Barbara asked, "or a one-night—call it a one-day-at-the-beach—stand?"

"I have no idea," I said. "They sounded pretty steamy."

"I bet they have a history," Barbara said. "No foreplay is one thing. No build-up is another. They didn't have time to make a connection that wasn't already there."

"But does it have anything to do with the murder? asked.

"We don't know," I said.

"We could find out." Barbara didn't qualify for Al-Anon because Jimmy drank a hundred years ago. She was hooked o minding other people's business.

Jimmy and I exchanged a resigned glance over her head.

"You don't have to quiver like a hunting dog," Jimmy said. "We don't even know it was a murder."

"But if it was," Barbara insisted. "We're the only newcomers. The others have been coming out here for years. And Oscar's house belongs to him. He wouldn't advertise shares, he'd invite people he knows, don't you think?"

"Okay, we're the newcomers. So what?"

"So we're above suspicion." Barbara bounced up and down. The lifeguard chair rocked.

"Whoa, there," I said. "It's a long way down."

"I wish we could see those notebooks of Clea's," she said. "Any of the others could have had a motive."

"I don't think the cops would want to share," I said. "The boyfriend wasn't even there."

"So he says."

Phil's shock when Lewis broke the news of Clea's death had seemed genuine. On the other hand, if he already knew b he'd killed her, he'd have rehearsed precisely that astonishment. The cops wouldn't take his word for just come from the city. He could have com before, gone back, and driven out aga suspect.

"Doesn't the conduct

"It doesn't pin dov off-peak. I checked. A date you travel either, ju

...we just leave it to the cops?" Jimmy asked. A rhetori-...ion, if I knew Barbara.

...nk of all the stuff they won't find out," she said. "The ...onships, the undercurrents—all the dysfunctional group ...se family stuff I bet is going on. And the cops don't go to ...eetings to investigate."

"Barbara!"

"I wouldn't break anyone's anonymity," she said with her best indignant frown. "But for background, you know we'll hear a lot—and when you go to meetings, you get a sense of who's reliable, who's really working the program."

"You think someone who works the steps can't commit a crime?"

"Not a *murder,*" she said. "Recovery is about integrity, you can't say it's not an indication of character. Besides, doesn't the thought of spending the summer with a murderer running around freak you out? I'll feel a lot better if we're trying to do something about it."

"What if it was an accident?" I scratched at my scalp with both hands. Sandy hair seemed to be a permanent condition at the beach. "Say whoever killed her didn't mean to."

"A program person would own up," Jimmy said. "Rigorous honesty. Making amends. 'When we were wrong, promptly ...mitted it.' "

..., yeah. Easier said than done."

... has got a point, Jimmy," Barbara said.

... his arm around her. She gave a little wriggle and ... him. I readjusted my butt into the extra inch or ...her other side. We sat in silence for a while as ...uted colors, antique rose and ochre and

She swung herself up off the seat and shinnied down the stilt-like struts of the lifeguard chair. Jimmy followed more cautiously, inching toward the edge, hooking his heels in as far down as he could, and then dropping to a crouch on the mounded sand.

"You guys go ahead," I said. "Take a little alone time."

"You sure?"

"Yeah, I need a smoke." I twisted around, swung my foot over the side of the seat like a cowboy dismounting, and clambered down backwards to the ground, my bare toes clutching at footholds along the way.

Jimmy took Barbara's hand. I watched as they plodded toward the hump of the wooden steps, almost covered by sand, between the bay beach and the pitted road that dead-ended there. Barbara looked back over her shoulder.

"Dinner's at eight-thirty," she called.

I raised an arm in a half wave, half salute. As they disappeared over the dune, I wheeled and started down toward the shore. The bay beach was a lot narrower than the ocean beach. Someone at the house had said they dredged most of the sand out of the channel that led from the open bay to the inlet that gave some of our neighbors waterfront property. In its natural state, the beach was mostly pebbles and small shells. I found out the hard way that many of the pebbles had sharp edges and many of the shells were broken. I limped back to the base of the lifeguard chair where I had dropped my sneakers when we climbed up for the balcony view. I stood on one foot, then the other, to put them on. I let the laces dangle. Barbara had been at me to get a pair of those rubber-soled mesh shoes you could wear right into the water. Maybe I would.

My toes and soles safe from impact, I scuffed my way down toward the water, lighting up and drawing deep as I went couple of kids with a dog pranced around on the big r at the far end of the beach. A boat or two, lights bobbing, putt-putted their way toward the inlet, trying to make dock before dark. But I was basically alone.

I'd been a champion liar in my drinking days. Of course I never called it that. Stretching the truth. Little sins of omission. Taking the path of least resistance. I'd never held myself accountable. But about eighteen months ago, I'd butted up against a choice between living and dying. In a weird way, it had still been about the path of least resistance. The door to living stood open, and I'd wandered through. Clueless. Not drinking is just the tip of the iceberg, they'd told me. Yeah, yeah, I'd said.

I still trusted hardly anybody except Jimmy, who'd been my best friend forever, and Barbara, who had worked her way into the glue between us and stuck through everything. I worked hard to keep it honest with my sponsor, a lawyer named Glenn with a radar for bullshit. But now I had a secret and a dilemma. Did I tell Jimmy and Barbara? Did I try to blow it off? If I did, would it go away? If I told them, would their endless tolerance for my screw-ups and stupidities finally crack?

I had met Clea before.

The truth sounded so implausible. Who would believe I'd had dinner with the woman, discussed her looks with Barbara and Jimmy, and kept a vigil over her body without recognizing her as a girl I'd almost, but not quite, had sex with at the age of fifteen? Although Jimmy and I were inseparable at that age, he hadn't met her. She'd cut me out of the herd at a party. We'd necked on the stairs for a couple of hours while Jimmy talked medieval history with a rare parochial-school intellectual girl with glasses, and everybody else danced their brains out and guzzled canned fruit punch spiked with cheap vodka. Even at fifteen, Jimmy and I despised any drink with fruit in it and tanked up in advance on whatever we could swipe from our dads or get an older kid to score for us.

I'd been hanging out in the doorway of Clea's room while Karen and the other women sifted through her possessions. The police had taken away the clothes she'd worn yesterday as well as her ID and everything with writing on it. They'd left the rest in chaos. Karen tut-tutted over the balled-up clothing. Jeannette sorted shoes and beach gear. Stephanie, the only skinny one, got down on her tummy and wriggled halfway under the bed to retrieve whatever had rolled there. She'd fished out a crumpled photograph.

"Hey, look at this. It's us, a couple of summers ago." Stephanie blew dust bunnies off the picture and handed it to me.

It was a group shot, taken on Oscar's deck with the ocean as a backdrop. Oscar dominated the group, his arms around four of the women. Lewis and Karen towered at the back. I spotted Jeannette trying to hide her bulk behind Oscar. I recognized Stephanie and Corky.

"Clea wasn't there?" I asked.

"Let's see." Karen plucked the picture out of my hand and squinted. "Sure she is. See? She had short hair."

Then it hit me. The toasted-biscuit skin. The green eyes that didn't come from contact lenses. And the honey-colored hair. She'd worn it short at fifteen. No wonder I hadn't remembered. The name hadn't rung a bell either. It had been the era of *Last Tango in Paris,* the Marlon Brando movie that everyone went to see for the X rating. Even fifteen-year-olds who couldn't get in to see it knew the girl won't tell Brando her name until the very end, when she shoots him. Clea was precocious. She said she'd tell me her name if I let her give me a blow job. At fifteen, I was still shockable. Also, my tolerance for alcohol had already started climbing. It took more than I'd had to drink that evening to abolish my half-Irish-Catholic inhibitions. I'd turned her down.

Was there any way the cops could trace the connection between Clea and me? The detectives had indicated that they'd time-travel through her life in the city as far as they needed to. I doubted Sherlock Holmes himself could find that party. But you never know. She'd known my name. She'd asked me on the breath right after the first tonguey kiss. Of course I'd told her. I didn't know it was the first move in a power play. I wondered if the grownup Clea who'd signed up for a summer in Deadhampton still played sexual games. I wondered if she'd kept a diary at fifteen. I wondered if she kept one now. If she'd brought one to the Hamptons, the detectives had it now.

She could have recognized me. Barbara always said I didn't deserve to look as good as I did after all those extra years of drinking. She claimed I kept the dissipated portrait version locked in a closet. The whole thing was a helluva coincidence, but I could be in trouble. I had an alibi for whatever time Clea could conceivably have drowned. Of course I did. I'd been with Jimmy and Barbara. And before that, I'd been blamelessly asleep with Stewie gently snoring in the next bed. That part wasn't such a good alibi. Maybe I'd better tell Jimmy and Barbara the truth. I needed all the backup I could get.

Chapter Seven

I don't know how I got roped into scrubbing the salt and dirt off a boat. Okay, I do know. Cindy asked me. She found a fourteen-foot plywood and Fiberglas rowboat half buried in the weeds behind the house and drafted me to help her drag it out to where we could contemplate it. Contemplation turned to cleaning a lot quicker than I wanted.

"How do you know this thing is seaworthy?" I rubbed at a persistent mass of crud on the hull with a Brillo pad soaked in ammonia. I might end up asphyxiated, but I wouldn't faint.

"I don't." Cindy grinned at me. She sat cross-legged in the only patch of shade in the vicinity, sanding an oar. Today her sweatshirt said, "Dolphins do it with a smile." "I don't see any obvious cracks, do you?"

"I wouldn't know what to look for. All I see is encrusted schmutz. Dirt. A Barbara word," I explained.

"The three of you seem pretty tight," she remarked. "Don't you have a girlfriend of your own?"

"Not since I got sober. How about you?"

"Too busy. Hey, watch out for the barnacles. You might need some kind of knife or scraper to get them off."

" 'It's me, it's me, I'm home from the sea, said Barnacle Bill the Sailor,' " I sang. "Hey, don't wince when I'm serenading you. These clingy little shell bumps around the pointy end here are barnacles? Who knew?" I rocked back on my heels, knees creaking, and drew the tail of my T-shirt up to wipe my sweaty face.

"Let's see." She swung the oar to vertical, stuck the blade in the ground, and used its six-foot length to pull herself up. "Yeah, yeah. I get it you're a landlubber. I suppose that makes me the press gang." She came around the bow to stand next to me. She put a light hand on my shoulder and leaned over to look. I could feel the warmth of her flushed cheek next to mine. "Yes, those are barnacles or something very like them. We need to scrape them."

"We? You really meant it about the press gang. So we get this thing in pristine condition and then what?"

"We take it out on the bay. It'll be fun."

I really liked her grin. Her eyeteeth were a little long. It gave her a predatory look that belied the sweetness of her mouth and the twinkle in her eye. Like a very charming vampire.

"How do we make it go?"

"That's the easy part. I give the orders, you man the oars."

I opened my mouth to voice my dismay. The heavy chomp of tires biting gravel and the purr of an engine interrupted us. A red Lexus swept past us. The car drew up in the cleared area to the side of the house. Phil emerged, slamming the door.

"Hey, Phil," Cindy called. "How's it going?"

He stalked over to us. Mirror shades hid his eyes, but the scowl above and below them expressed anger.

"Those bastards think I'm a suspect!"

"You had to talk to the police again? What did they tell you?"

"They didn't tell me anything. They asked a lot of damn insulting questions that I've already answered over and over."

"Sounds like they're treating it as a homicide. Did they do the autopsy yet?"

"I have no idea. They acted like it was my fault they had to work on a holiday weekend, so they had a right to give me a hard time. How long had I known Clea, were we living together, was I seeing anybody else, when did I leave the city that day, could I prove it. What's the sense of asking all those questions if they're not going to believe the answers?"

"What don't they believe?"

"When I got out here, for one thing."

"You didn't have a ticket for your garage?" I'd have been astounded if he didn't garage that car.

"Sometimes I throw it away." Phil pried a piece of gravel out of the tread of his fancy running shoe and threw it like a hardball. "Sometimes they stick it in my windshield and it blows away once I hit the highway." The pebble glanced off the hull of the overturned boat. Phil threw another. "But I didn't put the car in the garage the night before I came out."

"You parked a Lexus on the street?" The shiny red hunk of overpriced machinery looked new. Garage space in the city cost a fortune. But so did theft and vandalism, in money or in hassle with the insurance company. So did retrieving it from the pound if it got towed. Even Jimmy garaged his Toyota.

"I had a lot of gear to load in the car, and I didn't want the hassle of bringing it around to my building before I could take off."

"Where do you live?" I asked.

"East Seventies."

"Doorman building?"

"Of course."

I lived less than a mile from Phil, but my building was an old-law tenement without a lobby or elevator. The closest it got to a doorman was when the super's wife popped out in the hall in housedress, flip-flops, and curlers to see who was going up the stairs.

"Why can't your doorman confirm you had the car parked on the street?" Cindy asked.

"He didn't see it." If Phil had sounded this sulky with the police, I bet he hadn't endeared himself to them. "I parked around the corner."

"You didn't double park when you picked up your stuff?" That's what everybody else does.

"The doorman wasn't there. They're not supposed to leave the lobby, but they always do."

That left Phil with no alibi. He could have driven out to Dedhampton early in the morning. Or the night before. He might even have met Clea on the beach by prearrangement. If he killed her, he could have found someplace to hide out during the day and shown up at dinner time as if he had just come from the city. The red Lexus was a conspicuous car. Or was it? In the Hamptons, Lexuses and BMWs were a dime a dozen. He could have ditched it for the day, parked it somewhere it fit in. As for getting to the beach, his girlfriend was a runner. Maybe he was too. Maybe the fancy running shoes he kept picking gravel out of weren't just for show.

So Phil had opportunity, but what about motive? Phil was the boyfriend in residence, but it sounded like Clea played the field. Could she have told him she didn't want him with her after all? Would someone kill for a summer in the Hamptons? Or they could have quarreled about almost anything. He obviously had a temper and a streak of arrogance. She liked secrets and manipulating men, if she was anything like her younger self. She'd also chosen a profession that gave her license to be nosy. That could have given her leverage over a lot of people, including an uppity boyfriend she wanted to keep in control.

"You know, the autopsy could change everything," Cindy said. "In a few days, if we allow for the holiday slowing things down, we could find out it was an accident."

"Those bastards won't make it that easy," Phil said, "even if it does turn out she drowned. They asked if she'd ever tried to kill herself. Idiots. Nobody buys bagels and puts on their high end New Balances to commit suicide."

When Phil left, Cindy and I picked up our tools without comment and started working on the boat again. He'd broken the mood, and I wanted it back. I hoped she did too. The rising heat of the day brought out all the country smells: dirt and flowers, green things growing, a tang of salt. Also the stink of two-day-old lobster shells. No garbage collection in Dedhampton. A heap of well-filled black plastic garbage bags stood ready for a trip to the dump. Someone in the house had turned on the radio, and the strains of Vivaldi's *Seasons* floated out the window on an undercurrent of bees buzzing and birds twittering.

I was mulling over ways to get Cindy to talk about herself when the crash and clatter of someone carrying too much beach stuff in not enough hands announced Barbara's arrival. She dumped all but a tote bag with a brightly striped towel peeking out the top on the gravel near the Toyota and came over to survey our efforts.

"Wow, that's quite a project," she said. "Work—I could sit and watch it for hours. Wanna come to the beach?"

I looked hopefully at Cindy. She shook her head.

"Later. I don't want to lose the momentum. This is the kind of project that part-way gets you nothing."

"Like a PhD in psychology," Jeannette said, coming up behind her with Stephanie on her heels. "That's why I've got a master's in social work." Her red flowered muumuu billowed about her. Stephanie, scrawny in a black bikini, carried a boogie board under her arm.

"Bruce, why don't you come?" Barbara said. "Stephanie's going to show me how to use the board."

"If the waves are right," Stephanie said. "If it's too calm, you can't even body surf. And if there's an undertow, you may not want to risk going out past the breakers. We don't want another accident."

So Stephanie thought it was an accident. Or she wanted us to think it was. Could she have something to hide? What was her relationship with Clea? Who was she? I knew she had a tendency to push her food around on her plate and was afraid of getting fat. Now I knew she was at home in the ocean. If she'd left the house the morning Clea died, would we have known? Could she have slipped out early, when Clea did? Even if she had, she had come home before the police arrived, after we found the body. Or had she? All the rest who'd spent the night in the house were accounted for when they strung that damn yellow tape around it. Could Stephanie have gone out and slipped back in during the commotion? She was almost skinny enough to slither through the keyhole.

If it turned out Clea's death was a simple drowning, the police would drop the investigation. That would be better for all of us. But I wasn't so sure I'd be satisfied. Our housemates seemed to have a tangled web of relationships. When you added Oscar and his crew into the mix, things got downright knotty. To mix the metaphor, I sensed currents beneath the surface.

"Earth to Bruce," Barbara said. "Are you coming?"

"No, I'm going to stay and help get this boat seaworthy." I would have said "help Cindy," but I didn't want to kindle the matchmaking gleam in Barbara's eye. "I'll be along later."

"How will you get there?"

"Someone will give me a ride," I said. "Don't worry, Mommy. I can take care of myself."

"We can take Stephanie's car," Jeannette said. "Barbara offered to drive, but we could leave her car for you."

"Whatever." Stephanie shifted the board from one arm to the other. Her shell necklace jingled as she moved. "Let's make up our minds and get going."

"Here!" Barbara tossed me her car keys. I caught them on the fly. "Try to talk Jimmy into coming down. Tell him I left a whole tube of sun block on our dresser." Stephanie was already throwing the boogie board into the trunk of her sand-colored Chevy as Barbara scurried after Jeannette. "We'll be on the beach by Oscar's house," she called over her shoulder.

Clea had run the four miles to the beach that morning. She hadn't planned to get killed. She'd simply gone for a run. Still, she might have told somebody she'd meet them on the beach. Wouldn't anybody planning murder come by car for a quick getaway? Our car had been the only one in the Dedhampton parking lot. We hadn't passed any cars on the one throughroad from the group house to the highway. Clea had given us directions to Dedhampton Beach. It was the only public parking on that stretch of the beach. But Stephanie could have left her car at Oscar's or hidden off the road between the parking lot and where we found her. So could anyone else in the house who had a car.

Or maybe there was no car. Maybe the killer lived within walking distance of the beach. If the murder was premeditated, he could have checked the tide table and deliberately walked close to the water, where his footprints would soon be washed away. His or hers. Or in the shallows, leaving no footprints at all.

In the next hour, I learned how come the word *barnacle* is the usual metaphor for clinginess. I took off my shirt. Cindy took off her sweatshirt. She had a bikini underneath. I discarded my sweat-soaked bandanna. Cindy produced a dry one from the pocket of her cargo shorts. Karen and Lewis came out of the house and asked us if we wanted to go to the beach. We remained industrious.

I was filling a bucket from the spigot on the side of the outdoor shower, planning to dump the contents over my head and Cindy's if she'd let me, when a weather-beaten man in overalls came around the corner of the house. He had a farmer's tan—face, neck, and forearms—and wore a straw hat.

"I'm here to fix the shower," he announced.

I twisted the tap shut and stood up. We both listened to the showerhead drip.

"Be my guest," I said. I stuck out my hand. I don't know why. Working class solidarity, maybe. "Bruce Kohler."

"Dowling." His thin lips tightened in what might have been meant for a smile.

"Well, I'd better let you get to work." I picked up the sloshing bucket.

Dowling hefted a heavy wrench in his hand.

"I've got a boat," he volunteered. "If you folks want to go out for blues, let me know and we'll set it up."

"Fishing? Thanks, maybe we will." I nodded and started back toward Cindy.

"Any time you want a bucket of clams," Dowling called after me, "no problem either. We're right down the road."

Cindy and I were thinking about quitting for the day when a car came scrunching up the gravel.

"Damn, more company," Cindy said. "Want to talk to them while I make a break for that outdoor shower?"

"I don't think we get a choice," I said as Sergeant Wiznewski emerged from the unmarked car.

"Good morning, Sergeant," Cindy called out. "How can we help you?"

I was glad she'd spoken up. I might have led with "Go away" or "It wasn't me." I wondered if Cindy's stomach was fluttering inside. Mine was. She seemed cool as a debutante in spite of the dirt that streaked her legs from the knees down and the rivulets of sweat running down her cleavage.

"Afternoon," Wiznewski corrected. He squinted at the sun

rather than checking his watch before he said it. Show-off. "I'd like a word with you, Mr. Kohler, if you can spare the time."

Moment of truth. He'd figured out the tenuous connection between Clea and me. I couldn't imagine how. But why else would he want to talk to me? I wanted to puke. Feeling scared while sober sucked. I hoped it didn't show. I needed to look innocent to Wiznewski and brave to Cindy.

"Sure." My throat felt choked, but I sounded normal enough. "Uh, where?"

Wiznewski turned his head and squinted at the house. Maybe he needed glasses. I took a mini-break from the situation to wonder if I'd ever seen a cop with glasses.

"Anybody home?" he asked.

"They're all at the beach," Cindy said.

She'd forgotten Jimmy. That happened when he disappeared into cyberspace.

"Just one," I said. "He's probably got earphones on."

"Why don't we sit in my car," Wiznewski said comfortably, "just to make sure we're private."

I bet he'd meant us to talk in the car all along. His turf. And maybe transportation to the slammer if he didn't like my answers. I swear I hadn't even jumped a turnstile since I'd gotten sober.

"Wait for me?" I asked Cindy, hoping I sounded calm and not abject.

"I'll be on the deck."

"Thank you." I wouldn't be surprised if she disappeared. Cindy might seem well balanced to me, but she was still an addict of some kind, like everyone else in the house. She'd make sure she didn't leave herself too vulnerable in any situation.

"We found a contradiction in your statement, Mr. Kohler," Wiznewski said. He'd settled into the right front seat, leaning toward me with a meaty arm flung over the back of it so I felt surrounded. The only good thing about this was he had the air conditioning on.

I said nothing because I didn't know what to say.

"Talk to me, Mr. Kohler."

"What was the question? Sir," I added, so he wouldn't think I was being flippant.

"You told us you'd never met Ms. Hansen before the evening you arrived in Dedhampton. Would you care to amend that statement?"

I couldn't think.

"Ms. Hansen?" I said stupidly. "I'd never met any of them."

"The dead woman. Are you stating you didn't know her?"

"Clea's name was Hansen." Stupid, stupid, stupid. I cleared my dry throat and tried again. "Clea's name was Hansen? I didn't know that. I didn't know her."

Wiznewski started tapping a finger against the vinyl back of the seat. It would drive me crazy if he kept it up. I wanted to take his hand and still it, the way Barbara does with Jimmy's leg whenever he starts jiggling it. I didn't think touching Wiznewski would go over big. More likely to get me arrested.

"That's very interesting, Mr. Kohler, because she knew you."

I wished he wouldn't call me Mr. Kohler.

"We have evidence, Mr. Kohler."

"You think I had some kind of a relationship with her? I swear I didn't."

"I didn't say you did. However, we have evidence that you had a brief encounter, shall we say a romantic encounter, with Ms. Hansen at some time in the past."

"How could you possibly know that?" I blurted. Oh, God, I was in the soup for sure.

"It will interest you to know that we found Ms. Hansen's notebooks in her room on the premises. She made an entry the night before she died. The whole group ate together that evening. Is that correct?"

"Yes." Sullenness on my part would make him even less sympathetic and more suspicious. I sat up straighter and spoke louder. "Yes, sir, we did. I didn't even speak to her. I mean, pass the butter, that kind of thing. We didn't have a conversation."

"Maybe not. However, I would like very much to hear you explain why she wrote—" He whipped a smartphone out of his pocket, thumbed it a few times, and read from the screen, "Blast from the past—an old familiar face at dinner tonight. Bruce has changed. I wonder how much. It would be fun to find out. A woman scorned never forgets. I'll have to think up a way to embarrass him."

I could feel my cheeks and the back of my neck heat up, hotter than when I'd been out in the broiling sun chipping away at that damn boat. My face had to be brick red.

"Jesus Christ!" I burst out. "I was only fifteen years old!"

"Why don't you tell me about it?" He had a great poker face. I couldn't tell if he expected to believe me.

I stumbled through the story. If Clea had yearned to embarrass me, she'd succeeded from beyond the grave. Wiznewski listened in silence. At least he didn't smile. I hoped the stupid, inexperienced kid I'd been wouldn't become a joke that made the rounds to every cop in the Hamptons. I wouldn't be able to look so much as a meter maid in the eye.

"This information would have come a lot better from you at the first interview," Wiznewski said. "Why didn't you tell us?"

"I didn't recognize her! She had short hair when she was a kid. I didn't realize it was her until we were cleaning up after, uh, cleaning up her room and found a picture. Then I remembered her green eyes, and the whole thing came back to me."

"She'd changed her hair." Wiznewski repeated my words, hefting them in some mental balance. "She hadn't changed her name, though."

"I didn't know her name." I couldn't afford to get angry. But I couldn't help leaking exasperation. "It was part of the deal I turned down."

"What a pity." I suspected mockery, but the deadpan face was still in place. He must be thinking how he wouldn't have said no to a blow job when he was fifteen. He must think he would have been in heaven. "Did you tell anyone about this incident at the time?"

"When I was fifteen? You're going to track down someone I knew that long ago?" Maybe out here in the boonies—and the Hamptons were the boonies as far as the locals were concerned, all the chic was part-time or imported—you knew where all your teenage friends were thirty years later. But I was a Manhattan boy to the bone. I still had the apartment, but the neighborhood had changed beyond recognition. I had jumped up a class, too, by going to college. Mentioning the city, though, would be a dumb move. The locals must have a chip on their shoulder the size of a million-dollar beach house about the way New York City intruded on their country paradise every summer.

"Did you tell anyone at the time?" he repeated.

Duh. Of course I did. If I hadn't been so flustered, I would have remembered right away that I'd told Jimmy all about it. The odds were in my favor that he'd remember too. Neither of us had started having blackouts at that age. Not every time we drank, anyhow. Nor had the parochial-school girls we knew ever made that kind of offer.

"Jimmy knew," I babbled, feeling like a candidate for hanging reprieved with the rope around his neck. "You can ask him right now. He'll tell you. We were just kids, and I really didn't know her name."

"What a coincidence," Wiznewski said. "Did you mention it to Mr. Cullen when you realized who she was?"

Shit! Why hadn't I? Because I valued Jimmy's good opinion,

that's why. It wasn't my fault I hadn't done what you'd think an innocent person would do in the circumstances. Of course I should have mentioned it to Jimmy. He was my best friend. Oh, man, I hated this self-honesty shit. Digging a little deeper, I had to admit the real reason I hadn't told Jimmy was that I knew what he'd say. Even though I hadn't dreamed the cops could possibly find out, he would have told me to go and tell them.

Chapter Eight

I walked into the kitchen carrying a stack of greasy dinner plates piled high with bones and other detritus of an all-out barbecue. Barbara snatched two fingers out of her mouth and her other hand, dripping, out of a bowl of sticky chocolate oobleck. Stewie bent over the table with a blowtorch, welding crème brûlée. Stephanie and Jeannette peered over his shoulder.

"Hey! Easy does it on the chocolate pudding," I said.

"Leave her alone!" Stephanie and Jeannette chorused.

"It's brownies, anyhow." Barbara glowered. "Don't critique the process."

What did I say? Just joshing the way we always did. The others had only beaten me to the kitchen by five minutes, and alliances were already forming.

Cindy stood at the sink.

"Want to put those dishes down?" She smiled at me over her shoulder.

Hands encased in yellow latex gloves, she scrubbed at the crusty residue of baked beans that rimmed a Pyrex dish.

"Want some help?" I asked. "I can dry."

"That's okay," Cindy said. "But if you want to hang out, be my guest."

"Or you could make yourself useful," Barbara told my back. She stalked to the refrigerator, opened the door, and gazed at the packed shelves.

"Done!" Stewie threw up his hands like a rodeo cowboy

who's just roped the calf. He thrust two exquisite crème brûlées into my hands. The little fluted cups were still warm. "Here, Mary, take these in."

"Smile when you say that, buster."

When I came back into the kitchen, Barbara had grabbed a dish towel and bonded with Cindy. Stewie, Jeannette, and Stephanie had taken the rest of the crème brûlées to the table and hadn't come back.

"First year in a clean and sober house," Cindy said, evidently answering a question from Barbara. She turned the hot water on full and sloshed a big bowl of soapsuds from side to side. "I know Karen from the program. Last summer I didn't get much vacation. The summer before that I was getting clean and sober. And before that, well, I was a bit of a party girl. What about you?"

"I wish I'd ever been a party girl," Barbara said. "I always sat on the good girl side of the aisle."

Cindy laughed.

"I guess you'd call me a bad girl. Still, I've enabled my share of alcoholics."

"Yeah, well, I've got Jimmy and Bruce."

"Two guys sounds like a party to me."

"Not that much of a party," Barbara disclaimed. "Jimmy and I have been together forever. Bruce is kind of a fun add-on."

"Gee, thanks," I chipped in. "Don't mind me."

"He's kind of new in sobriety," Barbara said. Dammit, was she warning Cindy off?

"Handle with care, huh?" Cindy grinned at me.

"I know, mind my own business." Barbara took a dripping plate from Cindy's hands. "I have a long history of progress, not perfection, in that area."

"Especially with us," I said. I whisked a clean dish towel off the rack and held up my hand for the next rinsed plate.

"I think that's sweet."

"They like it," Barbara said.

"We humor her," I told Cindy.

"Like I said, sweet. So how did you all get in the house?"

"Oh, Jimmy knows Lewis from the program."

Cindy reached into the sink, released the drain, and watched as flecks of culinary debris swirled and vanished with a sucking sound. "Interesting how people connect."

"Did you know Clea?" Barbara asked. "I still can't believe this happened."

"Neither can I," Karen said. She paused in the kitchen doorway. "Do I smell brownies?"

Barbara squawked and leaped for the oven. Cindy produced and handed off a couple of oven mitts like a nurse in the operating room. Crisis averted, we made room for Karen in what actually had become a circle. Spontaneous group therapy.

"Karen, this must have been such a shock for you," Barbara said. "You knew her, right? You hadn't just met her like Cindy and me." She lowered her voice. "What's the story with her and Phil?"

Karen leaned her Amazon frame against the refrigerator door.

"It's kind of complicated. When Lewis and I decided we wanted to organize a clean and sober house a few years back, everybody told us we had to talk to Oscar. He's kind of Mr. AA out here. Clea was in Oscar's house last summer and the summer before. Two years ago, she and Oscar were an item."

As Karen spoke Oscar's name, Barbara shot me a look she no doubt thought was subtle. Luckily, Cindy had her eyes on Karen, and Karen was blowing onto a hot brownie.

"No kidding," Barbara said. "Serious?"

Karen laughed.

"Not serious at all. Oscar is a master of the summer fling. They call him the Dedhampton Jack of Hearts."

I frowned at Barbara to forestall another telling glance. I got the point. That was Karen's story. She was sticking to it, but we didn't have to believe her.

"Do they break?" Barbara pursued. "The hearts, I mean?"

"I don't think Clea's did. Last summer she was with another guy. Ted."

"Is he back this year?"

"I haven't seen him yet," Karen said. "Though extra people pop up at Oscar's all through the season. He's got a big house."

"What does Oscar do?" I asked. "Where does the money come from?"

"Real estate developer. He's got a lot of property out here. Land in the Hamptons went through the roof a long time ago, and even in a bad economy, it's a good investment."

Money made a great motive for killing someone. Oscar had as good an opportunity as anybody to meet Clea on the beach. His house overlooked the spot where we'd found her body. Maybe he took an early run on the beach himself. Maybe he had a telescope among his fancy toys. How could Clea have become a threat? She'd been a journalist, and someone had called her a crusader. Maybe preserving the environment had been one of her causes. Environmentalists considered developers the bad guys. But Clea didn't own property herself. Unless she was an ecoterrorist, the stakes wouldn't be high enough. For him, yes, but not for her. Anyhow, an ecoterrorist might want to kill Oscar for turning cornfields into McMansions, not the other way around. Unless she tried to stop him. If that's what he was doing. If she was an activist, it shouldn't be hard for Jimmy to find out online.

"So Ted was out and Phil was in this year." Barbara was still thinking about Clea's boyfriends.

"To tell the truth, Clea hadn't made up her mind when she signed up. She wanted dibs on the room with the double bed, and she paid for two shares."

"Ohhhh," Barbara said. "Now I understand why Jimmy and I are stuck in twins, like a couple in a Fifties sitcom."

"Sorry about that," Karen said. "Lewis and I took the master bedroom, and Clea asked first."

"I guess it's Phil's room now."

"He seems to think so," Karen said.

"You say that as if he's not your favorite person." Barbara always comes right out with it. In this case, I was curious too.

"He's okay." Karen shrugged. "He's a bit of an odd duck. She may have been seeing Ted in the city too. She played them off against each other. All I know is Clea wanted to control the room."

"Pick her guy at the last minute, you mean?"

"Yeah, or have the room to herself if she wanted."

"And now it's Phil's."

"But will he stick it out all summer?" Cindy asked.

"His girlfriend died." Barbara frowned and shivered. "That would put me off a summer of fun if it was Jimmy."

"So would getting arrested for murder," I said.

The phone rang in the other room. We heard the scrape of a chair and Lewis's deep voice answering. He listened, with an occasional murmur of assent.

"Thank you, sir," he said finally. "Thank you. I appreciate that. We certainly will. Goodbye, sir."

Lewis lounged into the doorway and leaned against the jamb, so those still at the table as well as the rest of us in the kitchen could hear him.

"Listen up, people," he called. "That was the detective. We're off the hook. They did the autopsy, and the findings were consistent with drowning. He said they won't trouble us again and wished us an enjoyable summer."

Karen clapped her hands. Cindy gave me one of her snaggletoothed smiles.

"About time!" Phil exclaimed in the other room.

"Hear, hear," I heard Jimmy say.

Barbara frowned and caught my eye.

"Findings, schmindings," she said. "So she drowned. I still say she could have had help."

CHAPTER NINE

The only thing wrong with a Sunday in the Hamptons was Barbara's passion for activity.

"It's the crack of dawn," I heard Jimmy protesting as she stuck her head inside my door and threw a shoe at me.

I sat up and rubbed bleary eyes.

"Hey, stop throwing things. It's the Sabbath."

"Not for me," she said. "Shh, don't wake your roommate."

Stewie in the other bed lay humped and invisible under a heap of blankets.

"You've got a funny idea of considerate," I grumbled. I yanked my legs out from under the tangled covers. "Ow!" I massaged the cramp in my left calf.

Barbara threw the other shoe.

"It's a beautiful day, let's not waste it. Come on, there's a farm stand down the road with a Pick Your Own Strawberries patch."

"Be still, my heart." I swung my legs to the floor and stuck them into the shoes. I left the laces dangling. How the hell did she think I'd pick strawberries when I couldn't even bend enough to tie my sneakers at this hour?

Barbara held the door wide for me. I marched past her. She closed it gently.

"And no bodies before breakfast," Jimmy said.

"Hear, hear," I said. "Coffee first, corpses later."

"Cut it out, guys."

"Aw, you know we're not hardhearted really," I said. "Are you going to revive us or not?"

"I'm not stupid—I put up the coffee in the automatic pot last night."

She knew how to get our cooperation.

Twenty minutes later, she was herding us down the road like a Border collie. Sparkling drops of dew glinted on blades of grass and tender leaves. A ton of birds sang their heads off all around us.

"Come on, it's not far," Barbara chirped. "The farm stand is our next door neighbor."

"The next door neighbor is our handyman. Mr. Dowling. Cindy and I met him the other day."

"That's them," Barbara said, "Mrs. Dowling makes great pies and runs the farm stand. Mr. Dowling is a farmer and a fisherman and a bayman and the guy we call if the toilet won't flush or a squirrel gets into the house. He also does the yard work. We might as well establish relations."

"Don't expect them to fall on your neck," Jimmy warned. "The locals here need the summer people, but they don't like them much. City folks in the Hamptons have so much money and such a different agenda."

"I'm glad to hear that nobody expects me to plunge the toilet or catch the squirrel," I said.

"Karen says it's hard for locals like them to make a living these days," Barbara said. "Up island, she says, developers are buying up property and putting up McMansions on land that nine or ten generations of a family like the Dowlings have farmed. If they don't watch out, in twenty years the whole East End could be suburbs."

"Get uprooted or go broke, huh? Tough for them."

"Oh, look, Jimmy." Barbara took a couple of skipping steps and waved her hand at a field of low, bunchy plants studded with dull white flowers. "Are those potatoes?"

"How should I know? I'm a city boy, remember?"

Barbara grinned at him.

"I don't know—by the pounding of your ancestral Irish heart, maybe. I'm sure I'm right, though. Long Island grows potatoes and corn, and those plants don't look like they could be as high as an elephant's eye by the middle of the summer. Anyhow, I know what a cornfield looks like. Oooh, I've never dug a potato, could we try?"

"If you want to start off on the right foot with the Dowlings," Jimmy said, "don't begin by stealing their potatoes."

"I guess you're right. I was thinking they're in the ground—the potatoes, not the Dowlings—waiting for us to dig in and pull them out." She waggled her fingers.

"It's hard to think of dirt as property."

"It's called land, pumpkin," Jimmy said.

"It might not even be time for new potatoes, anyway," Barbara consoled herself.

"If it is, they'll have them at the farm stand," Jimmy consoled her. "Or maybe there's a pick-your-own-potatoes season."

"It doesn't turn you on even a little?" she asked. "Plunging your fingers in the soil, feeling the weight of this smooth, round, mealy miracle of nutrition that fed your grandparents?"

"My grandparents left Ireland so their descendants wouldn't have to do that," Jimmy said.

The cough and growl of a motor broke the quiet. I saw a tractor on the far side of the field. John Deere green with yellow wheels. I'd had a toy one just like it as a kid.

"There goes Dowling," I said

"And there's the stand. Good morning!" Barbara called.

Mrs. Dowling nodded as she lifted baskets of strawberries from the bed of a pickup truck and set them on the shelves. She was tall and angular, with a high forehead and dull brown hair pulled back into a wispy bun. The frown stamped on her brow and mouth looked like it didn't come off easily.

"What beautiful strawberries!" Barbara exclaimed as we neared the stand. "Did you grow them yourself?"

Mrs. Dowling glanced at the field that stretched away behind the stand. I made a sound that was one nostril short of a snort. A corner of Jimmy's mouth quirked. Barbara babbles when she's ill at ease and a lot of the time when she's not.

"I hope you've got plenty left for us to pick ourselves. Oh, what gorgeous petunias! I'd love to get some for the deck if you've got some planters we could buy."

"Planters in the back," Mrs. Dowling said. "Strawberry baskets too. Three dollars a pound, weigh when you're through. You can eat 'em, but don't pick the green ones."

"Thank you." Barbara retreated to the back of the stand. "Oh, look, guys, the planters are old whiskey barrels! Aren't they cute? Let's get a couple and put flowers on the deck."

Jimmy and I followed her around the stand. The old wooden barrels would look kind of perky filled with the bright orange marigolds and pink and purple petunias arrayed in flats to one side of the stand.

"We'd have to leave them at the end of the summer," Jimmy cautioned her.

"They cost thirty-four ninety-five each." Barbara picked up the wooden sign, which had fallen to the ground. "Do you think it's too much?"

"No, no, petunia—" Jimmy hesitated.

I grinned.

"It's okay, marigold, knock yourself out."

"Shut up, you."

"How about one thing at a time," Jimmy said. "We came for strawberries, so let's pick strawberries."

"The baskets are over here," I said. "You want the big ones?"

"Might as well," Jimmy said.

I handed him a stack of quart containers. They weren't really baskets, just soft green cardboard with holes in the bottom.

"They'll fill up fast," Barbara said. "How are we going to carry more than two each?"

"How many strawberries do you need, pumpkin?"

"Lots," she said. "It's a short season. The ones we pick ourselves are bound to be the ripest and sweetest. We can make fruit salad and strawberry shortcake."

"Just say 'yes, dear,' " I advised.

"Look, here are some big flat-bottomed baskets." Barbara stuck her arm through the handle of one and dangled it from the crook of her elbow. "Line up the containers inside this and you'll still have both hands free."

"Yes, dear."

The field started right behind the stand. Barbara led the way toward the far end.

"The plants near the stand have probably been picked over already," she said. "We can each take a row, once we're not too close."

At first I couldn't see any fruit. I said so.

"Underneath," Barbara said. She dropped to her knees and parted the powdery green leaves. "See?"

Sure enough, a cluster of bright red pincushions peeked out at us, half buried in a tangle of stems. Barbara plucked the biggest one off its stalk.

"Ahhhhh." She took a bite. Chewed it slowly. Licked juice off her fingers. "Mmm. This is the real thing, all right, ten times the flavor of the ones you get in the supermarket." She held it out. "Take a bite."

"I'll pick my own, thanks." I dropped to my knees beside her and teased a berry out from its nest of straw mulch and reddish brown earth.

Jimmy knelt slowly, one knee at a time. He opened his mouth like a giant baby bird. Barbara popped the rest of her strawberry into it.

"Mmm," we said simultaneously. The strawberry was meltingly sweet.

"So this is what they're supposed to taste like." Barbara popped another strawberry. "I'll take this row. You guys go get your own rows." She shooed us off.

"There's enough for all of us, poppet. And don't forget to put some in the basket."

"Thank you for sharing," Barbara said. The program way of telling someone to go to hell. "Go pick a strawberry."

"Yes, dear," I said. I dropped a small strawberry down her neck as I inched past her. She yowched and swatted at me. She didn't really mind.

Being one with the earth felt kind of nice. As the sun climbed higher, my arms and face started to bake pleasantly. The fruity smell of strawberries and baked earth and something even sweeter, maybe wild roses around the edges of the field, tickled my nostrils. Companionable bees zoomed around the plants that were still in blossom. I ate one strawberry for every three or four I picked until my thumb was coated in juice. In the next row, Jimmy filled baskets, a model of industry. Every time I looked over at Barbara, she was chewing.

"How many baskets do we get?" I called to her.

"As many as we can till we get too hot."

"When my back gives out," Jimmy said, "I'm outta here."

"You know, we could have bought them from the stand," I said.

"What, and miss the experience?"

A faint shout from the direction of the stand made us all look up. I rocked back on my heels. Jimmy pressed his palms against the small of his back and flexed. Barbara popped another strawberry in her mouth and squinted toward the sound.

"It's Lewis and Karen. Last night I invited her along, but she didn't seem interested. I guess she changed her mind."

"Hi, guys!" Jimmy called out, raising his arm to wave. His shoulder cracked audibly.

Karen wore a hot pink tank and pants. A straw hat as big as a market umbrella topped the ensemble.

"Wow, she looks like a strawberry smoothie herself," Barbara said. "Yoo-hoo!" she yodeled as they marched toward us, Karen in the lead. Lewis carried the baskets. New century, post-feminist world, and men were still the porters.

When they got close enough for conversation, Lewis said, "I got drafted."

"I want to make jam," Karen said. "They've got the little jars and everything in the hardware store in Amagansett."

"I've never made jam," Barbara said. "I'll help."

"We'll do it this evening," Karen said, "so we won't get too hot in the kitchen."

Clearly experienced strawberry pickers, she and Lewis each took a row beyond ours and started efficiently stripping fruit off the plants.

"How do you stay so clean?" Barbara asked. "I'm covered with strawberry juice."

Karen laughed.

"Wait till we make the jam. I dress down for that."

The baskets filled. The sun climbed. Jimmy had a confrontation with a bumblebee. Sweat started getting in my eyes. Barbara handed me a red bandanna, which I tied around my forehead.

I was about to suggest calling it quits when someone called out to us.

"Oh, look!" Karen said. "It's Oscar."

Sure enough, Oscar led a little troop of his housemates

through the field.

"Surprise, surprise," Barbara muttered. We had reached the same point in adjacent rows, so I was the only one who heard.

"I hope you left some for us," Corky said. "We're going to make jam."

"So are we," Karen said.

"I've already picked up everything we need," Oscar said. "Pectin, sugar. And I got plenty of jars. Why don't we pool resources? Use my kitchen. It's a lot bigger than yours."

"What a great idea," Karen said.

Barbara was practically bursting by the time we got back to the car.

"They planned that!"

"Maybe, poppet, but so what?"

"You weren't there when she told us Oscar's affairs were never serious. Summer fling, my eye. Right, Bruce?"

I had to agree Karen seemed to be blowing smoke.

"But still, so what?"

"Romance and intrigue, for one thing. People go to Sex and Love Addicts Anonymous for that."

"Oh, come on, not everything is an addiction," I objected.

"You only say that because you've got the one everybody knows about."

"Why do you care, peanut?" Jimmy asked.

"Because I still don't think Clea's drowning was an accident," Barbara said. "You'd like to think nothing bad could happen in a clean and sober house. But where there's steam, there's there's hot water. Romance and intrigue and murder—is it so farfetched?"

"Karen and Oscar make a steamy pair," I said, "I'll vouch for that. I'm even with you on things we don't know about bubbling beneath the surface with this crew. But how does it connect with Clea's death?"

"I don't know," Barbara said. "Yet."

Chapter Ten

"It's hard to get information out here," Barbara complained. "Everybody's a lotus eater when they're on vacation, especially at the beach. Nobody talks about anything real."

"You mean like world peace and improving the economy?"

"No, you clod, like who slept with who last summer and who's got a motive for murdering Clea."

"If Clea hadn't died, maybe they would all be talking about who slept with who last summer," I said. "I think people are more spooked than they're admitting."

We huddled together on Jimmy's little porch, talking quietly when we remembered. Barbara had a tendency to bounce and get louder when she got a bright idea. The small space bristled with the tools of Jimmy's trade: laptop, wireless router, coils of cable, adapters, and what he called peripherals. He'd have told us what each one did, but he knew from long experience we didn't want to know.

"You have to cut them out of the herd," Jimmy said. His fingers flew on the laptop's keyboard, and he jounced on his seat to the music in his headphones, of which we could hear only a faint megabass boom. "Who'd be likely to know the most?"

"Oscar and Phil," I said. "They were her lovers. And this Ted guy, if he shows up."

"Stephanie and Jeannette," Barbara said. "Women who've shared a group house know a hundred times more about each other than any guy would."

"Sez who?"

"Feminist psychologists," she retorted. "Women are relational."

"Meaning?"

"Think about the last five women you slept with."

"I can only remember two," I said. "The others, I was still drinking."

"I can't remember anyone but you, pumpkin," Jimmy said. "It's been too long and I'm getting too old."

"The five most memorable, then," she said. "Do you know how they lost their virginity? How many D&Cs they've had? How they get along with their mothers and sisters?"

"You know all that about your friends?"

"I know all that about women I've sat next to on a plane."

"You win," I said. "Let's say we push a little harder, talk to all of them: Oscar, Phil, Ted if we can, Stephanie, Jeannette. How about Karen and Lewis?"

"Them too," Barbara said, "but they didn't share a house with her last summer."

"They went to meetings with her."

"They can't share what she said in meetings," Jimmy said. "Anonymity."

"But she's dead."

"It's still wrong," he insisted. "They're our housemates. We'll be sharing shampoo and tortilla chips with them all summer."

"The police don't even think it was murder," I pointed out.

"Then they won't get in our way," Barbara said.

"And if they're right?"

"So we won't find anything that proves it was," she said.

Barbara and I found Jeannette in the kitchen, stirring a double boiler full of crème anglaise.

"You have to stir it and stir it and stir it," she said. "It's supposed to thicken, but it hasn't yet, and my arm is killing me."

Barbara used her eyebrows to give me a wordless order. I took the long-handled spoon out of Jeannette's hand and got to work.

I thought they'd start schmoozing immediately. Nope. They both headed for the refrigerator.

"Narnia isn't in there," I said. "And my back is getting cold."

They each snagged a Diet Coke. Barbara closed the door with a regretful backward glance.

"How can you drink that swill?" I asked as they popped and glugged. "It's not mostly chemicals. It's *all* chemicals."

"Better chemicals than calories," Jeannette said.

Women. I didn't bother pointing out that crème anglaise has calories.

"This stuff is thickening," I said. I held the spoon upright in the thick goo of egg yolks, sugar, and cream and let it go. It subsided very slowly against the rim of the pot.

"Let's see," Jeannette said. "It should coat the side of the spoon."

She came up behind me and leaned over my shoulder. Tendrils of brown hair fell over her forehead. A few wispy curls tickled my ear. I could feel the damp warmth of her body and smell a powdery floral scent. As she reached for the spoon, the shell necklace she wore around her neck swung forward against my shoulder.

"Sorry!" She flipped it back with a practiced gesture, so it snaked around the front of her neck and dangled down her back.

"Oh, that's pretty," Barbara said. "Let me see."

Jeannette had taken command of the crème anglaise again. I stepped back and looked at the necklace, still around Jeannette's neck but the shells held loosely in Barbara's hand. It was more of a pendant, really. A very small but convoluted whitish shell hung on a gold chain so fine I had to peer closely to see the links. The shell had ridges and grooves that swirled around to a flourish at the tip. Something had lived and squirmed in there, but not recently. On either side hung a much smaller translucent half shell, one pale yellow, the other a light peach color.

"Did you make it?" Barbara asked. "It's so delicate, I'm amazed the shells didn't break when the holes were bored."

"Oh, no, I got it like this—that is, I bought the chain. The shells were on the kind of filament you put beads on."

"Is that scungilli? I live back to back with an Italian restaurant," I explained to Jeannette.

"The big one is. It's a whelk. They come in all sizes, I guess depending on how old they are. You can find them on the beach after a high tide, sometimes even at the bay, but it's hard to find an unbroken one. The seagulls catch them live and drop them from way up in the air to crack them open."

"The little pastel pearly ones are so pretty," Barbara said.

"Jingle shells," Jeannette said. "The bay beach is covered with them, in among the rocks."

"Well, it's beautiful," Barbara said. "Did you buy it? Where can I get one?"

"N-no." Jeannette snatched up a dish towel and dabbed at her forehand and the damp pink back of her neck. "It's hot in here. If you want, you can get one of those bowls of strawberries out of the fridge. You can put them in dessert dishes, and we'll pour the cream over them and maybe a little whipped cream on top."

"I can't get a necklace like that anywhere?"

"It was a beach thing a couple of years ago," Jeannette said. "Well, actually, Oscar collects the shells. But I don't think he's making any now." She took the bowl of strawberries from Barbara's hands. Setting it on the table, she began to line up glass dessert bowls.

"I'd love to have one," Barbara persisted. "I can ask him, can't I?"

"Not a good idea," Jeannette said.

"Why not?"

Jeannette shrugged.

What was the big deal? Barbara looked disappointed. She could string her own seashells if she wanted. But I could tell she felt Jeannette's rebuff.

"Didn't Clea have one too?" Barbara bounced back and took the subject up from another angle. "That first night at dinner, I noticed some of the others had them. I thought it was a house thing."

Jeannette switched off the burner and gave the cream a final stir, frowning in concentration.

"She didn't have it on when we found her," I said. I could see her on the beach, her jaw lax and skin already dingy. I'd checked her neck for signs of bruising and seen only a blackish coil of seaweed and a stray tendril of wet, sandy hair. "Maybe it broke and washed away."

"I don't think she'd run with it," Barbara said. She started dealing strawberries into the bowls. "We could search her room again. Maybe it fell behind the dresser or something. And if nobody wants it—I hope this doesn't sound too awful—but maybe there's someone who would get her jewelry. Jeannette, you've known her for what, three years? Did she talk about her family? Did she have any sisters?"

Jeannette's lips tightened. She scooped up a ladle full of cream and poured it slowly over a mound of berries.

"Clea didn't bond with women very well."

"How do you mean?"

Before Jeannette could respond, Stephanie came in, banged open the refrigerator door, snatched up a can of Diet Coke, popped it open, and answered for her.

"She was sexually competitive."

Jeannette kept her eyes lowered as she topped off each dish with a giant strawberry.

"Don't exaggerate, Steph."

"Come off it, Jeannie," Stephanie said. She tilted her chin up and poured down a slug of Coke. A little soda dribbled down her chin. She wiped it off with the palm of her hand. "As the beach got more crowded, Clea's bikinis got skimpier and skimpier. She never joined a group of women sitting together, and she only pitched in in the kitchen when at least one of the guys was helping too. And she couldn't leave a man and woman having a private conversation alone. She'd come strutting up and butt in."

"She sounds narcissistic," Barbara said.

"If that means 'me, me, me,' she was," Stephanie said.

"Was she in therapy?" Barbara asked.

"No," Jeannette said.

"Don't drink and go to meetings was as far as it went with Clea," Stephanie said.

"How long had she been sober?" Barbara asked.

"I don't know," Stephanie said. "Jeannie?"

"Five years."

"No step work to cut the narcissism," Barbara diagnosed. " 'I'm looking after me today.' "

"She had had a rough time," Jeannette said.

"The usual, I suppose."

I'd heard enough alcoholic women share to know she meant sexual abuse. I hoped they wouldn't get explicit. I didn't want to hear the R word or see the way women looked at the closest male when they used it.

"She was adopted." Jeannette shook up a can of whipped cream and started shooting as if the dessert were men.

"Is that bad?" I asked.

"Not necessarily," Jeannette said. She set a large strawberry on top of each dessert.

"You should know," Stephanie said. "Jeannette works in adoptions. She's a social worker."

"Really?" Barbara asked. "I'm thinking about social work school. Do you like it?"

"Most of the time I love it," Jeannette said. It seemed to me she seized the change of topic with relief. "Most of the adoptive parents are great. Every once in a while a rotten one slips by us."

"How did you happen to get into it?"

"My second year field placement in social work school was an adoption agency. When I graduated, they offered me a job. Actually, I thought the birth mothers didn't get much of a break. This was years ago, and some of the workers despised them. It's gotten better."

"Sure, open adoption and all that," Barbara said. "Did Clea know her birth mother?"

"I don't know." She picked up two bowls and started across the kitchen. "Can one of you run some water and detergent in the sink?"

"Bruce will do it," Barbara said. "Was she a sexual compulsive?"

"I don't know."

"She wasn't in recovery, that's for sure," Stephanie said. She picked up two bowls and crossed the kitchen in Jeannette's wake. "She didn't go to SCA. I heard Stewie invite her to a meeting and she turned him down. And when somebody mentioned SLAA, Sex and Love Addicts Anonymous, you know? Addiction to romance and intrigue? Well, Clea said romance was not her style, but she was all for intrigue."

"She sounds like a borderline to me. Histrionic too, the whole cluster."

"To me it sounds like she was showing off," I said.

"That's what I said." Barbara ran her finger around the cooling top of the double boiler, gave the crème anglaise a farewell lick, and plunged the pot into the sink.

Chapter Eleven

Barbara hitched up the straps of her backpack so the load rode a little higher on her back and wiggled her hips to center it. She and three other women from the house were bound for a secluded cove at the foot of the cliffs near Montauk. Karen, who knew the way, had announced that the beach there was "clothing optional" and that the men were not invited. Barbara grinned as she remembered the transparent look of relief not only on Jimmy's face, as expected, but on Bruce's too. Stephanie had agreed to come once she heard no men would join the party. Jeannette had been coaxed with assurances that most likely they'd have the beach to themselves and that she could wear her bathing suit, even her muumuu, if she wanted. Barbara hoped she'd get to know the three women better, maybe have a chance to ask them more about their relationships with Clea. But even if she didn't, she looked forward to getting sunlight on her bare skin.

The drive had led them past the high dunes of Hither Hills State Park and the lush landscaping of the resort hotels along Old Montauk Highway, through Montauk Village, and onto a half-hidden road past several parking lots crammed with the SUVs and pickups of surfers. They had left Karen's car in an unmarked, unpaved lot, shouldered as much day-at-the-beach gear as they could carry, trespassed briefly on a trailer park, and descended several flights of rickety wooden stairs. Now they picked their way over a narrow strand of rocks and tide pools at the foot of the cliffs toward an untenanted stretch of paradise. Karen led the way, her tall form nearly hidden by a bulging pack and a folded lightweight lounge chair,

"What a gorgeous day!" Barbara said. "I'm so glad I came, and we aren't even there yet."

"I can't believe you talked me into this," Jeannette panted. "We could have enjoyed the gorgeous day at Dedhampton, and I wouldn't be about to have a heart attack."

"Wait up a minute," Stephanie called. "Jeannette, you lost a towel."

"Can you pick it up? I don't bend that far." Jeannette clanked to a halt. "In fact, mop the back of my neck for me and then tuck it in there somewhere."

"Let's take a break," Karen said. She pulled a plastic water bottle from the utility belt slung around her hips. Raising it to her lips, she swigged, sloshed, and spat the first mouthful before taking a gulp and passing the bottle to Barbara. "Don't drink too much."

"Were you a Girl Scout, Karen?" Barbara said. Her own patchy outdoor lore came from long-ago scouting experiences.

"No, just a dedicated hiker. Lewis and I have done about half the Appalachian Trail."

"So this is just a stroll in the park for you." Jeannette eyed a large rock. "The question is, if I sit, can I get up again?"

"Better not," Karen said. "It'll only make it harder to go on."

"Now, that I can believe."

"Oh, wow, look!" Stephanie pointed out to sea. "Dolphins!"

The others picked their way over the rocks to join her at the water's edge. A pair of sleek gray dolphins flowed past them parallel to the shore in synchronized perfection. Their half-moon dorsal fins cut through the water. As the women watched, they arched and leaped out of the water, landing smoothly to continue on their way.

"That's what I call jumping for joy," Barbara said. "C'mon, Jeannette, admit you're glad you came."

"Ask me when I'm safely back at the house."

"Break's over, ladies," Karen said. "We need to move before our muscles start to lock up." She forged ahead and disappeared around a bend in the shaggy, eroded cliff. Her voice floated back.

"You're almost there. We've got it all to ourselves!"

Barbara increased her pace, rounded the bend, and stopped short. The cove nestled in the curve of the towering cliff between two headlands. The far end shimmered in a veil of haze. In the foreground, sea and virgin sand sparkled, every glint, grain, and droplet crisply delineated. Surf crashed intermittently on a broad border of flat, hard-packed beach the color of coffee cream. The lacy edge of the breakers formed a single rim with an unbroken line of high rollers behind it.

Karen dropped her gear on the ocean side of a magnificent weathered driftwood log as long as a telephone pole. Standing on one foot, she stripped to the buff without ceremony.

"I'm going right in! Come on, you must be sweltering. We can set up afterward." With a shrill whoop, she galloped down the beach and splashed into the water. Her tanned body flashed as she arched and dove through a breaker almost as gracefully as the dolphins.

"Woo-hoo!" she yelped, waving.

"Is it cold?" Barbara called back.

"Exhilarating!"

"I know what that means," Barbara said as the others drew up beside her. "Icy."

"Look, I'm standing." Karen waved her arms above her head, then let them fall to rest on the bright skin of a soaring roller. Her head bobbed up as she sailed over the wave, which broke with a crash against the shore.

"It looks like she's floating," Jeannette said.

"No, it's an illusion," Barbara said. "She jumped. I love jumping the rollers. For a moment, you defy gravity."

"That *is* an incentive," Jeannette said. "I've been fighting a losing battle with gravity my whole life."

"I'm a lot shorter than Karen," Stephanie said. "The water comes up to her boobs out where she is. I'll be submerged."

"If you can't get out that far, you can jump through the breakers," Barbara said. "That's fun too."

"Why are you standing there with forty pounds of paraphernalia on your backs?" Karen sailed over another wave and fell back into a float, shaking out her long hair like a mermaid and wiggling her toes just above the surface.

"Good question," Barbara said. She freed herself from the heavy pack with a quick twist of her shoulders. Kicking off her shoes, she hopped on one foot while she stripped off socks and shorts. She pulled a stretchy tank top over her head, laughing at the shock of cool air on her bare breasts. She slung her thumbs into the elastic that held up abbreviated panties and snapped them a couple of times. "Okay, I'm in." She drew her thumbs downward along her thighs, stepped out of the panties, and tossed them over her shoulder as she ran down the beach. With a triumphant howl, she dove through a breaking wave the color of celery crowned with a froth of foam.

An hour later, pleasantly exhausted, Barbara lay on her back in the sun, a thick towel under her and a smaller one rolled behind her neck, with the big log as a headboard. The other three lay beside her, equally relaxed.

"Like a row of salt sticks baking in the oven," she murmured. "God, it feels so good to be naked."

"I told you," Karen said. "Anyone need more sun block? Some of that skin hasn't seen daylight in a long time."

"After twenty years with Jimmy," Barbara said, "I couldn't

possibly forget. He'd be many times dead without it."

"You're more olive toned, though," Stephanie said.

"Yeah, and hopelessly codependent. I used to put the sun block on me to encourage him to do it."

"I had a skin cancer scare a couple of years back," Stephanie said. "So now I'm careful. But it's not like I spend the whole summer at the nude beach. I've let go so many addictions, I gotta let myself have a little pleasure once in a while."

"Me, I'm so pink and white you could use me to decorate a nursery," Jeannette said. "I slathered myself with the stuff, but maybe I should put on my muumuu."

"No!" The other three spoke in unison.

"You said you'd try it for an hour if nobody else showed up on the beach."

"Admit it feels good."

"And no lying."

"I hate people seeing my body," Jeannette said. "I've been ashamed of being fat since I was a kid, and that means a lot of years."

Barbara hesitated between assuring her she wasn't fat and asking how old she was. The first would be a codependent lie. She would have guessed Jeannette's age as close to her own, but maybe she was older. She had no wrinkles, but her eyes looked tired.

"I'm forty-five," Jeannette announced, "and sometimes I feel every minute."

"I was a fat kid," Stephanie said.

Three pairs of eyes flew open.

"You're kidding," Barbara said. "I can't believe you ever had a weight problem."

"Believe it. I ate constantly. I used to steal food all the time. My brothers called me The Blob. Then when I hit puberty, I became anorexic."

"They say you can't be too rich or too thin," Barbara said.

"They also say an alcoholic should just say no and try a little willpower," Karen said. "Wrong!"

"I know anorexia is an eating disorder," Barbara said, "but I don't get it."

"I got teased so much, I hated them all," Stephanie said. "I decided to starve until they'd have to admit I was thin enough. If I was perfect, they'd have to leave me alone."

"Fuck-you starving," Jeannette said. "Like fuck-you eating."

"Sounds like you've gone through it yourself," Stephanie said.

"Starving, no," Jeannette said. "But I could write a book on binges. Crunchy is fuck-you eating, and sugar is poor-me eating. I'm better at poor-me, which is probably why I look like a blimp."

"You don't!" Barbara sat up. "I think your body is goddessy."

"Yeah, right," Jeannette said. "Tell it to my mirror."

Stephanie rolled from her back onto her stomach. Raising her upper body onto her elbows, she shook sand from the top half of her towel.

"One reason I chose our house is because everybody is into food. I thought I wouldn't be able to starve. My period is still touch and go, and I worry about ever being able to have children."

"I'm starting to get hot flashes," Jeannette remarked.

"I never thought I'd get this old without having a baby," Barbara said.

"How old are you?" Karen asked.

"Going on forty—biological clock age, though it feels more like a time bomb."

"So why don't you?" Stephanie asked.

"Same reason Jimmy and I don't get married. Fear."

"Fear of relapse?"

"Not so much, after almost twenty years in recovery. It's hard to imagine it. But he could still pass on alcoholic genes."

"Lewis and I got married on our tenth sober anniversary," Karen said. "We met in rehab and went straight into AA together afterwards. But you keep saying 'one day at a time' and wondering how long it'll last."

"Doesn't Jimmy want kids?" Jeannette asked.

"He's not sure," Barbara said. "I think he'd make a fabulous dad. But he's an ACOA. I think he's scared of perpetuating the alcoholic family, even if he doesn't drink."

"Lewis doesn't want kids for the same reason," Karen said.

"And you're reconciled to that?" Jeannette asked.

Karen hesitated.

"Not exactly," she said finally. "It took me a long time to, well, embrace monogamy. Lewis got a vasectomy, but I need to know I have options."

Judging by the scene Bruce had stumbled onto at Oscar's, Barbara thought, Karen hadn't embraced monogamy yet. She rolled onto her side and raised herself on an elbow, turning away from Karen to hide her telltale face. They were all being very candid in this nudie women's group. Why wouldn't Karen admit she still had the occasional fling?

"I did get pregnant once," Karen said. "I had an abortion."

"Did the guy know?" Stephanie asked.

"Did Lewis find out?" Jeannette asked.

"Yes and no," Karen said. "I wouldn't have told Lewis unless I was ready to leave him. I thought I might be, but in the end I wasn't."

"Were you in love with the guy?" Stephanie asked.

"Was he in love with you?" Jeannette asked.

"Yes and no," Karen said.

Barbara wondered if the guy in question was Oscar. In her opinion, Oscar was in love only with Oscar. The veneer of geniality hid either a ruthless sexual predator or a sexual compulsive. This group had more than its share of charismatic narcissists. Oscar, Clea. Phil was equally self-centered, if not charismatic.

"So the guy didn't want the baby?" Stephanie asked.

"Actually, he did," Karen said. "He didn't care about me—not enough. But he was in recovery too. He reacted to being an ACOA the opposite way from Lewis."

"He didn't have a dysfunctional family?"

"Of course he did," Karen said. "But instead of not wanting to risk it, he wanted a do-over. He wanted us to have the baby, break the pattern, and do it right." She got to her feet, brushed sand off her legs, and marched down toward the inviting surf.

Barbara rolled over onto her stomach and arranged a towel in a kind of sun roof, held off the back of her head by her shoes stuck upright into the sand. Suppose the guy who wanted a baby had been Oscar. Had he made the same offer to Clea? Clea was a lot younger than the rest of them. Had she wanted children? And even if she had, would she have wanted to raise a kid with Oscar?

Chapter Twelve

"If we're having the meeting," Shep said, "let's have the meeting."

We all lay sprawled or propped on wicker furniture or cushions on Oscar's back upstairs deck. It faced west, away from the ocean but toward a spectacular fiery sunset. We were all stuffed with alder-smoked salmon and strawberry shortcake.

Barbara and I shared a piece of furniture that didn't exactly swing or rock but jounced pleasantly. Jimmy sat on a giant cushion at Barbara's feet, his head against her knees.

"We need to move the chairs." Lewis took off his Docksiders, shook sand out of them, and put them on again. He was inches too long for the wicker chaise longue. His legs were tanned and covered with golden hair that glinted almost red in the waning light.

"Are we doing it out here?" Barbara asked. "I don't think this rocker moves."

"Neither does this," Cindy said. She and Corky were perched on a teak chest topped with the kind of cushions you sit on in boats. "What have you got in here, Oscar? Rocks?"

"Rope. Fishing tackle. An anchor you could use for that boat I hear you're working on."

"Really? That'd be great!"

"Hey, wait a minute," I said. "When I signed up for the maiden voyage of this ship, I thought we weren't going anywhere I couldn't wade home."

"Too late, sailor. You've got an unbreakable contract." Cindy bared her incisors at me. Her eyes twinkled. I was getting addicted to that wolfish grin of hers.

"You can anchor in shallow water," Oscar said. "You might want to fish for fluke. I can show you on a chart."

"Come on, guys! Service!" Shep said. That's program speak for "cut the cackle and let's hold hands and say the Serenity Prayer." I'd never done it out in the open like this. I looked left and right and over my shoulder. Dunes screened us from the houses on either side. Oscar's property, which must be worth millions, was deep. The occasional car passing on the road could barely be heard. And twilight was falling on the beach. Most people who couldn't get enough of looking at water shifted to the bay side at the end of the day anyway. If they wanted sunset over the ocean, they should move to California.

In the end, everybody except Oscar took a hand in rearranging the chairs. They didn't quite form a circle. But everybody could see everybody else, more or less, without getting a neck spasm. We started with the Serenity Prayer. Then we went around the circle with names and labels.

"Hi, I'm Bruce, I'm an alcoholic." I didn't even grimace when I said it anymore.

Not everyone in this hybrid meeting was lucky enough to be a drunk.

"Hi, I'm Barbara, recovering in Al-Anon."

"Stewie, gratefully recovering in AA, ACOA, SCA, DA, and various other programs."

"I'm Ted. Addict and alcoholic."

Clea's last-but-one boyfriend had fair skin, a peeling nose, and a baby face on top of a beanpole body. I noticed he and Phil sat as far from each other as they could on the crowded deck.

Oscar volunteered to qualify—tell his story.

Barbara put her lips to my ear. I smelled strawberries as she whispered, "Principles before personalities."

One definition of anonymity. Or my sponsor once put it, "You can get something out of anyone's experience, strength, and hope even if you think they're an asshole."

All AA stories are the same, even when they're different. Oscar had been clean and sober for longer than Jimmy. Before that, he'd partied with the rich and famous. He'd done his share of stupid shit. Stumbled into the closet instead of the bathroom in the middle of the night and peed on his shoes. Dropped acid and set off the alarms in an art museum. That won him an unwilling grin from me. Jimmy, still propped up against Barbara's shins, reached up and grabbed me by the ear, pulling me down so he could whisper.

"See? I told you if you listen long enough you'll hear your story."

He released my ear. I grabbed him by the hair to whisper back.

"And here I thought we'd done something original."

"Hallucinogens and grandiosity—horse and carriage."

Then Barbara shushed us and we shut up.

When Oscar finished, they went around the circle so everyone could share. I passed. Playing it safe. Stewie talked about how he missed Clea and cried a little. Phil said how pissed off he was at the police for picking on him. Everybody listened to both of them in respectful silence, the way they do in meetings. I hoped Cindy would drop a clue or two about her outside life, but she didn't. She was pretty funny about how badly she'd screwed up while she was drinking. Ted said he was still in shock from Clea's death and wished he could have been here before she died. He and Phil kind of sizzled at each other, like electric wire in water. But neither broke the no-crosstalk rule. I thought we were home free. Then Barbara raised her hand. I have to hand it to her; she's good at weaving recovery jargon into whatever damn thing she wants to say.

"I need to talk about Clea," she said. "The police think it was an accident. I keep telling myself 'Let go and let God,' but I can't turn it over. I have a disease of not minding my own business. I know that. But is it so terrible to want more closure?" She might as well have said, "I plan to snoop."

I looked at Jimmy. He had slumped over with his elbow propped on his knee and two fingers held to the furrow between his eyebrows, as if identifying the location of the headache the woman he loved could be.

I slapped a supportive hand on his shoulder.

"Oy veyzmir," he murmured.

When the meeting ended, they brought out coffee, fruit, and a couple of Mrs. Dowling's pies. Everybody stood up to shake out the kinks and started milling around. We got Barbara in a corner, out of earshot of the others.

"What do you think you're doing?" Jimmy's voice was strained with the effort not to screech. "Hi, I'm Barbara, I'm nosy, and my inner T-shirt says 'Tethered Goat.' "

"I was just sharing," Barbara protested. "So I stirred the pot a little."

"What do you think will happen?"

"If it really was an accident, nothing. If it wasn't, you don't want a murderer running around getting away with it, do you?"

"Shoot me now, Jesus," Jimmy breathed. "If someone comes after you, who do you think will have to jump into the line of fire?"

Barbara waxed indignant, not a stretch for her.

"I don't need protecting! I can fight my own battles, thank you! Only there won't be any battles. You're just projecting."

It occurred to me that I was superfluous to this conversation. I cleared my throat, jerked a thumb at the other end of the deck, decided they'd already forgotten me, and fled.

I found Cindy perched on a rail with her feet propped against a big planter filled with marigolds and petunias. She held a Styrofoam cup of coffee in both hands.

"You never quite mingle, do you," I greeted her. "You're always a little apart. Are you one of those terminal loners they talk about?"

"I'm not alone, I'm with you. Have a perch." She shifted her butt along the rail and made room for my feet on the rim of the planter. "You didn't share."

"I still have trouble baring my soul in meetings," I said. "I didn't feel up to it tonight. Or playing the clown either."

"Is that what you do?"

"Yeah, that's my defense."

"What's your friend Barbara up to?"

"Nothing much."

"Bullshit. She still thinks it's murder, doesn't she?" She clamped a small hand on my jaw and swiveled my head around so I had to meet her eyes. I breathed a little harder. "How about you?"

I shrugged as her palm slid away from my face, scraping across my sandpapery cheek. I mostly didn't bother shaving out here. I caught up in the city whenever I went in to do a few days' work.

"Am I a suspect?"

I couldn't tell if she was kidding or not. But if an "us" and "them" got established, I didn't want her on the other team.

"You're new like us—the three of us, I mean. We don't know these people the way they know each other."

"Quite the clan. Is this your first group house?"

"Yeah." I fished in my back pocket for a pack of cigarettes. "Yours?"

"I had a share out in Montauk a few years back." She handed

me a large clam shell. "Ashtray."

"Thanks. House like this? What kind of people?"

"Not as upscale as Oscar's house. Montauk is more down home and working class than most of the Hamptons. Bunch of folks who liked to fish and drink beer."

"I guess you've left them behind, huh? Was one of them your boyfriend?"

"Nope. What kind of work do you do?"

"I temp." It sounded bald and unglamorous. "Pink collar all the way."

"It's okay to have a recovery job."

"I suppose you could call it that. Though it was my drinking job too. I'm still trying to figure out what I want to be when I grow up. How about you?"

"City government."

"Pushing paper?"

She shrugged.

A burst of laughter drew our attention. The main group, clustered in the center of the deck, consisted of Oscar and a harem.

"Sometimes charisma can be so annoying," I said.

Cindy laughed.

"You don't know you've got it too? Don't worry, not everyone is drawn to the Pasha of the Hamptons."

It sounded like she was sending me a signal, but I wasn't sure. To my own surprise, I got flustered. I guess flirting was one of those skills I'd never practiced sober. That meant I'd have to learn it all over again.

Before I'd figured out what to say next, someone came over and set a bowl-sized candle with a pungent scent on the railing next to me. Citronella. Twilight had turned to night without my noticing, and the bugs were out. I picked the candle up and toasted Cindy with it. The light flickered on her smiling face. I decided I didn't have to say anything. I edged a little closer till our shoulders touched. She didn't seem to mind.

The conversations of the others on the deck were just background noise until shouting broke out. Two angry male voices dominated the hubbub. The rest of them drew closer as if to pull the combatants apart, then fell outward, like a kaleidoscope shifting, to get out of the way as they started swinging at each other. I could see Ted's head, higher than the rest, bobbing as he tried to land a punch. I didn't see his opponent, but the string of curses identified Phil.

I slid from the rail and debated whether to jump in. I wanted her to see me be a hero. But with such a crowd, did they need my help to stop the fight?

I heard Shep bleating, "Come on, guys, break it up. Stop it. Work your program."

Oscar hovered well back of the action, shouting AA slogans.

"Easy does it! Live and let live!"

The twelve steps didn't work so well with fisticuffs. Shouts from the guys and squeals from some of the women indicated that the fight had brought out the arena hound in most of them.

Cindy jumped down from the rail.

"This is ridiculous!"

She shot forward like a cannonball, boring her way through the knot of spectators into the center of the ring. They froze in stupefaction long enough for me to slip through in her wake. I got there in time to see her chop their straining arms apart, upend Ted by hooking a leg around his, and stop Phil's furious rush with a head butt that could have cracked a coconut.

"Oscar!" Her command voice would have done credit to a starship captain. "Take this one in the house and clean him up. Someone give him a handkerchief and some ice."

Phil shook his head like a baffled bull. His nose streamed blood. But he went meekly into the house with Oscar and

Corky, who had whipped out what looked like a dish towel and scooped up the half-melted contents of the ice bucket.

Cindy caught my eye.

"Bruce. Good. You take this one." Ted knelt on his hands and knees. He looked like a disheveled table. His "Save the Whales" sweatshirt, ripped through in front, hung down on either side. He stumbled but eventually got himself upright. Cindy gripped his upper arm as if she were giving him the bum's rush, except that to hold him she had to reach up, like a toddler crossing the street. I had to smile. I turned my face away, though.

"Yes, ma'am." I stepped forward and put my arm around as close to Ted's shoulders as I could reach.

"You!" she snapped at the shaken warrior. "What's your name?"

"Ted," he said obediently.

"Do you know the rest? It's not a meeting!"

"Ted Mailer."

"Where are you?"

"Uh, right here."

"Where's here?"

"Oscar's deck."

"And where's that?"

"Dedhampton. Dedhampton Beach."

"What date is it? What time? And who's the president?"

"If you're checking for concussion," I said, "you should probably ask Phil those questions—and yourself."

"I'll go," Barbara said. "I know how to do a mental status. I'll make sure Phil's oriented times three and check that his pupils are the same size. Then, if he's okay, we'll drive him back to the house."

Jimmy put his arm around her, and they marched inside.

"Cindy?" I said. I'm in love, I wanted to say. I'm awestruck. "Your head took quite a crack too. Shouldn't you—"

"I'm fine!" she said. "And I know perfectly well where I am—in the middle of a pack of staring fools. Shoo!"

Sheepishly, the herd retreated.

"Just help him wash his face and make sure nothing's broken, Bruce," she said in a softer voice. As I started to lead Ted away, she called after me, "And find a different bathroom. Keep them away from each other. I don't want to have to make peace all over again."

Making peace, she called it. My face wore a foolish grin, and I didn't care.

"There's a bathroom next to my room," Ted said. I had forgotten about him and started wandering down the hall. He came up behind me. "You're headed in the right direction."

He pushed open the third door down, his arm passing easily over my head. It wasn't the master bathroom, but it was big enough, with cold mottled blocks of tile that had to be marble and a wall of mirror that stretched to the ceiling. Ted didn't have to stoop as he surveyed his face. A shiner was making a nice start around his right eye.

"Fuck, fuck, fuck," he said. "This wasn't supposed to happen."

"If you want to hear God laugh, make a plan," I said. I'd heard it in the rooms. "You could use some ice on that."

"There's an ice machine," he said. "In the kitchen."

"I'll get it. Back in a minute."

"And Bruce, is it? Thanks."

"Hey, no problem."

I'd already seen the kitchen. It was still a high-tech marvel, but I didn't linger. I grabbed a bowl, filled it with ice, and got the hell out before anybody came in and started talking. I even found my way back to Ted's bathroom without getting lost.

"This is so embarrassing," Ted said as he dabbed ice on his eye and tossed the ruined sweatshirt in the trash. Violence one, whales zero.

"You're not an alcoholic?"

"Sure I am," he said. "Why?"

"Never mind." Barbara had trained me so well that every time I heard "embarrassing," I thought "Al-Anon." "I guess you were upset about Clea, huh?"

Ted punched his right fist into his left palm and then winced. I guess his knuckles had taken part of the beating.

"I can't understand how she could have taken up with that twerp! If I thought he had anything to do with her drowning, I'd kill him!"

"Easy does it," I said. "The cops said nobody killed her. She did drown, you know. They couldn't make a mistake about that."

"Oh, God, the autopsy! I can't bear to think about them cutting her up. She was so beautiful!"

He clutched his hair in both hands and pulled it till it stood up, like a mourner in a Greek tragedy.

"So you and Clea were tight, huh?"

"I thought so." He sat down on the lid of the toilet seat and gripped his hair again, but didn't pull it this time. He rested his elbows on his knees like a big praying mantis. His legs stuck out so far that I had to lean against the door to fit inside the room. "We had such a great time last summer. But you could never tell with Clea. She was that kind of woman."

"Aren't you cold?" I asked. His naked white skin was blotched with red and dotted with goose pimples. "Have you got another sweatshirt?"

"In my room," he said, "first door to the right. On the bed. It's another 'Save the Whales.' Thanks. Again."

"Forget it. You don't have to keep thanking me."

I wouldn't be you, poor boob, I thought as I tossed the sweatshirt over my arm and ambled back into the bathroom. I figured group house shirts were a lot like motel towels. They migrated into your luggage and home without any conscious thought on your part. But two of them—"Save the Whales" must be his personal manifesto.

"Oscar's got quite a place." I pulled words out of my head at random. "You get to sleep within earshot of the ocean. Mother Nature's white noise machine."

"It would be great," Ted said, "if it wasn't so politically incorrect to build a house on a dune."

"The damage is already done," I said.

"That doesn't comfort me," he said. "But I like knowing the ocean can take it back any time it wants. Clea used to say that people like Oscar say, 'I own this dune,' and Mother Nature says, 'Sez who?' "

"I'm really sorry, man. I only met her the one night before it happened. She must have been quite a woman."

"She was. Listen, can we get out of this bathroom?"

"Sure. I was just keeping you company while you pulled yourself together. You want some coffee? I saw a spiffy machine in the kitchen that must make it in no time flat."

"I don't want to see anybody," he said.

I could understand that. Should I offer to go make the coffee? No. I wanted to hear more about Clea.

"Let's go and see if the coast is clear," I suggested. "If it's not, we can skip the coffee. Tell me more about Clea. What was she like?"

"Good question," he said. "Passionate. Fickle. Dedicated. Exasperating. Insecure. Cruel."

"Good words. I thought you'd say, 'A sexy alcoholic woman with codependency issues.' Are you a journalist like she was?"

"Ha! No, not me," Ted said. "I'm a counselor. I work at a clinic in Queens."

"What kind of stuff did she write?" I asked.

"Environmental stuff when she could get the assignments. She'd had articles in most of the neighborhood papers and once or twice in *Newsday.* Not the *New York Times* or anything like it. And if she had to, she did obits and baby showers or whatever they would pay for."

"So being out here was a working vacation for her?" Journalists had a thousand ways to get up people's noses.

"When I was with her last summer, she didn't go anywhere without a notebook or a digital recorder."

The cops had the notebooks, as I'd found out the hard way. This was the first I'd heard about a digital recorder. The detectives probably hadn't interviewed Ted. He hadn't showed up in Dedhampton till they'd already dropped the investigation. If the autopsy had turned up evidence that she'd been killed, they might have tracked him down in the city. Phil would have been eager to tell them about the rival boyfriend. But now they wouldn't follow it up.

Could the cops have her recorder tucked away? Maybe it had nothing incriminating on it. No reason to mention it to me. But when Wiznewski told me they'd found Clea's notebooks, he was trying to scare me into some kind of admission. It seemed to me if they'd also had her digital recorder, he would have said so. Besides, Ted said she'd taken it everywhere. If she wanted to jot down a thought while running on the beach, would she stop to write in a notebook? No. She'd take the recorder so she could keep running while she made her notes. She could tuck it in her cleavage. But if she went for a swim, she'd have to leave it on the beach. So where was it? We'd arrived on the beach before the cops. We'd seen her towel, her sweatshirt, her running shoes. No recorder. It should have been there—if she'd been alone on the beach. Okay, what if she hadn't been alone? What if whoever was there had taken the recorder? The odds in favor of murder got a lot shorter.

"Tell me more about what Clea wrote," I said. "For instance."

The kitchen was still deserted. I figured he was still hurting. He moved stiffly, and the eye was getting darker and more swollen by the minute.

"Sit," I said. "I'll make the coffee." I started opening cabinets. Found filters, mugs, and sugar. Ground coffee in the freezer, milk in the fridge. I could have ground whole beans, but there were limits.

"Clea liked to write about things she could get worked up about," Ted said. "Out here, that would be the vanishing baymen versus the rich sports fishermen, the surfcasters with their dune buggies versus the nesting piping plovers, that kind of thing."

"The embattled environment versus the developers?" I poured water, pressed a button, and watched the nectar of the gods start to drip.

"Oh, yes," he said. "She loved to pick on Oscar. She could be all over him, the way most of the women are, and then turn around and give him a hard time about greed and the land."

I needed a cigarette. I had a choice of ashtrays: a chunk of millefiore glass from Murano with a depression for the butts or a giant clamshell from the beach outside. I pulled out my pack and shook out a cancer stick.

"Want one?"

"Oh, hell, why not?" Ted said. "Another of the things I do that I don't approve of. Like loving Clea."

We smoked in silence for a while. The coffee pot hissed and gurgled.

"Was she a good journalist?" I asked.

Ted blew out a slow stream of smoke.

"Writing came easy to her, I know that," he said. "I'm no literary critic."

"I mean, as an investigative reporter. Was she good at putting two and two together? Did she ever dig up a cover-up or blow the whistle on a crime?"

"Maybe not as good as she thought she was," Ted said. "But those were her aspirations, all right. She was a bit of an adrenaline junkie, and that applied to her work as well as her, let's say, personal relationships."

How far would she go? I would have asked if I'd thought Ted could give me the answer. Far enough for someone to arrange for her to drown? Someone smart enough not only to set it up, but to fool the cops?

Chapter Thirteen

"It's our turn to go to the dump today," Phil announced. He had been hovering when I stumbled out of the bedroom and tagged along as I staggered into the bathroom. I did my best to ignore him.

My eyes in the mirror over the sink looked what an amateur would have called bleary. For an old alkie like me, this was bright eyed and bushy tailed.

"We have to sort everything for recycling," Phil said, "so we should get started right away. I've already had breakfast."

"Thank you for sharing." I bared my teeth in the mirror and wondered if the minty taste of toothpaste would refresh or nauseate me. "Now go away."

"You're my buddy," he informed me. "It's on the schedule."

I began to get the hang of Phil. He had no doubt made up the schedule.

"Oh, go and bag some bottles. Stack some newspapers." Damn, he already had me thinking about the task. I wasn't ready to think. "Or if you want to make yourself useful, bring me a cup of coffee."

The man actually went and did it. Then, while I drifted through the kitchen in slow motion, he went out on the deck and scrubbed garbage cans. Nuts. The smell of ammonia did not improve my Cheerios and blueberries.

Lewis, barefoot and bare-chested, banged open the refrigerator door. I sprayed Cheerios out my nose.

"Sneak up behind me, why don't you," I said. "I need a thrill or two with breakfast. If you're looking for the milk, it's here."

Lewis poured himself coffee and stared out at Phil, who had turned a garden hose on his handiwork and was whistling through his teeth.

"What the hell are you doing?" he asked.

"You gotta keep up with the chores, or the whole house will fall into chaos. These cans stank. We should do this every few days. And some people aren't sorting. I found smelly stuff, fish scraps and bones, in the paper garbage and tinfoil in with the bottles."

"Insane," I told Lewis. "Was he always like this?"

"Only since he got sober," Lewis said.

"So you did know him before."

"Oh, yeah. Clea invited him out a few times last summer. She liked variety."

"An active alcoholic?"

"Believe it or not, he had us all convinced he was a normie. Said Clea was the first woman he'd ever dated who was in a twelve-step program. Didn't seem to mind the house being dry."

"So what happened?"

"He got a DWI. She dragged him to a meeting, he decided he was a high-bottom drunk, and he turned into an obsessive-compulsive monster. Though if he wants to scrub the garbage cans, God bless him."

"Where's the dump? And do I have to?"

"That's one chore we have to keep up with. If you can't stand a twenty-minute ride in a car full of Phil and garbage, you could switch with someone and go another day. But you might as well get it over with."

"The dump. It's so country. Do the locals go there to shoot rats?"

"It's not like that at all. In fact, it's not called the dump any more. Recycling center. In fact, I may come along. I need to throw out a bunch of Clea's stuff and a broken chair that's been sitting on the deck for days."

"You won't fit that in Phil's car."

"I'll take my own."

"If I help you load, can I ride with you?"

"Sure. As long as we give Phil a hand loading up and help him when we get there, he'll be happy as a clam. More room for garbage."

The day was crystal clear. I rode shotgun. We headed west on Montauk Highway. Lewis made sure we pulled out of the drive ahead of Phil, so we wouldn't have to tail his stench all the way to the dump. Phil's rear seat was piled high with black plastic garbage bags. With his rear view blocked, he'd have to be very careful. The unscented junk in Lewis's car cleared the wide open windows. Once we got going, the prevailing scent was fresh-cut grass. Seagulls wheeled overhead, going our way. Lewis said they loved the dump.

I stuck my head out the window and looked back.

"Phil's stuck behind a tractor. Wanna lose him?"

"Better not. He's only been there once before. I promised I'd show him the way. He's even more anxious this year."

"Along with fanatical about garbage. He's got something to be anxious about, you've gotta give him that."

"I could never understand why she took up with him."

Lewis's hands gripped the wheel a little harder than necessary. I sorted through ways to get him to go on and settled on an encouraging grunt.

"The guy has zero charisma," he said.

"And Clea had a lot, by all I've heard. You knew her well?"

"Clea didn't drop the seventh veil for anyone." Lewis chewed on one corner of his lower lip.

"Did you ever sleep with her?" It came out very casual, nicely judged if I say so myself.

"Oh, what the hell. Yeah, it was impossible to be just buddies with Clea. She was steamy as a Turkish bath, and if she offered, you'd be a fool to say no."

"So you had a thing?"

"I had a thing, a bad one. Clea had one romp among many, just another roll in the hay. The dune grass, if you really want to know."

It sounded scratchy to me. And sandy. But according to Lewis, Clea made you forget all that.

"Did Karen know?"

"No." He bit it off so hard I saw tooth marks on his lip. "God, I hope not."

We both fell silent. A minute later, the car swung into a long road with what looked like a ticket booth at the end.

"I've got it." I reached in my pocket. Offering to pay was something I'd never done drunk.

"We have a sticker."

Sure enough, the guy at the booth surveyed our front bumper and waved us by.

"What's that big hill?" I asked.

"Mount Garbage," Lewis said. "When this was a real dump, people came and hurled their bags over the edge. The seagulls used to have a field day scavenging. When they built the recycling center, they let it grass over. We go this way."

We pulled up in front of a long shed with a corrugated metal roof. Lewis got out of the car and started unpacking bags and boxes with practiced efficiency. I guess I could have jumped in and given him a hand without waiting to be invited. My instincts hadn't changed that much yet.

A toot signaled Phil's arrival. He too immediately got to work.

"Here!" He tossed a giant black plastic sack my way.

I caught it before it knocked me over, but the jolt dislodged the wire twister holding it closed, and a cascade of soda cans clanked merrily around my feet. Oh, great. I flunked Dump.

"Oh, for God's sake!" Phil had to rub it in.

I started chasing the little buggers and flinging them back in the garbage bag. A few eluded me by rolling under Phil's car. Growling the Serenity Prayer under my breath, I lay down flat and fished them out. Lewis helped. Phil didn't.

"I think that's it," I said finally. "Now where did the twister go?"

"You don't need it," Lewis said. "You empty the bag right into the bin."

I dragged the bag, rattling and bumping, in the direction he pointed. He followed with a load of plastic soda bottles. Both bins were almost full.

"I haven't seen so many beer cans in one place," I said, "since I cleared out my apartment after detox."

"Just dump 'em in and throw the bag away," Lewis instructed.

Phil came up behind us with another bag of bottles, this batch glass. They clinked as he poured them into the appropriate bin.

"They used to make us separate them by color," Lewis said. "They keep changing the rules."

A battered dark green pickup truck pulled up next to us, shaving the flank of Lewis's car like a matador's cape. I didn't recognize the strawberry lady in a baseball cap and big padded gloves until Lewis called out, "Morning, Mrs. Dowling. Beautiful day."

"Rain this afternoon," she said as she started swinging well-filled garbage bags out of the bed of the truck. She marched into the shed with one in each hand.

We hung back long enough for Lewis to murmur, "I can

never tell if the locals are really weather wise or just trying to maintain a reputation."

"I guess we'll see this afternoon." I grabbed an unwieldy bag in each fist and do-si-doed around Mrs. Dowling coming briskly out. She wasn't the kind of woman you'd want to whack with a sack of garbage.

Mrs. Dowling drove off just as we finished. I walked over to Phil's car and peered inside. The back seat still held a couple of boxes of small appliances, beach paraphernalia, and girl stuff like makeup, a mesh laundry bag full of clothing, and a battered suitcase.

"I've cleared the trunk," Phil said. "This is Clea's stuff."

"Things like the electric toothbrush," Lewis said, "can go in the garbage bin. But maybe somebody could use the suitcase. There's another shed down at the end for items to swap."

"I don't know," Phil said. He sounded uncharacteristically uncertain.

"Karen talked to Clea's mother on the phone," Lewis said. "She lives in Florida. She didn't want it either. And none of this stuff interested the cops."

While Phil grumbled and Lewis coaxed, I idly picked things up and put them down again. I turned a couple of straw tote bags upside down and shook them. The police must have done the same. Nothing but a little sand fell out. The little suitcase was an old plaid canvas model with a couple of rips in it. Everybody used to have at least one of these before the kind with rollers and retractable handles came in.

"Nobody wanted this?" I tugged at the zipper. It had collected a little rust and didn't want to move.

"It's the kind of thing you pay two bucks for at a yard sale," Lewis said, "and are ready to throw out by the time you get home. But you never know. If it's free, somebody will want it."

"Not if it won't open and close," I said, tugging harder. "Got it!"

Past the stuck point, the zipper slid easily enough.

"I don't know if this is worth it." I stuck my nose inside the suitcase and sniffed. "The lining is mildewed." I ran my hand over the cheap, shiny nylon and poked a finger into the elasticized pockets on the side. "Hey! There's something in here."

My questing fingers had discovered a flat pocket inside one of the side pockets. Wedged snugly into it was a hard square shape. I drew it out. It was a small black notebook. Before I could open it, Phil snatched it from my hand.

"What the hell—"

"Not so fast!" Lewis's hand shot out.

Phil held the notebook up above his head. Lewis was taller, but Phil danced away from his long reach.

"If it's Clea's, I should get it. It's none of your business."

It might be Lewis's business. The notebook didn't look new. Clea might have recorded all the details of her love life. On the other hand, she could have used it for shopping lists.

Lewis's face turned a rich plum color. He clenched not just his fists but his whole body. I could see the muscles bunch in his neck.

"Give it back, you son of a bitch!"

"Like hell I will!" Phil's skin didn't change color, but he started to sweat. I could see the droplets spring up on his bald spot.

"Do you want another bloody nose, you bastard?" Lewis roared.

"Why don't we give it to the cops?" The devil made me do it. They both turned and glared at me.

"No way!"

"Forget it!"

I raised my hands in surrender and backed off a pace.

"Okay, whatever." I could feel the shit-eating grin on my face. I didn't want them throwing punches at each other or at me. I'd like to cut a heroic figure stopping them. Too bad I didn't have Cindy's moves. What could I say to defuse the situation?

"I wonder how come the cops didn't find it." I pitched my voice in a conversational tone. "I thought they checked everything. We sat out on the deck for hours before they let us in."

"The suitcase wasn't in her room." Lewis's face slowly faded to lavender. "It was in the big closet off the living room, stowed away with some of ours."

"So maybe they just zipped it open to the stuck point," I surmised, "and shook it around a little. When nothing fell out, they decided it was empty and not of interest."

"You may be right." Lewis pushed the words out reluctantly.

"A fistfight won't solve anything. We saw that ourselves, right?"

A car door slammed. While I had Lewis's attention, Phil had made his getaway. He'd abandoned the rest of his garbage.

"Shit!" Lewis turned purple again. "Come back, you little rat fink!"

Phil revved the engine. The exhaust emitted a derisive fart as he wheeled, burning rubber, and sped away.

"Easy does it," I advised.

The program slogan got through. Lewis took a few deep breaths, pursing his lips and blowing out on the exhale. Whoo, whoo, whoo. I think they teach it in yoga class.

"He'll go back to the house, anyhow," I said. "Maybe you can talk to him when you both calm down."

"It's only because of what I told you," Lewis said. "I want to know if she mentioned me."

"Phil probably feels the same."

"Do you think he'll give it to the police?" Lewis looked at me as if I had the answers.

"Why would the cops be interested? She drowned," I said. It seemed prudent not to mention that Jimmy and Barbara and I still thought she'd been murdered. "It might have been filled with negative stuff about him. He'll probably destroy it."

Lewis ground his teeth, ready to flare up again.

"I've got to see it first."

"Come on, man, let's finish up here and go back to the house. We can't do anything about it now."

I liked Lewis a lot better than I liked Phil. But I didn't want to side with either of them. One or the other might be a murderer. Anyhow, Clea was a journalist. Her love life wasn't the only potentially dangerous information she could have recorded. Scandal, corruption, lies, and secrets were her bread and butter. Even if her notes didn't point directly to her killer, they might cast a lot of light on various people's motives. I didn't want that notebook destroyed unread any more than Phil and Lewis did.

CHAPTER FOURTEEN

"Bruce! I'm doing laundry!" Barbara's shadow fell across my face as I lay basking on the deck, a pitcher of lemonade on a low table at my elbow.

I pushed my shades up to the top of my head and opened my eyes.

"Bully for you," I said. "You're an industrious woman. I can't tell you how much I admire that."

"Less sarcasm and more gratitude, please." Ice rattled pleasingly as she poured herself a glass of lemonade. "I'm offering to do yours."

"Does this offer involve any fetching and carrying on my part?" I held out my hand, and she refilled my glass.

"Not exactly."

That sounded ominous. I sat up.

"Don't tell me," I said. "You've got a cunning plan."

"I do." She perched on the edge of my chaise longue, shoving my legs over to make room for herself. "Does 'don't tell me' mean you want to hear it?"

"Do I have a choice? Lay it on me."

"The good news is I'll gather up your laundry." She settled her tush more comfortably on the seat, almost knocking my legs overboard.

"Saving me an arduous task." She knew as well as I did that all my dirty clothes and towels were in plain sight on the floor and other available surfaces in my room.

"I'm doing my good deed for the day," she announced, "as we used to call it in the Girl Scouts. I'll do everybody's laundry, the whole house."

"Wow, I am impressed," I said. "For people who go around practically naked from dawn to dark, we get a huge amount of stuff dirty."

"It's mostly towels and T-shirts," she said. "Easy enough to throw in the machine."

"And the purpose of this exercise?" I inquired.

"That's the best part." She drained her glass and set it down on the wooden side table with a triumphant bang. "It gives me an excuse to go through everybody's things, especially Phil's. And while I'm doing the wash, you can sneak into his room and look for that notebook."

"Oh, goody." I chugged the last inch of lemonade, put the glass on the table, and settled my shades back down over my nose. "Phil might have something to say about that."

"He isn't here." Barbara flashed me a broad grin. "He went off to see some art show in Southampton. That's what gave me the idea."

"How about the rest of them? It'll be hard to miss me tiptoeing into Phil's room."

"They're leaving in fifteen minutes to go to a meeting." She had all the answers. "I already told them you're helping me with the laundry. Bruce, we've got to find that notebook!"

Twenty minutes later, as I plunged my arm up to the bicep into the smelly socks and shorts in Phil's laundry basket, I thought that Phil would have been an idiot to leave the notebook in his room. Lewis had wanted to see it more than we did. I already knew the cops had the notebook in which Clea had mentioned me. She might have written anything in the one they'd missed. I hadn't told anyone but Barbara and Jimmy about the scene at the dump. Who had Lewis told? Not Karen.

He didn't want her to know he'd had a fling with Clea. If I were Phil, I'd either carry that little black hot potato around on me until I could take it into the city or lock it in the glove compartment of my car.

In the next forty minutes, Barbara and I went through every drawer in the place, the pockets of every shirt and pair of pants our housemates had worn since the last time they'd done laundry, the underside of every mattress, and as far as we could penetrate into every closet. No notebook.

"Do you think we should take down their suitcases from the tops of all the closets?" Barbara, a pile of sheets in her arms, appeared in the doorway of Lewis's room where I was nosing through a metal box of fishing tackle. It was marginally possible that Lewis had gotten the notebook away from Phil already.

"No way." I snapped the tackle box shut. It was bad enough we'd pawed through their underwear. I could imagine the hoopla if they all came back and caught us tossing their luggage around. "Give it up, Barbara. It isn't here."

"I guess you're right. We had to try, though." She thrust the sheets at me. "Here, follow me. We need to take the first load out, throw it into the dryer, and put these sheets in the wash. Then you can help me hang them on the line. They're too big for the dryer, and anyhow, clean sheets smell fresher when you dry them in the sun."

"What a treat," I said.

"Don't bellyache about it," she said. "It's a gorgeous day. Think of hanging sheets as a meditation."

Chapter Fifteen

"The fireworks don't start till dark," Barbara said, sniffing the air like a pointer as we trudged across the parking lot of the biggest public beach in the area. "Do you think we brought enough food?"

"Enough for a bar mitzvah," Jimmy assured her.

"It's a long wait," she said. "I don't want you guys to get bored." She looked up at the sun, still high in the sky, and flashed a glance over her shoulder at me. "Are you okay?"

"Just fine and wonderful," I said. She had loaded me down with chairs and blankets, extra layers of clothing for the Arctic night that might follow this tropical Fourth of July day, and a folding picnic table.

"Remind me why we had to get here three hours early." Jimmy shifted his shoulders beneath the weight of a giant cooler bag stuffed so fat, it made him look like Atlas carrying the world.

"We promised to save places for everybody. You were there when we talked about it, you just weren't listening. Besides, look what a great parking spot we've got. Corky told me that by seven-thirty they're parking people way down on the residential streets. Some people even walk the whole way from the village. Anyhow, I didn't want to miss anything."

I refrained from pointing out that all those cars that would have to park farther away would be ahead of us on the road out when the fireworks ended. You have to give Barbara points for enthusiasm.

"How come the rest couldn't get here early?"

"Some of the gang at Oscar's are making fried chicken, but it was so gorgeous at the beach this afternoon that they didn't get into the kitchen till late. Karen and Lewis decided they wanted to hike along the beach, if not all the way from Dedhampton, at least from Amagansett. They started this morning. The others should be here any time, they had to stop for gas."

"Or was that a rhetorical question?" I asked.

"Carrying all their stuff? Sounds like the Long March."

Barbara looked guilty.

"We've got their chairs and blanket and their food for the picnic," she said, "all except the fried chicken. I couldn't not offer, could I?"

We reached the weathered rail fence that separated parking from soft white sand. Families of picnickers streamed past the fire trucks, police cars, and ambulances at the head of the road. Firefighters and local cops directed traffic, collected contributions, or just hung out enjoying the festive occasion, greeting neighbors, and rescuing the occasional kid from running into a car. Long lines had already formed in front of a row of Porta-Potties.

Barbara led the way onto the sand. The beach was already crowded. Large groups had set up picnic tables, lit candles, built small pit fires, and broken out the six-packs. Screaming kids ran everywhere. Vendors made their way through the crowd selling glow-in-the-dark necklaces. Lazy rollers broke up into lacy surf that foamed and clung before receding. A faint white moon hung in the deepening sky. Up on the dunes, blades of beach grass with the western sun behind them gleamed like light swords.

"Hey, Barb, wait up," Jimmy called. "Where are you going?"

Barbara stopped and swiveled, waiting for us to catch up. Her flyaway hair whipped in the breeze. Her brown eyes sparkled. She wiggled her bare toes in the sand, dancing in place with impatience. She wore her backpack and carried her sandals in one hand and a plastic shopping bag with a bag of potato chips and two loaves of French bread sticking out the top in the other. She gestured behind her with the hand holding the sandals.

"There's room up by the fence," she said. "Let's sit in the front row. I love it when the fireworks go off right over my head and thump inside my chest."

"All that way?" Jimmy whined.

"Yup. C'mon, Jimmy, it'll be great."

"You can pretend it's artillery fire," I consoled him. Jimmy's the consummate military history buff, but he would have hated being in the army.

The sun was sinking in a pink and golden glow when we finally got settled to Barbara's satisfaction. She laid down a wide swath of blankets so that nobody would encroach on our encampment before our gang arrived. Jimmy and I plunked ourselves down into beach chairs. Barbara walked the perimeter, sniffing the air and nudging various bags and shoes in place to weigh down the edges of the blankets.

"What are you doing?" I asked. "You can't pee to mark our turf."

"I'd love to make our area a no-smoking zone, but with this crew, I'd get lynched, right? The wind's in the right direction, though, blowing away from us, and I don't see any smokers close around us."

"I'll exhale the other way," I promised. I'd probably get up and stretch my legs, maybe even go down to the edge and get my feet wet, when I wanted a cigarette. But I didn't want to make things too easy for her. She says herself we shouldn't enable her when she gets too controlling.

"Yo! Hey, guys!" Cries and hollers announced the arrival of

the rest of our party. Everybody bustled around setting up more chairs and finding room for an enormous quantity of food, including the still-warm fried chicken and a giant watermelon. Lewis and Karen came up from the water side only a couple of minutes after the others, slipping around the orange slatted fence that marked the point past which they didn't want unauthorized persons screwing around while they set up the fireworks. It didn't take long for everyone to dive into the food and start chattering away.

"Don't tell anyone," I muttered to Jimmy, "especially Barbara, but I'm having fun."

"Don't worry, dude. Your secret is safe with me."

"Who wants watermelon?" Oscar roared. He swung a chef's knife that was little short of a machete over the fat green-striped melon. He raised his arm and sliced downward. The blade bit into the taut rind with a satisfying crunch.

"Like a guillotine on an aristo's neck," Jimmy said.

"I dated a doctor once," Corky said. "He had great pills, and he could get hypodermic needles, too. Watermelon with IV vodka, mmm."

"Listen long enough and you hear your story," Lewis said. He sprawled on a sling chair like an unwieldy spider. Karen, on the blanket at his feet, used his knees as arm rests. "Raise your hand if you ever shot up a watermelon."

Hands waved, including mine. Jimmy and I used to go camping in New Jersey until it started interfering with our drinking. We'd had enough disasters that nowadays Barbara couldn't get either of us into a pup tent.

"We never laced a watermelon in Girl Scout camp," Barbara said, "but we made s'mores."

That got a mixed response of jeers and "Ooh, I love s'mores." Oscar started to hand around thick wedges of watermelon. A lot of clowning accompanied the spitting of seeds.

"Everybody got some?" Oscar asked.

I looked around.

"Where's Cindy?" I asked. She'd been seated on the far end of the carpet of blankets. We hadn't talked. But I had kept her in my peripheral vision. We had some kind of chemistry going, and I wanted to get to the explosion.

"Took a walk," Jeannette said.

"Save her some watermelon, Oscar," Karen said. "If she went to the loo, she won't be back for ages. The lines were endless when I went."

"Thank you for sharing," Lewis said. He gave her ear an affectionate little tug. She slapped his leg.

"Where's Phil?" Barbara asked.

"He stayed home," Lewis said.

"He said he didn't care about fireworks," said Stewie.

"His loss," Karen said. "He turned up his nose at picnicking on the beach, too."

Snotty of him. I didn't like sand in my food either. But I was making an effort to socialize sober. To tell the truth, it surprised me that I could do it at all.

"Damn! I wanted the house to be empty," Barbara muttered in my ear. "I thought maybe one of us could rush back early and search his room again."

I laughed out loud.

"One of us? Which one would that be?"

"Shh! You two, of course. Jimmy because he wouldn't mind missing the fireworks, and you because you're a lot more larcenous than he is."

"Well, it isn't happening."

I spat out the last slippery little seed and threw my watermelon rind in a plastic bag already bulging with accumulated garbage.

"My knees have locked up," I announced. "I think I'll take a stroll." I stood up and shook off sand. "And shut up, Grandma,"

I told Barbara. She knew perfectly well that I was going to look for Cindy.

It was hard to believe the beach could get any more crowded. But people were still streaming in from the parking lot and points beyond. Loaded for bear, too, even though these late arrivals had probably had dinner at home or in town before they came.

The kids, some already in pajamas, had gotten wilder. I tripped over several little screamers and runners. One almost pitched me into a roaring campfire. I thought fires on the beach were forbidden, along with alcohol, unleashed dogs, and loud music. I saw all those rules being broken as I wove through what Jimmy might have called a bivouac.

Once I reached the fence, I stopped to light a cigarette. It was twilight by now. A fiery but subdued red glow, like burning embers, lay low behind the dunes. People with glasses in their hands had popped up all along the grassy humps of sand. Tonight the prohibition on walking on the dunes went unenforced if it hadn't been suspended altogether. On the ocean side, the crescent moon had turned from translucent fingernail white to cantaloupe orange. It rode higher in the sky every time I looked.

I scanned the crowd. Amid the cheerful hubbub, Cindy's laugh caught my attention first. Then I saw her some distance away, near one of the parked police cars. She stood nose to nose with a stocky African American woman with close-cropped hair. Or maybe it was breast to breast. What was Detective Butler doing here? Did detectives do crowd control? Maybe they all pitched in for an event like this. Or she'd simply come to see the fireworks. Were they arguing? Most people tried not to provoke a cop. Those I'd known who did had been drunk, high, or otherwise out of control.

I moved cautiously closer. Cindy laughed again, then flung

her arms out and pulled Butler into a hug. Most people I knew didn't hug a cop either. Except in an AA meeting. Could Butler be in the program? If so, she'd had a tight grip on her anonymity when we admitted that we were all in recovery. Maybe she was Cindy's sponsor, or the other way around. We'd already hit a few AA meetings in the area, and I hadn't ever seen her there. But she might go up island for meetings so as not to meet anyone she might be called on to investigate or arrest. If so, I wished Cindy had told me. But I could understand if she respected Butler's anonymity.

Or maybe I was seeing something else. As I watched, Cindy ran a hand over Butler's hair. I would have said she ruffled it if there'd been enough of it to ruffle. Butler responded with a tug of one of Cindy's pigtails. They fell back a little, grinning at each other like there was no one else on the beach. Damn! Had I misunderstood when Cindy said that Oscar didn't appeal to her? Now Cindy punched Butler lightly on the shoulder and turned away. Was that a buddy punch or a lesbian punch? It seemed to me I ought to know the difference, but I didn't. Butler kept looking as Cindy marched straight toward me, an enigmatic smile on her lips. I wanted to believe she'd spotted me. But it wasn't that kind of smile.

She ran right into me.

"Whoa, there," I said. "What's your rush?"

"Hi, Bruce." Her smile broadened to a grin. "Are we having fun yet?"

"Now I am." Don't quit five minutes before the miracle. I swear to God, every time I had a thought these days, a program slogan popped up with a clang like the numbers on an old-fashioned cash register. I meant, if she'd been flirting with Butler, so what? I'd flirt better.

She looked up at me, close enough that I hoped my breath

smelled okay, but not so squashed together I couldn't read her sweatshirt.

"Born to party, huh? I guess you're having fun yourself."

She tucked her hand in the crook of my elbow and steered us back toward the gang and the picnic.

"Now I am." Was she putting me on or not? Did she swing both ways or what? For the moment, I didn't care.

Vendors crisscrossing the beach were making a killing on neon necklaces. When one showed up beside us, I bought us each a glow-in-the-dark choker, hot pink for her and bright chartreuse for me. They were only a couple of bucks.

"Buying me jewelry already?" She flashed her little snaggle teeth up at me. They still turned me on. "Should I let you?"

"Keep it. It's you," I said.

A firecracker went off almost at our feet. Some asshole do-it-yourselfer. We both jumped. It made a great excuse to grab her hand, and I didn't give it back. Her fingers closed lightly over mine.

"Do you really want to see the fireworks?" I asked. "We could make a U-turn and keep going."

Cindy laughed and squeezed my hand.

"I love fireworks, and Fourth of July comes only once a year. There'll be other nights."

"I'll hold you to that," I said.

When the fireworks started, I sat down near Barbara and Jimmy, separated from Cindy by piles of stuff and people. As the illuminations leaped and burst and shed streams of sparkles down the sky, she crept up behind me and put a hand on my shoulder. When I turned, she signaled to me to make room. Barbara, who can match-make even when riveted on something else, scooted her chair over. I pushed mine back, sliding down onto the blanket. Cindy snuggled in beside me. We held hands. Is it Faust who sells his soul to the devil for one perfect moment? In a million years, I wouldn't have predicted that booze would not be part of mine.

The fireworks ended on a prolonged high note, to communal cries of pleasure as if the occasion were an orgy and the beach one big happy bed. Then everybody started scrabbling for their shoes, separating leftovers from chicken bones and watermelon rind, and flapping and folding blankets. Someone said how nice that the rich Hamptons could spend so much on bread and circuses. Someone else, dragging addictions into it as usual, said we have a disease of "more." Or maybe they meant our whole society, not just addicts.

"I don't know if I'll ever have *enough* fireworks," Barbara said, "but forty-five minutes is pretty darn good."

"I'm glad you're happy, pumpkin," Jimmy said.

The contented crowd eddied around us as we headed toward the road. Parents carried sleeping toddlers. Young guys we might see in AA in a few years chugged the last can of beer.

Cindy disappeared into the swirling mass of people, yelling, "See you at the house!" as they carried her away. Barbara still clung, hanging on to Jimmy's shirttail with one hand and my sleeve with the other.

"Glad you came?" she asked me.

"Tonight or the Hamptons?"

"Both."

"Yes, I am," I said. "I'm even glad I came in out of the cold."

"Good." She reeled me in and kissed me on the cheek with a smack loud enough to make Jimmy turn around.

"No horseplay, children," he said. "Focus, or we'll never get out of here."

"The old horse feels the pull of his stable," Barbara said.

"Computer withdrawal," I said.

We finally made it back to Dedhampton after a long crawl. We passed the East Hampton village green, almost too pretty, with its pond and ancient graveyard. The resident pair of swans, rumps in the air and elegant necks invisible as they dabbled for whatever swans find to eat in the muck on the bottom of ponds, saved the scene from an unnatural perfection. Traffic thinned out some before Amagansett and melted away on the home-stretch.

Our housemates all arrived almost simultaneously in spurts of gravel and a mighty slamming of car doors. Jimmy headed straight for his laptop on the porch. Everybody else piled into the kitchen. More food came out of the refrigerator than went into it. Watching fireworks on the beach is hungry work. Cindy tossed spoons from the drawer with the dexterity of a juggler. Karen passed pints of ice cream back from the freezer. Within minutes, the whole crew was eating out of the container, some propped against various appliances, others sitting on the counter with their legs dangling.

"Shit!" Jimmy's voice exploded from the other room.

"What happened, baby?" Barbara called. "See if he wants any ice cream," she said to me.

Cherry Garcia in hand, I ambled into Jimmy's sanctum. Something major, like a computer crash, would have evoked prolonged curses rather than a single expletive.

"What's up, bro?"

Jimmy swiveled in his chair to look at me.

"Our friend Phil isn't out there, is he?"

"No, not a sign of him. His door is closed, so he's either in or out."

"I know how he spent his evening," Jimmy said.

"How? And so what?"

"Look at this." Jimmy clicked his mouse a few times, and websites started flashing on the screen. "Online casinos."

"He used your computer?"

"Everybody else was at the fireworks with us."

"He didn't delete what he did?" I asked. "Dumb question," I answered myself. "He did, but Jimmy Cullen, boy genius, tracked him through cyberspace anyway."

"He played deep," Jimmy said, "and he lost big. Phil may be a high-bottom alcoholic, but he's a heavy-duty gambler—way out of his depth and sinking fast."

Chapter Sixteen

I inspected my freshly shaven face in the mirror.

"Oh, you handsome devil, you," I said.

"Cut it short, Narcissus." Barbara's voice startled me. "Other people need to use the bathroom."

"What part of a closed door don't you understand?" I inquired.

"The part where you didn't make sure the latch snapped."

"Don't be a smartass," I admonished her as I opened the door. "Hey, you look pretty."

"Do I really?" She looked down at herself and twirled. "Let me at the mirror."

We were getting ready for a party at Oscar's. I'd dressed up to the extent of smooth cheeks, long pants, and a blue denim shirt. I had rolled my shirt sleeves up and down twice and changed the number of buttons open on my chest three times. The chemistry between Cindy and me had been bubbling quietly since the Fourth of July, and I was more than ready for an experiment.

Barbara did look nice. Her usually intractable hair fluffed attractively around her face. Intricate webs of gold wire and crystal dangled from her ears and on her chest above a deeply scooped black tank top. Gold sandals peeked out from beneath a long turquoise skirt. Her tanned olive skin glowed with health.

"Nice skirt," I said. "Very sixties."

"It's batik." She stuck out a foot and wiggled her toes at me.

"Like my toenails?"

"They match the skirt. A little weird, but in a good way."

"Do you think I'm too dressed up? It is the beach."

"Hey, it's a party," I said. "Let yourself go."

"It'll be a big evening if I can get Jimmy to dance," she said. "But let yourself go, yourself. You look terrific." She stepped forward and buttoned the lowest open button. "There. Now you're perfect."

Oscar's house looked like a cruise ship in full regalia sailing against the sky as we walked up from the road on the land side of the dunes. The parking area near the house was packed solid. I'd heard that every recovering person on the East End from Southampton to Montauk came to Oscar's parties. Festive strings of lights draped the structure, twined around the rails of the deck, and garlanded the nearby trees against a backdrop of inky midnight blue. Fireflies did their bit to light things up. The night air felt soft against my skin. In contrast, my perception felt sharpened. I seemed to see the gaily decorated scene and hear the music, the laughter, and the roar of mingled voices as we approached with exceptional clarity. Well, of course I did: I used to arrive at parties fuzzed over by preliminary drinking.

What do you do at a party when you don't get wasted? Talk, talk, talk. Eat, eat, eat. Dance, dance, dance. Barbara started pawing the floor and shaking her fanny the second we got in the door.

"Come on!" she said, jerking her head toward the dance floor, though surely not expecting us to obey.

I shook my head. I wondered if Cindy liked to dance.

Jimmy, the pusillanimous coward, said, "Later!"

Barbara shouted something I couldn't hear. The music, with its thumping bass, and the roar of multiple conversations drowned her out. Still dancing, she wiggled her way over to the marble kitchen counter, heavily laden with food, to put down the tray of homemade brownies she had brought. I hadn't eaten a brownie that wasn't laced with pot or hash since the sixties. But this clean and sober crowd was into chocolate in a big way.

Barbara reached the middle of the floor and ratcheted up the motion, shimmying to the beat all by herself with her eyes closed and a smile on her face. Jimmy watched her, a big goofy grin on his own face. I still felt uncomfortable in company without a glass in my hand. I skirted the edge of the crowd, some watching the dancers in the center and others jigging along. Spotting a regiment of soda bottles at the far end of the marble counter, I worked my way over to it. I helped myself to an oversized plastic cup of seltzer, squeezed half a lime into it, and fished a few cubes out of a nearby ice bucket to plunk into it. Now I was as ready to socialize as I'd ever be.

I couldn't see Cindy, so I looked around for other familiar faces. The first one I spotted was Corky's. She swung her hips and touched down twice on each foot, dancing her way toward me. I raised my glass to her.

"Have you seen the whole house?" she asked me when she got close enough to shout. Her voice was hoarse, as if she'd been attempting to converse in this hubbub for hours. "Oscar designed and built it himself. Well, his architect did, but it was Oscar's vision."

I shook my head.

"Not all of it." I doubted she'd show me Ted's bathroom.

"Come on, I'll give you the grand tour." She looked around for a place to put her glass down and finally stowed it under the drinks table. She held out her hand.

I waved her ahead of me.

"Go on. You lead and I'll follow."

She led me out of the crowd and down the same dark corridor I'd explored clandestinely the day I'd found Oscar and Karen in bed together. She flicked a switch. Track lighting illuminated a gallery of photos I hadn't even noticed that day.

"We're all here," Corky said. "Take a look. They're not just snapshots. Oscar's a terrific photographer, you know. Way back, he used to do it professionally—portrait photography and photojournalism. See how many faces you recognize. Not just us—celebrities, too. Oscar really does know everyone."

She was right. I spotted a number of famous faces known for hanging in the Hamptons: Spielberg, Vonnegut, Paul Simon, Billy Joel. The Clintons. Puff Daddy. Nobody had mentioned Oscar was a world-class portrait photographer. I was impressed, not by the celebrities, but by the photos themselves.

"These are great," I said. "Why did he stop doing it for a living?"

"He says he found he could make more money with less effort in real estate," Corky said. "But that's not the real reason. There was an incident right before he got clean and sober. His bottom, in fact. Here, look at this."

She pointed to a black and white photo of a young woman. It wasn't a studio portrait. He'd taken it on the beach. She stood in the water with surf foaming around her ankles, wearing a filmy gauze kind of dress with the skirt bunched up in her hand to keep it dry on one side, wet and clinging to her legs on the other. She laughed up at the camera. Her pale tangled hair flew up and away from her face in the wind. Her even lighter eyes managed to be huge, sleepy, and crinkled with amusement at the same time. Even in black and white, she was luminous.

"Who is she?" I asked. "An actress? A model?"

"No, she was a local girl," Corky said. "You know the farmer down the road from the house you're in?"

"Sure. He fixed our plumbing, we picked his strawberries. What about him?"

"Believe it or not, she was his daughter."

"You're kidding. American Gothic produced this goddess?

You said 'was.' Did she die?"

"Yes," Corky frowned at the picture. "She's dead."

"How did it happen? Did Oscar get drunk and drive her into a tree?"

"No, that was Jackson Pollock over in Springs, way back in the fifties. In that case, Pollock died and the girlfriend lived. Maybe if Oscar had died, his photographs would be world famous now. But then he'd never have gotten clean and sober."

"What did happen?"

"He turned her on to drugs."

"She was his girlfriend?"

"Oh, everybody's Oscar's girlfriend for at least ten minutes."

"A townie/summer people thing?"

"Yeah, but more so," she said, "because of who summer people in the Hamptons tend to be. He ran with a star kind of crowd—of course he was dealing, he had amazing contacts—and he liked having groupies."

"She was dazzled." I found it easy to imagine.

"She fell in love with him," Corky said. "The stupid little cunt."

I detected some strong feeling there. Contempt for the farmer's daughter? Bitterness about her fate? Protectiveness of Oscar?

"How did she die?" I asked.

"She OD'd," Corky said.

"Suicide or accident?"

"They were never sure. Oscar went into a depression, though. It's not like she was important to him. But he did blame himself. He stopped taking pictures, and he got clean and sober. So I guess it wasn't a total waste."

"What was her name?"

"Huh? Oh, the girl. Amalie, Emily, something like that. Amelia."

"Oscar didn't tell that story when he qualified." You weren't supposed to pretty things up when you shared.

"Sometimes he does." Corky sprang to his defense. "He twelve-stepped a lot of his old customers to make amends for dealing. It's not his fault that it was too late for Amelia. Oh, never mind about her. Let me show you the rest of the house. You've gotta see the master bedroom, Oscar's room. It's got a sunken hot tub."

I didn't tell her I'd seen that room before. I'd missed the sunken hot tub. Too busy goggling at the couple in the king size bed.

When Corky and I returned to the party, we found Oscar engaged in talking everybody into skinny dipping in the ocean.

"We'll never have a better night for it," he said. "The moon is full."

"The better to see you with, my dear." Cindy suddenly appeared at my elbow.

"Hey! I've been looking for you all evening."

She flashed the vulpine grin at me.

"Plenty of towels for everybody," Oscar said expansively.

"I've heard that Oscar likes to look at naked ladies," Cindy said. "I think I'll pass."

The clamoring crowd of groupies around Oscar didn't seem to mind. And a few of the guys joined in, probably because they realized it was their chance to look at naked ladies too.

I heard a familiar coaxing voice at my back. "Aw, c'mon, Jimmy, it'll be fun."

I turned.

"Give it up, Barbara," I said. "Jimmy wouldn't go bare-ass even when he got wasted. If you painted him blue, maybe."

"Not even then," Jimmy said firmly. "You heard the man. Stop trying."

"Then you come with me, Bruce. You can't both leave me

without any moral support."

"I'm going for a walk with Cindy." I raised my eyebrows at her. "At least I hope I am."

"Sure," she said. "You heard the man. We'll never have a better night for it."

"There you go," I said. "We won't stub our toes on any driftwood or step on any icky jellyfish."

"So what are we waiting for?"

"Well, I don't want to miss it," I heard Barbara say as we turned away. "Okay, if you don't want to come and watch, I've got another idea."

Barbara's always got another idea. I thought of saying so, decided not to. I found I wanted Cindy to think well of Barbara.

"Barbara's a good friend," I said.

"She seems to be," Cindy said. "And Jimmy too. You're lucky."

It was only a few steps and down a flight of wooden stairs set into the dunes to the deserted beach. It was almost as bright as day. The skinny dippers dropped their towels and streaked down the beach with whoops and shrieks. Oscar and Corky, in the lead, hit the water with a splash. Others followed. Inevitably, someone called out, "It's not cold once you get used to it."

"Famous last words," I commented. "Want to watch? Or change your mind and go in?"

"No, let's walk."

The night was even balmier on the beach than on Oscar's deck. We took our shoes off and walked almost in the water. Our toes squidged at every step. I rolled up my pants legs. Cindy wore a little black dress so short the hem didn't even get wet when a breaking wave splashed her legs. The moon spilled a bright trail onto the water and cast our elongated shadows on the sand.

"I saw you with that cop the other night," I said.

"What cop? Oh, you mean Butler. She's a detective. I didn't know you saw me. You got a problem?"

"No! No, not at all!" What had I expected? Reassurance? "I just wondered how you knew her."

"We met out in Montauk a few summers back."

"Was she one of your housemates?"

"No. She knew people who were."

"Was it a clean and sober house?"

"No," she said. "I wasn't in the program yet."

"All women?" I knew I should stop asking questions.

"No, only a couple. The rest were a bunch of guys who liked to fish and drink beer."

It didn't sound like a gay and lesbian house, but what did I know?

"Look, it's ancient history. Let's not talk about it, okay?" Cindy bent down, picked up a large clam shell, and got very busy brushing sand off it.

"Okay, okay." This was not how I'd hoped our stroll in the moonlight would go. We paced on awkwardly, maintaining a frozen zone of about a foot between us.

"Bruce! Bruce! Wait up!"

Barbara trotted toward us, a towel wrapped around her, and wet hair plastered to her head. We stopped and waited for her.

"Sorry to barge in," Barbara panted, "but I need support."

"What happened?" Cindy asked.

"Where's Jimmy?" I asked.

"He went back to the house, our house, I mean, or I wouldn't have bothered you, I know you wanted some alone time."

I watched her expressive face as her brain caught up with her tongue a little too late, as usual. Oh, well, the whole evening had already gone down the toilet anyway.

"What happened, Barbara?" I asked.

"That slimy bastard Oscar made a pass at me!"

"Naked? In the water?"

"Yes!" She shook her wet hair out of her eyes and wiped her nose on her sleeve.

I fished in my pocket for a red bandanna.

"Here."

"Thanks." Barbara blew her nose with vigor. The towel around her started to slip, and she clutched at it. "Damn!"

"Are you hurt?" Cindy sounded ready to spring into action if necessary.

"No, I'm furious! I'm not exactly an expert on nudism, but I know there are rules! You're not supposed to come on to someone when you both have no clothes on!"

"Really? I guess it's an unstated rule, like the alcoholic family rules."

"Don't trust, don't talk, don't feel," Cindy supplied. "In this case, don't touch. What did he grab? Your ass or your breast?"

"He goosed me! And don't you dare laugh, Bruce! It isn't funny."

"I'm not laughing," I protested.

"It's plain hostile," Cindy said. "You think sexual violence is always dramatic?"

"This was so invasive. It felt like a mini-rape."

The two of them glared at me.

I wished they wouldn't look at me that way. I'd never goosed a woman in my life.

Cindy put her arm around Barbara.

"Come on. Let's go back to the house. Is Jimmy supposed to come back to pick you up?"

Barbara shook her head as they started walking.

"Then we'll find ourselves a ride home with one of the women."

Oh, well. I'd wanted them to bond.

"Just don't let Oscar get anywhere near me," Barbara said.

"I'd like to break his neck. He started flirting with me the second we got into the water. He thinks he's God's gift to women."

"Couldn't he take a hint?" Cindy asked. "I assume you blew him off well before the incident."

"I didn't handle it all that well."

"Barbara is incurably honest," I told Cindy. "It's one of her most lovable qualities. Can I guess what happened?"

"Yeah, yeah," Barbara said. "Go ahead."

"She's a chronic codependent," I explained. "She was afraid to hurt his feelings."

"I didn't mean to encourage him," Barbara said, "just keep things from getting sticky. Unfortunately, the situation escalated. In the end, I told him off but good. He got nasty too. I don't want to see him again this evening. I'm damned if I'll make amends to that self-satisfied sexist pig."

We had almost reached the house.

"Look, I didn't mean to break up your evening," Barbara said. "I can get myself a lift home. I'm okay, really. You two can go ahead and take your walk anyway."

"No, that's okay." Cindy and I spoke in unison, not looking at each other.

This party was over.

Chapter Seventeen

When I staggered out of my room in search of coffee the next morning, I found Jimmy alone in the kitchen. He sat on a high stool at the kitchen counter, his nose in a mug and the Technology section of the *New York Times* spread open in front of him.

"Good morning." He put down the mug. "How was the rest of the party?"

"Barbara didn't tell you?" I asked, pouring myself a shot.

"Tell me what? I was asleep when she came in, and she was gone when I woke up this morning. I know she was there because her side of the bed was still warm and my pillow had migrated out from under my head, but we haven't had a chance to talk yet. Did I miss something?"

"Nothing too dramatic." I didn't want to make too much of it. "I'll let Barbara tell you."

"How about you, dude? How did it go with Cinderella?"

I took a sip of coffee.

"It was going fine until she turned into a pumpkin." I didn't want to blame Barbara. Certainly not to Jimmy. "Just a setback, not a permanent bust." As I said it, I was relieved to find I believed it. There was no reason for Cindy to write me off just because Oscar behaved like a scuzzbag. On the contrary, maybe. That felt good. During the last year or two of my drinking, I had trouble comparing myself favorably to anyone. "Why did you leave, anyhow?"

"I am *not* addicted to the Internet."

I laughed.

"Right, bro. Now write that a hundred times."

"If I lie, may I be attacked by nuns with rulers. Look, I'm even reading the *Times* in hard copy. I was getting bored, I don't dance, and I didn't want to see that bunch in their skin." He shuddered.

"You had that right."

He lowered his voice. "Phil's been at my computer again."

"Not last night. He was at the party."

"Earlier yesterday, then. I didn't get back online between coming back from the beach and party time."

"You're sure it was him?"

"Oh, yeah. He left footprints."

I must have looked blank.

"Electronic footprints. Delete doesn't always mean delete."

"Gambling again? Did he win this time?"

"What do you think?"

"Sarcasm? That's more my department."

"I don't like anyone fooling with my computer."

"He'd be broke by now if you went to the beach more often."

"I doubt he's grateful. But enough about that." He'd seen the door behind me open. I heard the creak and turned. It was Stewie, clad only in Hawaiian-print boxer shorts. He looked disheveled and coffee-deprived.

"Good moooorning," he said on a jaw-cracking yawn. "Did you have a good time last night?"

"Did you?" I asked. I had seen him dancing up a storm with about six of the women.

"Not bad for a party with girls," Stewie admitted. "At least I wasn't tempted to break my abstinence."

Thank you for sharing, I thought. Oh, what was the use?

The telephone rang.

I was the nearest. I picked it up.

"Yeah."

"Bruce? Is that you?" I barely recognized the squeaky voice as Barbara's. "Is Jimmy up? I need him."

"He's right here. What's up? Where are you?"

"I'm at Oscar's, oh God, can you both come right away?"

Jimmy looked up from his paper.

"Is it Barbara?"

"Where's Jimmy?" she gabbled. "I need to talk to Jimmy."

He saw my face and put down his coffee mug so fast it bounced as he reached for the phone.

As I passed him the receiver, we both heard her squawk, "Oscar's dead! I found him on the beach just like Clea."

"Now, hold on, petunia," Jimmy said. "Take a deep breath, say the Serenity Prayer, and then tell me what happened."

Recovering alcoholics! Jimmy meant it about the Serenity Prayer. I danced with impatience as he soothed Barbara and made encouraging noises into the phone. Then I realized I'd be better occupied in throwing on my pants, some shoes, and a sweatshirt. When I returned, he was saying, "Don't worry about it. We'll get somebody to drive us. We'll be there in ten minutes."

More squawking.

"If they tape up the car, we'll deal with it. And if they won't let us in, we'll be right outside. Don't worry, peach. We'll get onto the beach somehow. Just sit tight. If they get there first, we'll be right behind them. Hang in there, pet. Just tell them what you saw. It'll be okay, I promise."

"What?"

"What happened?"

"What's going on?"

Jimmy had acquired an audience. The whole house sat or stood in various states of undress, waiting for him to finish. I eyed Cindy, who looked fetching in a pink sleep shirt. I hoped she had forgiven me overnight for our bungled walk in the moonlight.

Hanging up the phone, Jimmy shook his head.

"Bad news," he said. "Oscar is dead. Barbara found him at the foot of the steps leading down to the beach from his house."

They all clamored for details, shouting questions at him like a bunch of news reporters on TV. He answered Cindy's first.

"No, the police aren't there yet. But she called them first."

"What was she doing there?"

"She'd gone for a run along the beach. She took our car. She said she parked at Dedhampton Beach and ran from there." He added, "I don't know why she didn't park at Oscar's."

Jimmy didn't know about the showdown between Barbara and Oscar at the party. Someone was bound to tell the cops. It would look bad, taken with the fact that she'd parked the car half a mile away.

"I'll drive you," Cindy said. "Let me get my keys and throw something on, I won't be a minute."

"Karen or I could drive you," Lewis said. "Karen?"

He looked at her, and so did I. Karen didn't answer. She looked stunned. Her eyes darted back and forth, as if she were reading off a teleprompter. What was she thinking? I wondered if Lewis knew or guessed that Karen and Oscar were lovers. He had a puzzled frown on his face. If I'd killed Oscar, I would have put on just that frown.

"Maybe we should all go over there," Jeannette said. "I feel so bad for Corky."

"Why Corky in particular?" I asked.

"He was her brother. Didn't you know?"

"I didn't."

"Neither did I," Stewie said.

"I did," Stephanie said. "Half brother. She's a lot younger. They didn't like to make a big thing of it."

"Actually, they owned the house together," Karen said. "It was his money, but her name is on the deed."

How did she know? Pillow talk? I watched her guarded expression and couldn't tell if she was devastated or relieved.

"There you go," Phil said with a nasty sneer. He pulled his bathrobe tighter around him and helped himself to coffee. "She probably inherits a bundle. All in the family, and she's got the motive. It has nothing to do with us."

"The police will want to talk to all of us soon enough," Cindy said, coming back into the room fully dressed in jeans and a plain black T-shirt with a gray sweatshirt tied loosely by its arms around her neck. "Once they hear about the party last night, they'll want our fingerprints, too. That party will be a headache and a half for them."

"They'll track down everybody who went to the party?" Stephanie asked.

"If they can." Cindy turned to me and Jimmy, jangling her ring of keys on one finger. "Ready? Let's go."

As we followed her down the stairs, I heard Phil say, "Who does she think she is? Anyhow, that makes the second body Barbara has found. I think the three of them are in trouble, not the rest of us."

What a skunk.

In the car, Cindy and I filled Jimmy in on the fight between Barbara and Oscar. Then we had to persuade him that since Oscar was dead already, getting fighting mad at him was neither necessary nor wise. Jimmy has pretty good anger management skills. I could see him shutting the fury down.

"Maybe we shouldn't have told you. The cops are bound to hear about it. Phil, for one, was in the skinny dipping contingent. If you didn't know about it, you didn't have a motive."

"No," Jimmy said. "I'm glad you did. I might have had

trouble controlling my reaction if I'd learned about it from the cops."

"If you think the detectives won't realize you're her knight in shining armor," Cindy said, "you'd better not count on it."

Jimmy, in the front seat beside her, turned his head to stare. "Her knight?"

"Aren't you?"

"Hell, no."

I couldn't help laughing.

"Barbara would kill him," I told Cindy, "if he thought she needed him to fight her battles."

"But he does anyway. He's galloping to her rescue now."

"That's different. We're being supportive."

"If you say so," Cindy said. "Tell us what she said on the phone."

"She decided to take an early run along the beach," Jimmy said. "Now you've told me about last night, I can see why she parked at Dedhampton Beach. She didn't want to see him again."

"And now she won't," Cindy said. "Believe me, that will interest the detectives."

"She'll tell them that herself," Jimmy said. "It would be ridiculous to think she'd kill to avoid a little social awkwardness."

"It was more than that," Cindy said.

"I'm not minimizing what happened," Jimmy said. "But Barbara wouldn't fan the flames. She'd try to let it go."

"The program says that if you pray for someone you resent every day for two weeks, the resentment will lift. I bet you anything she was praying for Oscar's health and happiness and prosperity, and that she's already told the cops that."

"They'll think she's nuts," Cindy said.

"I know," he said.

Except if Detective Butler was in the program, she'd understand. If Cindy was blowing smoke about that, I wished she'd stop.

"Barbara wasn't going to stop at Oscar's," Jimmy said, "but as she passed the house, she saw what she thought was a pile of clothes heaped up at the foot of those steps that go from the deck down to the beach. She went over to take a look, and it was him."

"Last time she thought it was a log," I said. "I hate to say that rat bastard Phil was right, but the cops are not going to like the coincidence. Finding one body is bad enough, but finding two will make them very, very suspicious."

"They might reopen the first investigation," Cindy said.

"The two deaths must be related," Jimmy said. "But Barbara had no reason to kill Clea. None of us did. We'd barely met her. The cops already know that. But a lot of the others had motives."

"Don't forget opportunity," Cindy said. "The law doesn't take motive to court. It takes opportunity and means. Evidence."

"Everybody in the area has access to the beach," I said. "Both Clea and Oscar were killed early in the morning. They should look for somebody who gets up early. That lets us out."

"But it doesn't help Barbara."

"How did she know he was dead?"

"She said someone hit him on the head."

"Sounds messy," I said.

"The blow could have broken his skull," Cindy said, "or started internal bleeding. You wouldn't necessarily know by looking."

"You mean he could have been alive when she found him?" Jimmy sounded appalled. "Oh, my poor Barbara." He thought for a second, then shook his head. "She didn't mention blood or brains. If she'd seen them, she'd have told me."

"We don't know enough." Cindy said. "No point speculating."

"You seem to know a lot about this kind of thing," I said.

"Oh, I've seen the inside of a lot of emergency rooms."

She meant in her drinking and drugging days, no doubt.

"So have I," I said. "So have I."

"Never mind that!" Jimmy's head bobbed as he rocked back and forth in his seat with impatience. "Let's just get there. I can't stand the thought of her sitting there alone with the body."

Chapter Eighteen

By the time we arrived at Oscar's, everybody in the house had trooped out onto the deck with Barbara. Someone had flung a sheet over the corpse. Uniformed officers were lifting the sheet gently as we scrambled over the dunes and approached the house. Cindy had parked her car down the road from Oscar's, far enough so we wouldn't get turned back. I recognized Officer Mike from the day we found Clea's body. No detectives yet. We were lucky we'd beat higher authority to the scene. A white wooden trellis with morning glories climbing up it lay flat against the wall right next to the deck, its crossed diagonal slats providing footholds. Barbara swung over the rail of the deck and clambered backward to the ground and into Jimmy's arms before the cops could stop her.

Shep leaned over the railing. I'd noticed his tendency to corral people. He beckoned and yipped, trying to get her back. Officer Mike swept him out of the way. Jimmy looked up at the cop over the top of Barbara's head.

"Have a heart, Officer," Jimmy said. "She's told you everything she knows. We're not going anywhere until you say so."

"All right, all right." Officer Mike flapped a dismissive palm at us and turned away. "Stay put, people!"

The crew at Oscar's was giving the cops a harder time than our house had when Clea died. They popped in and out of doors like the cast of an old-fashioned farce. More sense of entitlement to go with the rich-folks' location on the beach?

Longer collective sobriety and therefore a better sense of self-preservation? Whatever.

Corky took advantage of the kerfuffle to sneak away. She puffed and panted as she slid down the dune a hundred yards down the beach and made her way back through the heavy sand at its base to join us. At first I thought her dash for freedom had left her out of breath. But as she got closer, I could see her face was streaked with tears. The heaving breaths demonstrated a barely controlled hysteria.

"They've already interviewed her too," Barbara said, gathering Corky into her arms. "Did you know she was Oscar's sister?"

Corky rocked and wept.

"Poor bunny," Barbara crooned. "I'm so sorry, I'm so sorry."

"He was always there for me," Corky sobbed. "He'd say, 'Big Brother is watching you.' " If she found that line comforting, she'd probably never read George Orwell's *1984*.

"He was the one who always kept me safe." Corky's voice, muffled on Barbara's shoulder, rose to a wail. "What'll I do?"

"You don't have to do anything right this moment," Barbara said. "And when you do, you'll take it one second at a time. Go on, let it out. It's okay to grieve."

"What'll I do?" Corky howled. "I'm all alone!"

Barbara's voice fell into a lullaby rhythm as she continued to rock Corky.

"That's right, let it out. It's okay, go ahead and let it out."

"Ms. Rose, can you spare us a moment, please." Sergeant Wiznewski stood over us.

I looked over at the house and saw Butler. She stood on the deck, sorting out the remaining housemates with a no-nonsense air.

"Talk to me, Ms. Rose," Wiznewski said. "It seems you've found another body."

It didn't take much to uncork Barbara. And when you did,

she bubbled up like champagne.

"I didn't do it on purpose this time either," she said, "I just happened to be there."

Jimmy drew her away from Corky and put his arm around her shoulders.

The sergeant held up a meaty palm like a traffic cop.

"Hold it. Let's get ourselves some privacy, and then you can tell me all about it."

"Now, look here—" Jimmy began.

"Mr. Cullen, were you present when the deceased was found?"

Jimmy shook his head.

"No, sir."

"Then you can wait for her here," Wiznewski told Jimmy. "And you, Mr. Kohler?"

I didn't much like being known to the police. And I'd gotten used to AA, where my last name stayed safely in my wallet even on the rare occasions when I spilled my guts.

"I just got here, sir," I said.

"You wait too," Wiznewski said. "I'll get to both of you in due course. The deceased was known to you."

It wasn't a question.

"Yes, sir." Jimmy and I spoke together.

"Then I'll see you later."

I had lost track of Cindy as soon as we'd arrived at Oscar's. As we waited for Wiznewski to finish with Barbara, I spotted her in the thick of things. This time she wasn't hugging Butler. They were arguing. What was with Cindy? What was her agenda? She made my blood heat up, but I didn't know a damn thing about her. I never used to care about an attractive woman's history or what she was thinking. AA promised it would get different. I was changing, whether I wanted to or not.

It was hours before Jimmy and Barbara and I had a chance

to talk. We pulled a couple of deck chairs and a chaise longue to the far end of the back yard of our house, near the scraggly garden. Barbara lay back with her legs up, a bowl of cherries in her lap. She munched steadily. Jimmy and I reached out for an occasional cherry and competed, without discussion, over who could spit the pit farther.

"Wiznewski seemed pretty annoyed that everybody downplayed the close ties between our house and Oscar's after Clea died," Barbara said.

"They could have figured it out," Jimmy pointed out. "We found Clea within yards of where Oscar died. It was the first house they hit when they started asking questions in the neighborhood."

"They know all about it now," I said. "Who told them?"

"Us, I'm afraid," Jimmy said. "The moment we went rushing over there, we were all connected."

"It was too late from the second I found him," Barbara said. "Sorry, guys."

"Hey, peanut," Jimmy said. "You didn't plan to find them either time. Anyhow, we're the newbies in this crowd."

Jimmy slapped at a mosquito. One reason he doesn't like the country is that when mosquitoes have a choice, they go for him.

"I wish we knew what the cops are thinking," Barbara said.

"What can you find out on the Web?" I asked.

"I can't hack into police files," Jimmy said.

"Won't," Barbara said.

"Forget it. But I can look through the local newspapers and also see what *Newsday* and the New York papers picked up."

"Anybody in Oscar's house might have wanted to point the cops at our house," Barbara said. "Nobody wants to be the prime suspect in a murder. On the surface, all of them were closer to Oscar than we were. But if you look back before this summer, there's been a lot of mix and match. Somebody is bound to have said to hell with anonymity and talked about how incestuous the program is out here."

"In the city," Jimmy said, "the program really is anonymous."

"Yeah, yeah," I said. "Yay city, boo country."

"Who would want to make the cops put Clea's and Oscar's deaths together?" Jimmy asked.

"Anybody who had slept with Oscar," Barbara said. "Karen, Stephanie. I've been thinking—was Oscar a sexual compulsive?"

"We could ask Stewie if he went to meetings," I said only half sarcastically. "Or if Oscar ever made a pass at him."

"We could rule it out," Barbara said.

"I'm not happy with you being the only one the cops know Oscar made an unwelcome pass at," Jimmy said.

"Neither am I," Barbara said.

"Who told them?" I asked.

"We did," Jimmy said. "Both of us. Better us than someone else. They were bound to wonder if I got into a rage and knocked him on the head."

"I told them you don't fight my battles!" Barbara said, the light of combat in her eye.

"I'm sure that impressed them," I said.

"Besides, Jimmy wasn't there," Barbara said. "So what about that little black notebook Phil found? I don't think the cops know about it. If it was a real diary, a thoughts and feelings diary, it would make interesting reading."

"If I were Phil, I'd take it to the city," I said.

"He might have given it to the cops. Or he might not have, but now they're interested in Clea again, he might."

"If she said bad things about him," Barbara said, "he might have destroyed it already."

"Why would she?" I said. "She picked him for that second share. She must have liked him."

"But why?" Barbara asked. "He's such an asshole."

"Define your term, my pet." Jimmy reached out and scooped up the last handful of cherries.

"Phil's not really in recovery," she said. "He's not trying to become a better person. He's got no empathy or loyalty. He's not nice."

That about covered it.

"Why don't we try again to find that notebook?" Barbara said. "Maybe it's in his room."

"We looked in his room," I protested.

"So maybe he hid it somewhere else and brought it back when he thought we must have given up."

"I guess it's possible," I said. "He had to hide it somewhere. Clea collected information. If she'd written down something damaging about one of them, Phil's just the kind of scum who would enjoy holding it over them."

"Watch it!" Jimmy said sharply.

I looked around. Phil himself and Dowling had just come around the corner of the house. They were probably too far away to hear us talking. But everybody knows the sound of your own name can carry over a remarkable distance. No harm being careful.

Phil's voice carried because he adopted a high, hectoring tone, as if the handyman were deaf and not too bright.

"I've scrubbed all these garbage cans with ammonia," he announced. He demonstrated by rolling out and tilting forward the nearest of a row of olive green plastic bins tucked behind a trellis-like wooden screen under the deck. "That needs to be done regularly, after they go to the dump. We don't want to attract flies. And it wouldn't hurt to double bag the garbage."

I couldn't see Dowling's face. He hunched his shoulders and pawed the ground a little, like a bull getting ready to go for the matador.

"Doesn't like being told how to do his job," Jimmy murmured.

"Nobody does," Barbara said. She sat up and shook out her hips, shifting from buttock to buttock. "I'm getting *shpilkes*. Let's go for a walk."

"No more cherries," Jimmy said. "Ergo, you don't want to sit here anymore."

"Shut up, you." She flung the cherry pits from the bowl in a backhanded arc, as if she were throwing a Frisbee. "Instant cherry orchard."

"Yeah, in about twenty-five years. Where do you want to walk?"

"I don't know. Down the road. How about to the deli? It's only a mile or so."

"You know what?" Jimmy said. "You guys go."

"The mouse is calling, huh? You'll come with me, won't you, Bruce?"

"Sure," I said.

At that moment, Cindy came out onto the deck.

"On second thought, maybe I won't."

Barbara laughed.

"Okay, I'll let you both off the hook. I can walk a mile by myself."

"Just be careful," Jimmy said. "There is a killer out there."

"Not between here and the deli," Barbara said. "I'll take my cell phone, okay?"

She gave Jimmy a quick kiss, set the empty fruit bowl on the deck, and started down the driveway.

"I'll bring you back some ice cream," she said.

"Do you think Barbara is eating more than usual?" Jimmy asked.

"Barbara's always liked her food," I said. "And this is a foodie house. No matter what's going on, from cheatin' to sudden death, we eat well. You don't think she's pregnant, do you, bro?"

"Hell, I didn't even think of that," Jimmy said.

Chapter Nineteen

Barbara turned left out of the drive. Open fields, stands of scrub oak and pine, and an occasional farmhouse, its cedar shakes so weathered they had darkened to the color of burnt toast, lined the narrow road on both sides. A hawk wheeled overhead. A flock of gulls landed in a field where some dark-leaved vegetable was just beginning to develop. Maybe broccoli. The gulls took off again. A monarch butterfly sailed by ten inches from Barbara's nose. She walked briskly along the shoulder of the road, where dried grass crunched underfoot, releasing its sweet, dusty smell. Spiky blue cornflowers, deep pink beach roses, Queen Anne's lace, and purple clover tickled her ankles as she brushed past them.

Not a car passed. A small plane hummed overhead on its way toward the airfield in Westhampton. A rustling in the brush startled her. Two squirrels burst out of the leaves and chased each other up the trunk of a fat oak. She laughed aloud when one paused to scold and the other dropped an acorn on its companion's head. Walking with her eyes on the treetops, she stumbled. She looked back at the road, still empty except for a solitary box turtle making its dignified way across.

"Hey, little guy," she said. "Aren't you a handsome one?" She approached it cautiously. "Don't shell up on me, now, let me help."

She squatted down and picked the turtle up. Its lizard-like orange head arched up in outrage, its legs churned comically as she held it suspended by its black and yellow shell.

"Don't worry, little guy, I won't send you back where you came from." She had heard that if a turtle was returned to its starting point, it would invariably turn and start making its laborious way across again. "I know you want to get to the other side. I'm just speeding up the process so you won't get hurt." Hurt was a euphemism. The wheel of a speeding car could crush the shell, kill the turtle instantly, and continue on its oblivious way.

"There you go, little guy. Bye-bye. Have a nice day."

She set the turtle down on the far side of the road, watching with satisfaction as it began to plod forward, still in the same direction. She dusted her hands together, although the turtle's shell had felt pleasingly clean and dry.

"It *is* a nice day. Good afternoon. Doing your good deed, I see."

The voice, a man's and unfamiliar, startled her. But one of the things she loved about the country was the way people greeted each other when their paths crossed. So she turned with a smile, ready to be friendly.

"Hi. I always cross a turtle when I get the chance. Look at him go."

The stranger grinned back amiably. He was a tall man, perhaps in his early sixties, loose-limbed as the Scarecrow in *The Wizard of Oz,* with a lived-in face seamed with laugh wrinkles and pale blue, disillusioned eyes. A shock of silver hair flopped over his forehead. He wore a pair of faded but not disreputable jeans. Both the pants and the lightweight tan blazer that hung open over his clean white T-shirt sagged as if thoroughly familiar with his body. His scuffed brown work boots looked like old friends of his feet.

"Nice to see a fella who knows what he wants," the man said.

They both watched the turtle until it disappeared into the

brush. Then Barbara flashed a quick glance left and right along the road. Where had he come from? She couldn't see a vehicle parked along the roadside, at least as far as the nearest curve in both directions. Her hand reached down to pat the cell phone at her belt.

The man stood at ease, thumbs hooked in the pockets of his jeans. His eyes crinkled with amusement as he watched her. He unhooked his right hand and held it out.

"Jeff Bushwick," he said. "I'm harmless."

For whatever reason, she believed him. She shook.

"Hi, I'm Barbara."

"I know," he said. "You're the young lady who finds bodies."

A cricket chirped in the silence. Barbara spat out a small flying insect that paused on her lower lip to investigate.

"I'm not usually speechless," she said.

"I just missed you back at the house. You can check if you like."

Barbara started thumbing in Jimmy's number.

"So what are you, anyway, Mr. Bushwick? What do you want?"

"Call me Jeff," he said, responding to her suspicious glare by somehow melting into an even more relaxed stance. "I'm a reporter for the *Dedhampton Deeds.* I just want a few words."

Jimmy's voice squawked in her ear as the man waved a press pass at her.

"Hey, pumpkin. Did that reporter catch up with you?"

"Jimmy! You told him how to find me?"

"Well, he seemed like a nice guy. And he wasn't going to go away. His car is blocking the driveway. Do you want me to come? I'll have to walk."

"No, forget it. I'll handle it." She scowled at the reporter, who grinned. "Okay, Mr. Bushwick, five minutes. What do you want to know?"

The pale blue eyes twinkled.

"Jeff. Come on, I'll buy you an ice cream cone."

Barbara found herself strolling beside him as he made a shaggy dog story of his search for the best ice cream in the Hamptons.

"The Dedhampton Deli came in third," he told her. "My cholesterol went up twenty points, but we scooped the competition."

Barbara snorted.

"I hope your questions are better than your puns. How did you find us, anyhow?"

"Us?" He left it there, a technique Barbara recognized from counseling.

"How come you're interested?" She could play the ask another question game too.

"How much did you know about Oscar Ainsworth?"

Not even his last name, she thought. People don't have to be introduced properly to kill each other, though. She wondered if Jeff Bushwick considered her a suspect. She wondered if he was a local—well, obviously he lived here now, since he wrote for the paper—but whether he'd gone to school with all those cops.

"Are you city or country?" she asked.

"Oh, I've knocked around some. I tell you what, Ms. Rose. I'll give you some answers if you'll give me some. Oscar Ainsworth was news. He was a big man around here. He didn't have to die to get his name in the paper, but his death could make a difference to a lot of people."

"I know he was a developer," Barbara said.

"That's an understatement. He was a mega-developer with strong opinions about land use."

"That seems to be a hot issue around here," she said.

"That's an understatement too. Do you read the *Deeds*?"

"Lewis—the guy who organized our house—says the farmer next door calls it fish wrap."

"Don't kid yourself. They call it the *Dirty Deeds,* and everybody reads it, whether they admit it or not."

"I've skimmed it. So what about Oscar and development?"

"He wanted to buy up as much farmland as possible and turn it into houses for yuppies with families. Some folks thought he wouldn't be satisfied until the whole East End became a suburb."

"And the locals are against that?"

"The *town* is against it. Most of the owners of the farmland would rather sell it off at a million bucks an acre than break their backs trying to turn a profit on corn and potatoes."

"When I was a kid," Barbara said, "I used to hear about Long Island ducks, but I haven't seen a duck since I've been out here, not a domestic one, anyway."

"That was the environmentalists. The ducks used to shit in the streams. The whole eastern end of Long Island is a case of 'water, water everywhere,' but there's only one aquifer to supply fresh water. It doesn't help that we're more or less at sea level and that the seafood industry depends on the wetlands."

"So the environmentalists and the town are on the same side?"

"Nope, it's much more complicated than that," he said. "Town government consists of locals, and the voters are the all-year-rounders who don't care what happens in New York City and are out here on a Tuesday in November. The old families are not only farmers. They're baymen too. They don't want the land and sea destroyed, but they don't want it regulated, either. They can barely make a living as it is."

"And the tourists and summer people come out here for the country. They don't want it turned into suburbs."

"Yep, but they want their conveniences too. And they want to lie on the beach half nekkid, but they also want to protect the piping plovers. They don't want the locals to go surfcasting with their dune buggies slashing up the beach."

"Okay, so Oscar was news. I get that. Our housemate Clea was a journalist. How come you didn't care when she died?"

"I cared, all right." Bushwick's face set. The grim look sat like a mask on his amiable features. "How about a bargain? If I tell you a few things, how about you tell me all about how you found both Clea and Oscar? I mean details. Deal?"

"Maybe." Barbara thought hard. "When you say a few things, do you mean things I couldn't possibly know? What makes you so sure you've got 'em?"

"I have my sources."

"And do you write the headlines?"

"Sometimes they change them," he admitted. "But I can try. My editor usually listens when I say it's important."

"So nothing that makes me and my friends look bad."

"All your friends? All the people in that group house you've got back there which is illegal by the way—and Ainsworth's house? That might be difficult, especially since one of them could be a murderer."

"No, my real friends—Jimmy Cullen and Bruce Kohler. They were with me when I found Clea's body. I assume you want to hear more about that."

"Okay, no sensational headlines. No 'Death Trio Makes a Habit of Finding Bodies.' "

"That's exactly what I meant," she said. "So talk. No, first buy me an ice cream cone and then talk. Three scoops."

The center of Dedhampton consisted of a crossroads with four-way stop signs, the deli, a two-pump gas station, and a pizzeria. The deli had all of Barbara's favorite flavors. Within minutes, she and the reporter were sitting on a slatted bench outside the deli door.

"Okay, Mr. Bushwick, talk," Barbara said. "So you did know Clea. Did you sleep with her like everybody else?"

"Jeff. Have you ever thought of being a reporter?"

"I'm a counselor," Barbara said. "I'm thinking about going to social work school so I can be a real shrink. If I'm going to turn people inside out, I'd rather end up making them feel better. You didn't answer my question."

"Yes, I knew her," Jeff said. "She was a journalist. Everybody who writes for the various local rags knows everybody else."

"So why wouldn't her dying make a big story? We found her too, but nobody bothered us."

"They ran a big obit in the *Deeds.*"

"You don't have to get defensive."

"I'm not defensive. Do you want to hear this or not?"

Barbara grinned at him.

"You're the one who didn't answer my question."

"I'd like to say that we soft-pedaled the sensation of how she died out of respect for a colleague," Jeff said. "But the truth is, on the East End, south of the highway is news. North of the highway isn't. At any rate, it has to be spectacular to make the front page of the *Deeds.* From what I've heard, they're treating it as a homicide, but they aren't a hundred percent sure it was one, even now. The autopsy was inconclusive."

"How do you know? And what do you mean?"

"I told you, I have my sources." Jeff spooned up ice cream. "She drowned, and they can't prove she had help."

"What do you mean about north and south of the highway?"

"South of the highway's for the rich and the celebrities: what people think of when they hear 'the Hamptons.' "

"Oh, I see," Barbara said. "Mansions on the dunes—and high tech beach houses like Oscar's. North of the highway is regular people, like us. In fact, we're so far north I never even heard it mattered."

She opened her mouth to add that south-of-the-highway Oscar and his crowd had treated them like peers. But she stopped herself in time. She didn't want Jeff wondering how come they were so egalitarian, because the answer lay in the principles of twelve-step programs. Barbara might be guilty of a little boundary crossing now and then, but she knew better than to break her anonymity, or anyone else's, to a journalist.

"That's it," Jeff said. "Something happens north of the highway, it's just a blip on the hometown radar, like 'soccer captain breaks a leg' or 'local merchant gets DWI.' Oscar was a player. Real estate is one of the major preoccupations around here, and the environment is another."

"One of Clea's old boyfriends told my friend Bruce that she wrote about the environment," Barbara said.

"She did indeed. Clea was young and ambitious. She wanted to become a world-class investigative journalist."

"I thought she cared about the environment—the water, the air, the land, the fish, the birds. Wow, when you add it up, it's amazing how much of that stuff there is out here."

Jeff threw back his head and guffawed.

"A whole planetful, lady."

"You know what I meant!" Barbara held her hands up to her hot cheeks, then gave in to his infectious laughter.

"Sure, there's land and sea and fish," Jeff said, still smiling. "But not enough, according to the conservationists. Clea did care. Her pieces were good because the issues mattered to her. Oscar wasn't her only target, you know."

"Do you think she slept with him to get on the inside track of his development plans? By the way, you never answered my question about you and her."

"I wouldn't dare to speculate about why any woman sleeps with any man." He scraped the last of his ice cream out of the cup. "My hunch? She had more than one agenda."

"How come you're not writing anything down?" Barbara asked. "Don't you use notebooks? So how do you keep track of a conversation like the one we're having now?"

Jeff sat up straight on the bench. Barbara watched with fascination as he went on alert, the sags and wrinkles smoothing out of his face.

"I use a digital recorder," he said. "I don't have it on now because so far, we've confined our conversation to what I already know. What made you mention notebooks? Clea used both, did you know that?"

Should she say yes or no? Better not to admit anything. They had to find that notebook.

"You know something," he said.

Barbara smiled.

"I hardly met Clea before she got killed," she said. "All I saw her do was eat lobster." If Bruce and Jimmy refused to search Phil's room again, she'd do it by herself. She ran her tongue around the perimeter of the cone. The ice cream was beginning to melt. "You said Oscar wasn't Clea's only target—you mean when she investigated what developers are doing out here?"

"Ainsworth wasn't the only prominent developer," he said. "The rivalry could get pretty fierce. There isn't an unlimited quantity of open land."

"That's the whole point, isn't it?"

"Smart girl," he said.

"Woman."

"I'm too old to feel guilty about air bubbles in my political correctness," he said. "But I tell you what. I'm invited to a big mid-season party south of the highway. Want to come along? You can meet some of the rival developers and some of the big-money environmentalists who disagreed with Oscar's views and disapproved of his influence on the town."

"I can't decide which to say first," Barbara said, " 'I have a boyfriend' or 'I have nothing to wear.' "

"You've just said 'em both. One of the two gentlemen I met at the house, I assume. The big one or the other one? And if you don't care what a bunch of rich women who can spot a designer dress without reading the label think, you'll look fine whatever you wear."

"The big one is my significant other," Barbara said, "Jimmy—we've been together for a hundred years. The other one, Bruce, is our friend."

"Bring them along," he said, throwing out his arm in an expansive gesture.

"I'm a codependent," Barbara said. "I care what everyone thinks. But I can act as if I don't for a couple of hours. Would long black polyester and a lot of bling do?"

"Sure. And for the guys, a blue blazer and khaki pants with a decent shirt will pass muster if they've got good shoes."

"Jimmy has the right clothes in the city," Barbara said. "I don't know about Bruce, but we'll think of something. When is it?"

"First week in August. I take it that's a yes."

Barbara threw her head back and sucked at the tip of her cone, where the last of the melting ice cream had worn a damp spot rapidly becoming a hole.

"I'm glad you enjoyed your ice cream," Jeff said. He fished in the hip pocket of his jeans and drew out a slim digital recorder. "Now it's time for you to tell me all about your experiences finding dead people on the beach. We had a deal."

"I know," Barbara said. "Can I have another ice cream?"

Chapter Twenty

"I wish you were coming with us," I said.

Cindy and I were stocking up on fruits and vegetables at the weekly farmer's market.

"I'm not the dress-up type." She was wearing "Beach Blanket Babe" again today.

"Neither am I," I said. "I've been told I don't have any choice. Are you the dancing type?"

"Not for years. I can just about remember when disco died. Since then, I've had other things to do."

"Like what?" I picked up a giant melon, its rough beige hide warm between my hands, and pressed my thumbs down on its belly button, the way Barbara had ordered me to. It gave a little, a slight springiness, the way she'd said it should. "Look at the size of this cantaloupe."

"It's a musk melon." She pointed to a hand-lettered sign perched on top of the pyramid of melons. "What are you doing? Feeling it up?"

"Seeing if it's ripe."

"That's not how you tell. Let me smell it."

She bent her head and sniffed, sticking her nose between my thumbs. Her honey-colored hair, swinging free of its usual pigtails, tickled my wrists and fingers.

"Mmm. Smells ripe to me."

"Here, hold it a second," I said.

She held up her hands and I dropped the melon into her

palms. That freed my hands. Before she could straighten up, I took her head between my hands. I bounced my thumbs against the spot where she'd have had a round depression if she'd grown on a vine on the end of a stem. Bending close, I breathed in deeply.

"Mmm. Smells like seaweed."

"I'm a mermaid in disguise. I should get a sweatshirt that says, 'My other legs are a scaly tail.' "

Impulsively, I planted a kiss on the top of her head. We both jerked back, surprised.

"How many corns do you think we need?" she asked, backing up until she ran into a rustic cart piled high with tasseled ears. Not exactly a smooth segue.

"Barbara said this reporter guy told her there'd be a big spread at the party," I said, "so don't count on us for dinner."

"You'll miss Mrs. Dowling's blueberry pies," she said, pointing to the stand where the farmer's wife was doing a land office business in baked goods and bunches of flowers.

"I'm tied to the mast with cotton in my ears," I said with regret. "Barbara won't go without Jimmy, and Jimmy won't go without me."

"What makes me think it goes like that a lot with you guys?"

"Your exceptional insight and perceptiveness." I trotted after her as she piled local tomatoes, eggplant, and peaches in a giant basket.

"Here." She thrust a bag of corn at me. "I think that's it. Come stand in line with me. Tell me what's so important about this shindig."

"Barbara's already swatted me over the head with a newspaper for suggesting she's in it for the caviar and lobster salad. Jeff Bushwick, the reporter guy, said he'd introduce her to all the real estate honchos and save-the-seafood activists who might have had it in for Oscar."

"You are amateur-sleuthing, aren't you?" she marveled. "Why don't you leave it to the professionals?"

"I wish we could. But they don't seem to be getting anywhere. The people we'll meet tonight have motives that could take the pressure off us."

"You don't think the cops have already thought of that? Anyhow, a murder investigation isn't all about motive."

"Well, that's the part where we might have an edge. That and alibis. Besides—"

I stopped short, not sure how much I should confide in her.

"Besides, what? Don't stop now," she said.

Those last three words rang sweetly in my ears. I cut short the erotic fantasy that sprang to mind. Did I trust her enough to tell her about the notebook? Better not.

"Nothing. Never mind."

"Come on, Bruce, what?" She heaved the basket of fruit and vegetables onto the counter. "You do know it's a crime to withhold evidence in a homicide?"

"I don't have any evidence. I swear. And before you ask, neither do Jimmy and Barbara."

"Should I believe you?" She pulled a bunch of bills out of her wallet and forked them over. "And two blueberry pies."

"Yes. Scout's honor." I hoisted two heavy shopping bags off the counter. "Are you mad at me?"

"I don't want to see you get in trouble," she said.

"It's a good thing you didn't meet me a few years ago," I said. "I did nothing but get in trouble."

She laughed.

"A few years ago, I'd have been getting in trouble right along with you. I'd have *been* the trouble." She handed me another filled shopping bag. "Make that three blueberry pies." To me, she said, "There's bound to be some left. You might get hungry in the middle of the night."

The party was okay. It would have been more fun if Cindy had been there. Besides Barbara, the only other girl I knew there was one I had to stay away from: Veuve Clicquot. The Merry Widow had married a guy named Ponsardin since the first time I kissed her, but she could still take my breath away. Too bad my sobriety would go with it. I ate a lot of lobster salad to console myself.

Many ritzy parties in the Hamptons were benefits for one thing or another, charities or political candidates, but this wasn't. I guess that's why Jeff Bushwick was able to bring three guests. Tickets for the charity bashes cost hundreds or even thousands. The purely social nature of the event also explained how come environmentalists and developers were rubbing shoulders, if not toasting each other with champagne. Bushwick admitted he was covering the party for his paper, but I think he was also an old flame of the hostess, a three-chinned lady dripping in diamonds that were definitely not cubic zirconia. I saw her flirting and him playing up to her a couple of times. Apart from that, he worked the room like the pro he was. Much of the time, he steered Barbara by the elbow, introducing her to the fat cats and ecomaniacs with motives for killing Oscar. Maybe Clea too, depending on what she'd written or could have written about them. Jimmy and I were on our own.

The band wore tuxes and played a mix of ballroom and get-down music, or at least a dignified facsimile. I waltzed with our hostess, mostly to get a better look at those diamonds. Their fire nearly burned my eyeballs out. I guess high quality gems are like single-malt Scotch or Napoleon brandy. You can't mistake the real thing. I tried not to stare. I didn't want her to think I was casing the joint or getting fresh. To tell the truth, I was surprised she agreed to dance with me. But I'm relatively young and not so bad looking. Half the men there were geezers with style that said old money and broken-veined red faces that said,

"Hi, I'm an alcoholic." And I know how to waltz. A girl down in the Village taught me when I was seventeen, young enough so the lessons weren't what Barbara called state dependent. In other words, I didn't have to be drunk to remember how. The girl was a runaway debutante with a trust fund who played at being a hippie like Marie Antoinette pretending to be a milkmaid. She'd said knowing how to waltz would give me a big edge with women in the right circumstances.

Jimmy didn't dance. When I got twirled away from him, he gravitated toward the food tables along the walls. The catering was extreme: guys in chef hats carving giant hams and loins of beef to order. Fifteen minutes later, I spotted him talking with a knot of men, the group farthest from the bar. Jimmy has had a lot of practice avoiding active drunks. I could see him talk as well as listen. Very animated, using his hands, a trick he'd picked up from Barbara. Traditionally, meaning before Riverdance, the Irish kept their hands down at their sides even when they danced. The guys he'd clicked with were probably computer people, maybe investors. Jimmy could hold his own in that company. He fit in.

After my courtesy waltz, I ate some more and then insinuated myself into a group of skinny young blondes from Southampton, dancing with one after another when the music changed to something the kids could dance to. They all had tans I bet didn't stop at their underpants and did their best to shake themselves out of their very short, very low-cut dresses. By the time the last of them had danced herself out and headed for the bar with a flick of her fanny, I had sweat rolling down my face. I wondered if I'd get thrown out for hauling out a red bandanna. Before I could risk such a faux pas, Barbara arrived at my side. She handed me a white linen napkin.

"Thanks." I mopped my forehead gratefully. "Having fun?"

"Yes!" She'd been dancing too, in between squirreling away

information that might be relevant to the murders. But she was still full of beans. Barbara bounces. "You looked like you were doing okay. I don't suppose you heard anything useful?"

"Nope, I left that to you. Would it be sexist to call those little ladies chicks?"

"Yellow, fluffy, and not a brain among them, huh? I'll give you a dispensation."

"Good. They were all only about eighteen, anyway, off to college in the fall. They hadn't even heard about the murders. They think a paper like the *Dirty Deeds* is fish wrap, and they don't wrap fish."

"Not even Oscar?"

"One of them admitted Daddy mentioned he had died. Daddy didn't shed too many tears. Oscar was the competition."

"Did she tell you Daddy's name? Maybe I met him."

"No, but she pointed him out." I scanned the room. The band was taking a break. Everybody was talking, eating, or drinking, or all three. Chatter and laughter swelled until it filled my ears. For a moment, it became surreal, like getting stoned and sitting on the beach listening to the breakers crash. "There."

"The guy with the bright gold hair like Robert Redford? Yes, Jeff introduced me."

"Short like Redford too. Not as pretty, though." The man she indicated had a puffy red face and a bulbous nose. As we watched, he lifted a tall glass of amber liquid—no plastic cups at this fiesta—and poured it down his throat in a smooth stream. I could do that. I just didn't any more.

"Your lips are moving," Barbara said. "Say the Serenity Prayer and move on."

"Yes, dear. What's his name?"

"Morton Day. He said he was celebrating. He just got the contract for a huge new golf course. There must be a dozen golf courses in the Hamptons. Why do they need another one?" She answered her own question. "For the people who wouldn't be caught dead in the other ones, like the synagogues in the shaggy dog story about the Jewish shipwreck survivors on the desert island—though come to think of it, they couldn't do it if it really was a desert island, that means no water, doesn't it?"

Barbara digresses almost as often as she breathes.

"You're drifting."

"Yes, dear." She grinned at me. "But I do have a point. Oh, and for the people who the other people wouldn't be caught dead letting into the golf courses—country clubs, I guess you'd call them—they're already in. I always think it's so silly to say country clubs, don't you, when what's all around them is already country?"

"Morton Day," I reminded her.

"Sorry. He was celebrating. When Jeff introduced us, he couldn't shake hands because he had a bottle of Veuve Clicquot in one hand and a flute in the other. And now he's moved on to whiskey. I don't suppose you or Jimmy could twelve-step him?"

"The program is for those who want it, not for those who need it," Jimmy said as he came up behind us. "Attraction, not promotion."

"Yeah, yeah."

"I know." Barbara tucked her arm through his, jostling the glass of club soda with lime he held. "Hi, I'm codependent, and ooh, how I itch to fix that guy."

"What was he celebrating?" Jimmy asked.

"The deal to build the new golf course. He said the competition had dropped out. I bet he meant Oscar. He didn't exactly gloat—that would have looked bad, considering—but he sounded kind of smug. You know, just a few wisps of canary feather hanging from his lip."

"I talked to a stockbroker who sides with the environmentalists," Jimmy said. "It sounded like he's managed to make a bundle on socially responsible stocks. He told me all about what a threat new golf courses are to the Long Island water supply."

"The single aquifer—I remember," Barbara said. "Somebody asked Morton Day if he'd keep the whole golf course green."

"Right," Jimmy said. "Franchetti—my stockbroker—told me if they can't keep it out, they try to regulate it, make them leave a certain percentage of it natural. They can do that by planting wild grasses and letting them turn brown in the summer rather than all that emerald stuff that has to be watered constantly."

"I wonder if Clea ever interviewed Franchetti," I said. "He would have been a terrific source for her."

"I'll look," Jimmy said. "This was an ongoing crusade for her, from what we've heard."

"I can ask Jeff, too," Barbara said. "He can find stuff in the files of the *Dirty Deeds* and tell me how to check the other local papers, if not everything's online. But I bet any really dirty deeds got buried."

"A developer who'd screw the planet wouldn't blink at suing a newspaper for libel," I said. "But to win, he'd have to make sure they couldn't prove what they said about him was true."

"So one, he'd have to get rid of anyone who had proof," Jimmy said. "Two, he'd have to make sure nobody who might be more cooperative about the environmental agenda outbid him. And three, he'd have to lobby or bribe his way to making sure things went the way he wanted. Not every rich guy out here is like Franchetti. If they golf, they want the greens green."

"And screw the planet," I said.

"I can picture Morton Day in that scenario," Barbara said. "When they asked him about cutting back on the green, he said, 'That will depend on the politicians, won't it?' And I could swear I smelled canary on his breath."

Chapter Twenty-One

Barbara stood on one foot in the dark hallway, waiting to see if the creaking floorboard woke anybody up. Wobbling, she reached behind her to steady herself on the door handle of the room where Jimmy lay sleeping. The bolt snicked shut behind her. She had left the door cracked open to avoid making that very sound. Lowering her bare foot gingerly to the floor, she waited another minute. Jimmy's even snores were muffled by the closed door and the pillow he clutched to his head. In his dreams, she thought, it was probably a sandbag on a Civil War battlefield. No sound came from the other rooms. One cautious step at a time, she edged toward her objective: Phil's room down the hall.

Her fingers curled around a sliver of plastic: the LED light from her keychain, the only light she dared carry. She hoped she wouldn't need it to search Phil's room. With luck, his digital clock would provide enough ambient light for her to find the notebook. Bruce had only seen it for a minute, but he had described it: square, about a half inch thick, with a stained and faded cloth binding. If she felt it, she'd know what it was. That was how he'd found it in the first place.

Was she crazy to search Phil's room again? She and Bruce had looked high and low. The notebook hadn't been there—or anywhere else in the house. Obviously he'd taken it away. But she'd had a brainstorm. She couldn't get out of her mind that Phil might have brought the notebook back once he knew everybody had given up on finding it. Since they'd hunted for the notebook, Oscar had been killed. What if his death made what Clea had written mean something to Phil that it hadn't before? Suppose he wanted to make trouble for someone? It would fit his character. Maybe before Oscar's murder, all Phil had meant to do was keep the notebook hidden. She didn't think he would have destroyed it. Having it gave him power, and Barbara was sure that Phil liked having power. But now, what if he'd brought the notebook back to threaten somebody with? She knew it was just a theory, but it had a convincing ring. What if the notebook was sitting in plain sight in Phil's room, and the only reason she didn't get it into her own hands was that she didn't go and look? She couldn't take the chance.

She groped for the edge of Phil's door and found it, as she had hoped, not shut tight but emitting a sliver of greenish blinking light. She eased the door farther open, slipped through, and pulled it almost shut, praying the hinges wouldn't squeak. They didn't. A snatch of dinner conversation came back to her: Jimmy, Phil, and Lewis debating the merits of WD-40 versus Vaseline. Men! Only Bruce had abstained. She smiled to herself, wondering at what stage of sobriety, if ever, a guy like Bruce developed handyman skills. In this case, Phil's obsessive-compulsive tendencies worked to her advantage. He must have oiled the door hinges to prove his point.

She'd forgotten to check the time before she'd left her room. She couldn't stay too long. A glance at the digital clock showed her it wouldn't help her. The glowing green digits read 12:00, blinking on and off to indicate that some time during the night there had been a momentary power outage. The clock would need to be reset before it would tell time again. The flickering light fell on a mound of covers, with Phil presumably asleep beneath them. Didn't people hide things under the mattress? Surely he would wake if she ran her hand along the box spring.

She and Bruce had done that before with no success. Maybe beneath the mattress was where he *wouldn't* hide the notebook, because everyone knew to look there first. If she had to, she would. But she would start somewhere else.

She looked around the room. Her eyes had grown accustomed to the dim light. She slipped the little flashlight into the pocket of her robe, leaving both hands free. Phil really was a neat freak. His shoes lay lined up in an orderly row at the foot of the dresser: expensive running shoes, sandals, rubber-soled mesh water shoes, Docksiders, and polished dark lace-up dress shoes that he must have worn out from the city. Jimmy, with prodding, stuffed his socks into his shoes. Bruce crumpled his and threw them on the floor. Phil's were not in sight, but a bulging laundry bag hung from the knob of the closet door. Might he have stuffed the notebook in with the laundry? At least it would make no noise if she dug her arm in and felt around for it.

First things first, as they said in the program. On the purloined letter principle, she scanned the visible surfaces: the window sill, the empty chair—the one in her room was piled high with half-worn clothes, both hers and Jimmy's—the dresser top. Phil's wallet, watch, and keys were arranged with finicky neatness. He'd even pooled his loose change in a giant clam shell. No notebook. How about the closet? Plenty of hiding places there: tossed casually to the floor in the dark depths at the back or tucked into the pocket of a shirt or pair of pants on a hanger. He must have a suitcase or at least some kind of travel bag in there. If so, she'd already failed. No way could she lift down a suitcase and unzip it without waking him. Searching the dresser drawers would be almost as difficult, unless he'd oiled them too. Maybe this had been a bad idea, she thought, not for the first time.

But she was here, and she had to give it a shot.

The easiest place to start, she decided, was with the shoes. She didn't have to move them. In fact, she'd better not. She'd simply slip her hand inside each one—except the sandals, which obviously concealed nothing. No flip-flops, she observed. Too plebeian for Phil with his red Lexus. No bedroom slippers either. That surprised her. She wouldn't have expected him to allow a grain of sand to touch the soles of his feet, much less a germ-laden dust bunny. She crouched, maintaining her balance by anchoring the fingertips of her left hand while her right crept out and worked its way inside the right-hand dress shoe. Nothing. The notebook might not even fit. Bruce had said it was small, but how small? Phil sure was a silent sleeper. He hadn't stirred or expelled an audible breath.

Now the left. She caught her breath on a near-gasp as her fingertips touched an obstruction. It had to be the notebook! It was wedged tight inside the shoe. She couldn't bunch her hand enough to wiggle her thumb under it and get a good grip to pull it out. She'd have to scissor it between her index and middle fingers and pluck it out like a hair in a pair of tweezers. She'd have to be careful and work it out little by little. If the notebook remained stuck, pulling it too hard might flip the whole shoe over and send it flying across the room. No way Phil could sleep through the kind of clatter that would make.

She held her breath as she tugged at the notebook, gradually working her fingers deeper into the shoe and the notebook farther down past her knuckles until she had a firm two-finger grip on it. One more jerk and it came free. She shifted her grip, finally able to use her thumb, and twisted it out without scraping or moving the shoe. She had it!

"What the hell do you think you're doing?"

She whirled, still on her knees, and found herself crouching at Phil's feet, which were clad in leather scuffs. No wonder there'd been no noise from the bed or slippers in the lineup.

Some Nancy Drew she was!

"Get up!" He clamped a vise-like hand around her wrist and hauled her to her feet. "Bitch! I ought to slap your face! Give me that!" He plucked the notebook from her hand.

Shaking with fear and humiliation, Barbara couldn't find a word to say. Her arms tingled, and her knees went loose and weak. Phil slipped the notebook into his pocket without letting go of her wrist. He too wore a robe. He must have been in the upstairs bathroom off the kitchen when she came down the hall. And then she had been too absorbed to hear the sound of flushing or his footsteps on the stairs. He grabbed her other wrist and shook her hard. Her head swam. Her teeth clattered against one another. It felt as if her very bones rattled.

"Listen to me, you snoopy little cunt! You stay out of my business, do you hear? Do you?" He shook her harder. "Answer me!"

"Yes," she gasped. Should she scream? If she did, Jimmy and Bruce and probably all the rest of them would come running, and there would be the most godawful scene. She hated scenes. She might be codependent, but she didn't have a death wish. If he hit her, she would scream. "Let me go!"

He released her wrists in an abrupt motion that flung her away from him. She fell back against the dresser. Its rim dug into her back. He glowered at her, and she shrank away from him. He raised a menacing hand. She tucked in her jaw and shielded her face with her forearm. She needed a weapon. His keys! She groped behind her on the dresser.

"If you touch me, I'll scream the house down," she panted.

"Like hell you will," he jeered.

"I will too!" She took a deep breath and opened her mouth as his hand hovered above her head. It looked enormous. His face was set with fury, his neck cords bunched.

She braced her arm and scrambled for the keys.

"Oh, fuck it! Get the hell out of here!" Instead of landing on her face, his open palm slammed down on the dresser. She flinched and ducked as his arm thrust past her ear and shoulder. He caught the keys before they fell. "You stay out of my way from now on! And if you try to set those two little dogs of yours on me, you'll be sorry. You'll all be sorry!"

He pushed her out of the way and jerked the top drawer open. As she stood stunned and trembling, he snatched up a T-shirt and a pair of boxer shorts. He banged open the closet door, yanked a pair of jeans from a hanger, and threw them on the bed.

"I said get out!" He shoved her toward the door. "And keep your mouth shut, or else! Scram!"

Barbara fled.

She couldn't go right back and climb into bed next to Jimmy. Tottering as if the confrontation had aged her by twenty years, she pulled herself up the stairs and made her way onto the deck. In the dark of the moon, the sky blazed with stars: the dippers, the couple of other constellations she could recognize, the wide ribbon of the Milky Way, big steady Venus down near the horizon, and the meandering pricks of light that she knew were satellites. She heard a scuffle, squeak of fear, and hoot of triumph off in the brush. An owl pouncing on a chipmunk or young rabbit, she guessed. Predator and prey, like Phil and her. She had cut a sorry figure in there. She hated the loss of her dignity even more than not getting the notebook. She had been terrified. She could talk the talk of a militant feminist, but long exposure to kind Jimmy and easygoing Bruce left her ill prepared for encounters with violent men.

She heard the slam of a screen door, footsteps crunching on the walk, and the heavier slam of a car door. Phil! A motor revved. She saw the headlights of the Lexus come on. The car made a sloppy K-turn, spewing gravel, and raced down the drive. Brakes squealed as the car racketed onto the road. Gone! And the notebook with him, no doubt. He wouldn't leave it around the house for someone else to find. Barbara drew a deep, unsteady breath.

What if Phil had attacked her? He'd been on the brink of losing control. She'd seen him go off that time he fought with Ted. She couldn't tell herself he wouldn't really hit her. That was probably why she'd showed what Jimmy would no doubt call a grain of sense for once and not mouthed off at him the way she usually did when provoked. Phil was scary. He wouldn't have felt guilty if he had beaten her up, even if it had brought the whole household down on him. Why hadn't he hit her?

For one thing, he didn't want to call attention to the notebook. Somebody else might try to take it away. Or somebody might tell the police about it. What had Clea written? Something that incriminated Phil? Information that gave him power over someone else? Why hadn't he destroyed it? And why had he driven away? It was the middle of the night. Where would he go? Maybe he simply wanted to get the notebook out of the house—and make sure he wasn't around if she did wake Jimmy and Bruce up and tell them he'd attacked her. He couldn't be sure she wouldn't. His threats hadn't sounded too specific. She doubted he had a plan for what he'd do if they confronted him, tonight or in the morning. Maybe he'd just drive around and cool down. Or drive to the beach to think. Nice people didn't have a monopoly on the soothing power of the ocean.

Come to think of it, why hadn't anybody woken up? The walls of the house were thin. You'd think someone would have come running in. The two of them had banged around and yelled at each other for quite some time. Or had they? What had they actually said? Thinking back, Barbara realized she hadn't said one word above a gasp. She'd been too completely taken off guard and then too frightened. As for Phil, even while he cursed and bullied her, he must have cared enough about whatever secrets the notebook held to keep his rage in check. They had conducted the whole furious conversation in a whisper.

Chapter Twenty-Two

I woke up to pounding on the door. I squinted past the crusts on my eyes and ran a hand over the bristles on my face. They felt stiff enough to leave scrape marks. An alarmed babble floated down the stairs. Everyone else was up—awake and in the second-floor living room—probably just coming to. That left me closest to the door. The pounding sounded urgent.

"Hold your horses," I grumbled as I stumbled down the hall. My brain was still on automatic. *Wake Duncan with thy knocking! I would thou couldst.* I'd played the king in *Macbeth* in college, my one foray into acting. I'd enjoyed hanging out during rehearsals to see how everybody took my death, so a lot of the lines had stuck with me.

Everybody said you could leave your door unlocked out here. But some of us, notably Jimmy and I, were such city boys that we couldn't. I slid back the latch and let it dangle from the chain. Wiznewski and Butler pushed their way in. I barely had time to step back as the door swung past my nose. The detectives looked angry and bigger than normal. I knew I hadn't done anything. But thanks to all those years of drinking, my guilty conscience was on speed dial.

Behind me, the gang came pounding down the stairs. It sounded like they all were barefoot, but agitated enough to shake the steps anyway. I kept my eyes fixed on the police, so I didn't know if anyone was missing.

Wiznewski thrust his jaw forward, drew down the corners of

his mouth, and pushed his pursed lips out and in again. His gaze bored into mine and moved past me to the gang clogging the stairwell.

"There's been another fatality."

The twittering behind me consisted mostly of, "Who? Who?" They sounded like a nest full of owls. But one sharp cry rose above the chorus.

"What, in our house?"

That was downright weird. I wondered which of the women, like me, had *Macbeth* on her internal hard drive. As they herded us up the stairs, I remembered that the line was Lady Macbeth's. It was the wrong thing to say on first hearing Duncan had been killed. And she said the wrong thing because she was guilty. She already knew.

Once he'd rounded us up, Wiznewski didn't screw around.

"Your housemate, Philip Kersh," he said, "was the victim of a hit-and-run collision this morning. He's dead. We're treating it as a homicide, and you can consider this house a crime scene."

"Couldn't it have been an accident?" Barbara blurted. She shook off Jimmy's restraining hand on her shoulder. "A coincidence."

Wiznewski looked grim enough to grind enamel off his teeth.

"At this point, we're not treating a hangnail in this house as a coincidence."

Cindy squeezed in beside me as he herded us into the living room. I perched on one corner of the couch, and she sat on the floor with her knees drawn up. I could feel the warmth of her side, upper arm, and shoulder all up the length of my leg.

"Mr. Blaney, you're first," Wiznewski said. Lewis jumped to attention. If this killer kept going, I thought, we'd learn everybody's last name. None of us would be anonymous.

"Butler," he snapped. "Kersh's room." They knew where that was—same as Clea's.

"We'll talk—" He looked around at the open-plan space as if he hadn't seen it before. Everybody looked out the window. It was a dismal day. It was raining so hard that I could see silver raindrops bouncing off the sodden deck furniture, like the school of mackerel we'd seen leaping in the bay one day.

Barbara leaned over and whispered in Jimmy's ear. He gave one of his big, gusty ACOA sighs and raised his hand. Wiznewski's heavy eyebrows went down for frown, then up for interrogative.

"What, Mr. Cullen?"

"Your best bet is the little porch in back where I keep my computer." He sighed again. "I suppose I can't bring it out with me."

"Not till we examine it." Wiznewski turned to a uniformed officer who had followed the detectives in and started to unroll the yellow crime scene tape. "Perotsky, you do Kersh's room. Butler, check out this porch he's talking about. Set it up for interviews. See what's on the computer."

Jimmy looked agonized.

"Can't I just go in and show her? I make my living on it."

Wiznewski thought about it.

"Okay, you can go in and give her any verbal help you need to," he said grudgingly. "You don't touch, is that clear? Not the computer, not the screen, nothing."

Jimmy squawked.

"Is it clear, Mr. Cullen?"

"Yes, sir."

I looked from Jimmy to Barbara. I expected to see steam wafting out of her ears. But she was remarkably subdued this morning.

"You said it was a hit and run," I said.

"It was," Officer Perotsky said. "He was tossed on the side of the highway like road kill."

Wiznewski bared his teeth and growled. Perotsky scooted out of the room, trailing yellow tape.

Wiznewski pretended the little Keystone Kops moment hadn't happened.

"We'll examine all your cars, and we'll want to see everybody's driver's license."

He looked at our motley dishabille. Not a soul had shoes or pockets, much less a wallet or a handbag. "An officer will escort you one by one to collect them when we're ready."

Oh, shit. I had been concerned on Jimmy's behalf and wondering what had gotten into Barbara. Three bodies in a row had knocked her for a loop. At least she hadn't found this one. I hadn't liked Phil enough to be unduly troubled he was gone. I wasn't scared they'd pick me as prime suspect. If they linked this death with Oscar's, they'd question everyone over in the other house. Someone would tell them about Phil's fight with Ted. I didn't even own a car. But here came Wiznewski's curve ball. I had been relief-driving Jimmy and Barbara's Toyota whenever they needed me to for about a year now. I hadn't gotten into any trouble on the road. I'd simply omitted telling them I'd lost my license years ago. I didn't have one.

Chapter Twenty-Three

I held out for three days. By that time, I felt too depressed to fend off Barbara's solicitous attempts to find out what was wrong. She wouldn't leave it alone, but followed me around pressing emotional chicken soup on me.

When I told her, she screeched, "How could you *do* that?"

"You're right," I said. "I did a bad thing. Look, both of you, I'm sorry I lied to you."

"I'm disappointed," Jimmy said.

I hate disappointing Jimmy.

"If you need a brush-up for your road test, I'll be glad to help," he said. "I'll pay for lessons or take you out myself."

Even worse. I felt like a worm. I'd fucked up plenty in the many years between when Jimmy put the bottle down and when I landed up in detox on the Bowery. Since I got sober, I had tried to convey to them that I knew I'd been an asshole. They didn't stand over me waiting for me to cop to my shortcomings. But they had thought I'd changed my behavior. It was never too early in recovery to stop breaking laws.

The worst part was that by driving their car without a license, I'd put them at risk. If a cop had stopped me, what would they have said? That they didn't know me and I'd just hijacked the car? Jimmy would have tried to take responsibility. I didn't know what the law did to someone who let an unlicensed driver drive his car. But what I'd done sure made it look like I didn't care. When I was drinking, I did stuff I couldn't help. I drank too much because I had a disease. A disorder. A compulsion. I acted stupid and crazy because that's what alcohol does to your brain chemistry. I ran away from relationships and my own feelings. But I was sober now. And I had gone on driving because it was *convenient.* I wanted what I wanted. I hadn't told a soul, either, because then I would have had to stop.

It was a little easier to be around Cindy. She showed no inclination to coddle me and didn't say a word about my mood. Also, she didn't know. But it was hard to keep up the act of devil-may-care Romeo that I was afraid to drop for fear the real me would turn her off. Part of me was disgusted with myself for finding it so hard to be genuine. What kind of a relationship would we have if I couldn't stop faking it? All in all, Bruce was not my favorite person right now. Meanwhile, the desire to have a real relationship with Cindy, not just get her into bed, kept getting stronger. Taking it slow was an experience that kept surprising me. And it would serve me right if it turned out she was a lesbian all along.

I did manage to notice that my internal angst was not the most important thing going on in Dedhampton. Over the next week or two, the atmosphere in the house got more and more tense. Oscar's place was no better, though Corky tried to maintain the anything-goes ambience. Everybody escaped to the city periodically. But nobody who'd paid for a house in the Hamptons wanted their investment to go to waste. My roomie Stewie came out to Dedhampton every weekend but took his couple of weeks' vacation in Fire Island. Cindy popped in and out on an irregular schedule that had nothing to do with weekdays and weekends. Whenever I asked, she would blow it off and say, "Oh, it's crazy busy at work." I got the message: she didn't want to be asked about her city life. I hoped she wasn't married.

When Barbara ran out of vacation days, Jimmy suggested she

call her boss and ask for some unpaid leave. That was an act of love, since as we all knew, Jimmy would always rather be in the city. But Barbara's heart didn't seem to be in her summer in the Hamptons any more. So they started going back and forth as well. I went with them a few times. But the city was hot and sticky. The offices where I temped were air conditioned and freezing. The work was boring. And every day I spent in Dedhampton was a day I might have a chance to spend with Cindy.

Among those who stayed, and on the weekends, when almost everyone showed up, invisible barriers went up. Karen moped around the house with puffy eyes or took the car and disappeared. She and Lewis barely spoke. Jeannette spent endless hours in the kitchen. We ate like we'd been given a free pass to a four-star restaurant, and it all tasted like cardboard and ashes. Jimmy dove into cyberspace. Everybody else spent long hours on the beach. Dark glasses, a beach chair inclined all the way back, and an open paperback face down on the belly made a very effective No Trespassing sign.

We all made endless trips to the town police station. When it was my turn, Barbara drove me, making a noticeable effort not to comment on the fact. The detectives remained polite as they asked the same questions over and over. I figured they were trying to fit together the three deaths, Clea's, Oscar's, and Phil's, like a Sudoku puzzle or one of those Rubik's cubes from the eighties. We all had connections, if not convincing motives. I had to tell the story of my pathetic teen-sex moment with Clea until I wished at least I'd let her give me head. Okay, add crudeness to the list of my nastier defenses. I had no way to prove I hadn't seen her from that night till we'd both shown up in Dedhampton.

Barbara was equally displeased to have to keep repeating the events of that nude group swim. On top of the embarrassment, the cops' assumption that Jimmy might have killed Oscar for putting uninvited hands on her made her furious. It shook even Jimmy's equanimity enough that he told the cops about the missing notebook. He was ready to throw Lewis to the wolves to take their attention off Barbara. They gave all of us hell for not telling them before. Neither Barbara nor I admitted that we'd looked for it. To judge by the cops' persistent questions and the edge of annoyance I detected when the subject came up, they hadn't found it either. Jimmy pointed out that the police now had access to Phil's car and his apartment. Barbara said that must mean he'd destroyed it. Burned it or shredded it or taken the subway out to Canarsie and tossed it into a Dumpster. Maybe we'd never know.

The interviews all took place in an undramatic small room like the untenanted offices that various companies had stashed me in as a temp. The lobby was the intimidating part of the police station. It was a big, high, very dark, empty space with two blank walls and two glass windows, no doubt bulletproof. The one to the right shielded the receptionist's desk, at which nobody ever seemed to be sitting. Behind the one straight ahead as the visitor walked in, the ordinary workplace life of the cops went on. I'd been in a police station or two in New York City in my time, and they allowed much more drama. Sometimes I'd been entertained. Sometimes I'd been the entertainment.

Coming out into the glare of the parking lot my third or fourth time there, I ran into Cindy. I blinked.

"What are you doing here?"

Cindy was the only one with absolutely no connection to Clea, Oscar, or Phil.

She laughed.

"Lost umbrella."

She meant it was none of my business. I could take a hint. That didn't mean I chose to. Instead of pressing her, I was sneaky enough to wait till she went in. The heavy door swung closed behind her. I counted to fifty, then cracked it open. As I'd hoped, she was still negotiating entry through the microphone. The strip of light I let in fell behind her in a diagonal on the floor. She didn't notice. Neither did Butler, who was scowling at her through the glass.

They didn't encourage visitors to state their business discreetly. Maybe the gloomy barrenness of the lobby was intended to make it unlikely that more than one member of the public would want in at any given time. It was the exact opposite of a hospital emergency room waiting room, where the lights are never off and the uncomfortable chairs are never empty. I'd been both spectator and show in some of those too.

"Dammit, Butler," Cindy said as I laid my cheek against the jamb, "stop treating me this way!"

"You lied to us, Cinders." Butler's deep voice coming through the speaker system sounded like Darth Vader's. "Face the consequences."

What had she lied about? Most likely, someone had told the detectives about Cindy's role in busting up the fight at Oscar's. What was she supposed to do? Call 911? I thought she'd done the right thing. One black eye and one bloody nose weren't worth breaking the anonymity of the whole meeting. But if Butler was her friend, I guess she saw it differently. What was with those two? I still couldn't figure out if they'd been lovers or if one was the other's sponsor. Maybe they'd fought in Iraq together. They both were tough enough. I wanted to hear Cindy's answer. But Butler caught sight of me. Her voice boomed out.

"Hey!"

I scuttled backward, letting the door fall shut. I hoped that whatever their problem was, they were mad enough at each other that Butler wouldn't tell Cindy she'd seen me snooping.

When Cindy stormed out five minutes later, I was leaning idly up against her car. She spotted me a couple of rows away and checked her furious dash. She slipped between two cars about four down in the row and strolled toward me.

"Find your umbrella?"

Her mouth twitched as she scanned my innocent face. Trying not to laugh. So not too annoyed with me.

"Nope. They had a pile of them, but not mine. Where's your car?"

"Barbara said she'd pick me up. But if you'll give me a ride back to Dedhampton, she won't need to." A quick call to Barbara on my cell phone, and we were in business.

Traffic was on my side, slow and thick enough to give us a little time. I meant to get her in the mood to talk. "Get in" and "Seatbelt!" didn't count. I buckled up, but left the belt loose enough so I could twist onto one hip, get an arm across the seat back, and watch her profile as she drove. Her jaw was very square from this angle. Expressions came and went across her face as she engaged in some interior tussle. Frustration: the brows crawled toward the bridge of her nose; the lower lip came out in a pout. Scorn: the corners of her lips curled; the oversized incisors crept out. Those bouncy little pigtails were still cute as hell. I wanted to tweak them.

As we hung a left into East Hampton village, the one with the swans and the old graveyard, she broke the silence.

"Why would somebody kill Phil?"

Ha! She was amateur sleuthing too.

For Clea's notebook. But Cindy didn't know about that. If I hadn't told her, Jimmy and Barbara certainly hadn't. Nor would Lewis have brought it up. He hadn't even mentioned it again to me.

"Uh, because he was a tightass? Nah, not worth a hit and run."

She looked sideways at me, keeping both hands steady on the wheel. A giant digital readout to the side of the road told us we were going fourteen miles per hour.

"Cut the crap," she said. "I know you've thought about this. I want to hear what you think."

I ticked them off on my fingers.

"One, he knew something about Clea's and/or Oscar's death." There. I'd said it without mentioning the notebook.

"Killed because he was a threat?"

"Maybe even blackmailing someone."

"Blackmail's kind of old-fashioned, don't you think? What used to be juicy secrets are just fodder for bloggers these days."

"Murder is still a secret any killer would go a long way to keep," I said. "Maybe somebody was blackmailing him."

"Why?" she asked. "He killed Clea and somebody knew?"

Come to think of it, I knew two secrets about Phil. Oh, what the hell.

"Phil was a compulsive gambler."

"In recovery?"

"No, but please don't ask me how I know. I found out the night of Oscar's party." I played the anonymity card because if she knew he'd left traces on Jimmy's computer, she'd say it was evidence and want us to tell the police. Then they'd take away Jimmy's computer. I couldn't do that to him.

"Did Phil go to the party?" she asked. "I didn't see him, but then, I wasn't looking."

Our gazes locked briefly and skittered away from each other.

"No," I said. "He was home alone the night of Oscar's party."

"That means we don't know where he was," she said. "He could have killed Oscar as well as Clea."

"What about this?" I said. "Oscar couldn't have been killed till after everyone had left the party. Phil could have waited for us to get back and go to bed. Then he could have driven to

Oscar's. Say he parked somewhere inconspicuous. He finds Oscar on the deck and pushes him down the stairs. Then he races to make it back to our house before anyone realizes he's gone."

"Somebody could have seen him. That red car is conspicuous."

"Maybe he got lucky," I said. "He was a gambler. He'd take the chance."

"You got that right. If a gambler *feels* lucky, to him it's a fact." She skirted a line of cars going left of the windmill at the far end of the village and speeded up. "My dad was a gambler."

"Oh, shit."

"Right response. Gamblers are even better rationalizers than alcoholics. If they're winning, they feel lucky, so they go on playing. If they're losing, they have to chase the luck until it turns, so they go on playing."

"Did you love him?"

"Unfortunately, yes. My mother was the penny pincher, so she's the one I rebelled against. My dad had charm to spare."

So she'd be extra wary of a charming guy like me.

"I adored him," Cindy said. "When he won, it was like Christmas. When he lost, she yelled and nagged and cried, but he would cuddle me and paint pretty pictures about how great life would be when the Big Win came along." She leaned over, stretched an arm across me, and fished a cassette tape out of the glove compartment. "When I stopped believing him, that's when I started drinking."

She popped the tape in, and a guy started singing about how the lady was a lot like Reno.

"You like country music?"

"I collect gambling songs. But that's as close as I get."

We passed through Amagansett. My cell phone rang.

"It'll be Barbara," I said. "Jimmy never calls me, and nobody else has the number."

I flipped the phone open.

"Yes, dear."

"Where are you?" Barbara quacked in my ear.

"On the way back. Why?"

"Jeannette just called the house, hysterical because Wiznewski put her through the wringer, and she needs a ride home."

I made roll 'em motions with a forefinger for Cindy's benefit.

"She got a lift there, and I was going to pick her up when I came for you, I forgot to tell you, but if you and Cindy can swing around and get her, that would be great. The poor thing needs some moral support as much as a ride."

"Breathe in," I said. "Breathe out. We're almost at Napeague, but let me ask Cindy." I explained the situation.

"No problem," Cindy said. "I wonder why Wiznewski put pressure on her."

"I guess we'll find out." To Barbara, I said, "We've got it. See you later."

I flipped the phone closed.

"Did you get Jeannette's cell number?" Cindy asked.

"I don't think they've locked her up yet. Barbara would have said."

"Clown," she said.

"Barbara will call her back. We both forgot to mention it, but she will."

Cindy flicked on her turn signal and made a quick, tight U across the highway. We rolled back through Amagansett and East Hampton, not exactly speeding but not wasting any time, either.

We found Jeannette in the parking lot. The sun rode high in the sky, and there wasn't any shade in the lot. Jeannette's creamy pink face was moist with sweat, like a peach that's been run under a faucet. She mopped at it with the edge of her sleeve.

"Oh, thanks so much for coming for me!"

"No problem," Cindy assured her. She clicked open the door locks.

Jeannette climbed awkwardly into the back seat. She really was a big girl.

"Let's get you home," Cindy said.

I twisted around in my seat so Jeannette could see my face.

"What happened?"

"They suspect me. I don't have an alibi. Well, I do, sort of, but it's almost worse than not having one. I'm so scared."

"Where's your car?"

"It's in the shop. That's part of why they're so suspicious."

"How come?" I asked. "When did you bring it in?"

Jeannette put both hands up to her damp cheeks and stroked downwards with her palms, wiping or maybe just comforting herself.

"That sergeant asked the same questions."

"Sorry!"

"No, that's okay."

"Tell us," Cindy said.

"The morning Phil got run over, I had already been out when the cops arrived. I got up early because my inspection sticker was about to expire. I couldn't wait till I got back to the city. I wish it didn't come due in the summer, but that's when I bought the car. It's a real hassle getting your car inspected out here. You have to bring it in really early and leave it all day. All the gas stations and repair shops are so busy in the season."

"So your car wasn't at the house. They'd want to go over it. Their next step would have been to send someone to the shop."

"I didn't tell them about the car until now." Jeannette wrung her hands, as if she were shaking down a thermometer. Two thermometers.

"That was bad," Cindy said. "Wiznewski must have been furious."

"He was," Jeannette said miserably.

"But why is your car still in the shop?"

"They found a problem. The mechanic explained it to me, but I can't keep car stuff in my head. I'm hopeless with it. He had to order a part, and we're still waiting for it. They have a car wash in the back. There aren't too many of those on the East End. So as long as the car was sitting there, I had them give it the full treatment."

"Waxing, buffering, detailing?"

"I just said yes to everything."

"And you didn't admit this to Wiznewski until today?" Cindy shook her head. "No wonder you're in trouble. They'll go right over there, you know. Even if the car's been cleaned, they can find traces of blood. Move it, asshole!" This last was addressed to an old fart in a pickup truck who eased up to a changing traffic light with exquisite timing, so that he made it through and we didn't.

"Only if she killed Phil," I pointed out. "No murder, no blood."

"I hit a deer!" Jeannette wailed.

"Oh shit! When?"

"The day before. It ran across the road so fast!"

"You could have been killed yourself."

"I know," Jeannette said. "So I slammed on the brakes. I'd just seen an article in the *Deeds* about how there are more deer every year and everything is so built up that they don't have enough habitat."

"I read it," Cindy said. "That's why you see them on the roads and even in the streets sometimes. Did you kill it?"

"No," Jeannette said. "I hit it, and I think I hurt it, but it ran away into the woods."

"That's good," I said.

"No, it's not," Cindy said. "If the deer had been lying dead on the side of the road, somebody would have seen it, and it would confirm her story."

"Oh."

"That's what the sergeant said," Jeannette agreed. "And I didn't report it, because there was nothing to report except a few dents."

"You left the scene," Cindy said. "But it sounds like you only brushed it. If you'd hit it hard enough to kill it, it would have been like any collision—a bloody mess. Did you get the dents fixed?"

"No, the shop I went to doesn't do bodywork. Besides, bodywork is so expensive. I wasn't sure whether or not to bother. I was thinking it over."

"Girl, you are in trouble," Cindy said.

"Won't they check the blood?" Jeannette asked in a small voice. "I couldn't ask back there, because I didn't tell them about the deer."

"If they find traces, they'll send them to the lab," Cindy said. "It could take time, though."

"Still," I said. "If she didn't kill Phil, they won't find human blood on her car. So sooner or later she'll be in the clear."

Jeannette started crying again.

"They think I killed Oscar too. And I didn't have any reason to kill Phil, but I did for Oscar."

Jeannette sobbed. Her nose began to run. She swiped her sleeve along her upper lip without much impact.

"Box of tissues under your seat, Bruce," Cindy said.

I found them and passed them back. Jeannette snatched two or three tissues out of the box and blew her nose, honking like a Canada goose.

"Sorry," she said. "I didn't mean to inflict all of this on you.

But if they arrest me, everyone will know. I could lose my social work license."

"Only if you're convicted," Cindy said. "And in that case, losing your license would be the least of your worries."

"What happened with Oscar?" I asked.

"Now or before?"

"Whatever you want to tell us," Cindy said.

Jeannette blew her nose again.

"If I tell you all of it, maybe I'll feel better. You know, I'm not a therapist like a lot of social workers. I've done adoption work ever since I got out of school. I deal with people, but it's not clinical. It's concrete. When you do a home study, you don't ask the prospective parents how they feel, you look at how they live."

"How about the moms who are giving up their babies?"

"That's why I got into adoption work in the first place," Jeannette said. "Some of my colleagues see themselves as advocates for the adoptive parents and despise the birth moms. I hate that. They're scared. A lot of them are too young to parent their babies, but it still takes guts to let them go. Even the crack babies. I'm in recovery myself. I know you don't have to be a worthless person to get addicted or an evil one not to get help."

"What about you and Oscar?"

"I'm getting there," Jeannette said. "You know those shell necklaces we all wear?"

"Uh-huh. Oscar made them, right?"

"They had a meaning," Jeannette said. "You got one for fucking Oscar. We all walked around with Oscar's sexual abacus around our necks. He kept score."

"The son of a bitch," I said. For a change, it felt good to be me.

"A sexual compulsive," Cindy said, "and not in recovery."

"Yes, Mr. AA had a few character defects," Jeannette said.

"Not that I realized that. I was just another stupid codependent who thought sex could be a short cut to love and commitment. How many trips to the hardware store do we have to take before we get it that they don't sell oranges?"

"You're not alone," Cindy said.

"Men aren't immune from relationship addiction either," I said.

We gave each other a sidelong glance. She wanted to hear more as much as I did. But now was not the time.

"Go on, Jeannette," Cindy said.

"Not every man wants to sleep with a woman as fat as I am."

"That must hurt."

"Oh, it does. Even in the personal ads, do you know how many men stipulate that they want to meet a woman who's thin? And when they ask for a picture, that's not just so they can reject anyone who isn't pretty, even if they're not good looking themselves. They want to make sure you're not fat."

"Some men think lush and voluptuous is beautiful," Cindy said.

"Not the men I've met."

"But you—"

"Don't say it!" Jeannette snapped. "If you want to cut a fat woman to the heart, tell her, 'You have such a pretty face.' "

"That's not what I was going to say," I protested. I lied. Who knew?

She calmed down, her high color fading.

"Sorry. But everybody says it. We're supposed to take it as a compliment, but they're really saying, 'You're fat and that's unacceptable and it's all your own fault.' "

"How about Oscar?"

"He was a practiced seducer," Jeannette said. "I was a pathetic, flattered, desperate fool. I thought he actually liked me until he'd fucked me twice, tossed me a necklace with two pretty little jingle shells on it, and walked away."

"I'm so sorry," I said.

"Clea's necklace had a lot of shells," Cindy said.

"So does Karen's," I said.

"I understand the alleged motive," Cindy said. "Did you have an opportunity to kill Oscar?"

"I didn't," Jeannette said, "but I can't prove it. I didn't go home that night."

It took me a moment to get it.

"You went home with someone else?"

"Not home. Into the dunes with a guy I didn't know who turned out to be a smirking self-centered chubby chaser. To him, I was just a soft pillow-top mattress for him to sink into and congratulate himself on giving a loser a thrill."

"But where did you spend the night?"

"On the beach," Jeannette said. "I'd let Stephanie take the car because I thought he was taking me to his house. I guess I could have walked home when he dumped me. I could do four miles if I were desperate. But I was feeling so vulnerable. I didn't want to move. With my luck, I'd get hit by a drunk driver or raped by some guy in a pickup truck on those lonely roads. So I stayed put. We'd taken a throw from Oscar's house to lie on, and I grabbed it when I stalked away, so I was a little damp but not cold."

"You were on the beach when Oscar got killed," I said. "I bet the cops got excited about that."

"I don't know when he got killed," she said. "I told them and told them that. We had walked quite a way down the beach, you know, fooling around and holding hands the way you do when your hormones are all fired up and you don't know yet that the guy is a jerk."

I sank down in my seat in as close as I could get to fetal position without removing the seatbelt.

"Men!" Cindy said. "So you didn't see or hear anything."

"No, and even if I'd known the asshole's name and where he lived, even if he'd still been with me when it happened, why would he bother to give me an alibi? All he has to do to stay out of it is deny the whole thing."

"They will look for him," Cindy said, "going on whatever information you could give them."

"I hope so. They said they would. But even if they find him, it may not help."

"You do have the deck stacked against you," Cindy said. "They've got you for motive and opportunity on Oscar and opportunity on Phil. I suppose they also think you killed Clea. If someone tells them what the necklaces meant, they'll know she had no trouble keeping Oscar, who'd dumped you almost immediately. You could have killed her out of jealousy, or she could have taunted you or given you a hard time in some other way."

Maybe Jeannette had killed them, I thought. Cindy's hypotheses were plausible.

Jeannette sat up straight with such a convulsive movement that the box of tissues on her lap fell to the floor.

"I would never have killed Clea!" she cried. "She was my daughter!"

Chapter Twenty-Four

"You've got to be kidding," Barbara said. "Clea was adopted, and Jeannette was her birth mother?"

"Uh-huh."

We lay on the beach with the sun beating down. To be accurate, I lay on a towel with my arm over my eyes. Barbara had been lying beside me, her towel spread neatly over the sand bed she'd made for herself with a hump at the head for a pillow and a scooped-out depression for her butt. But she sat bolt upright when I passed on Jeannette's revelation.

"How did they find each other? They didn't just happen to wind up in the same group house in the Hamptons and somehow figure out that they were related, did they?"

"God isn't quite that anonymous."

Program people love the saying that a coincidence is God's way of remaining anonymous. They see a Higher Power in everything that happens. All these dead bodies suggested HP had a bad day here and there.

"They found each other on one of those websites," I said.

"They were both looking? Sometimes the mother doesn't want to be found, and sometimes the child is too mad about being abandoned to look for her."

"They must have been," I said. "Otherwise, they wouldn't have been listed. I thought the whole point was to give the children control over what happens."

"It is," Barbara said. "How old was Clea? Twenty-four or

twenty-five, maybe? I think open adoptions started in the early or mid-eighties, so that would make it about right for neither of them to start out with any information about the adoption, without necessarily believing that never the twain shall meet. And Jeannette worked in adoptions, so she'd have known how to go about it. I guess that's why she went into that field, huh?"

"That's what she said. When she had Clea, she was very young. She grew up in a small town upstate where they treated what they still called 'unwed mothers' like criminals."

"Not sinners?"

"That too. The father was black."

"Oy vey. So that was where she got that gorgeous ginger snap complexion, and the ringlets didn't come from an expensive hair salon."

"Yeah, well, her family didn't see it quite that way."

"Did they have a relationship?"

"No, it was a one-night stand. She met him at a party. The nearest city had a university, and she said the high school girls used to dress up to look older and crash their mixers. She spent nine months not only being regarded as a tramp but knowing the baby was going to come out what her family called 'colored.' They were some kind of fundamentalists. Abortion was not an option."

"Oh, God, poor Jeannette," Barbara said. "So she gave the baby up right away?"

"Yeah, and felt like shit about it." I sat up to catch the cool breeze that blew steadily off the ocean. It was hot down there at sand level.

"So how did they connect?" Barbara pulled her hair up off her neck and slapped on some sun block. "And how did they get to Oscar's?"

"They emailed first and then talked on the phone. Then they decided to spend some time together and see if they wanted to take it any further. They thought shares in a group house would be a safe way to get to know each other."

Barbara shuddered and hugged her knees.

"It wasn't safe for Clea."

"It wasn't so hot for Jeannette, either. She slept with Oscar, hoping for romance, and guess what?"

"It turned out to be another one-night stand."

"Two."

"But who's counting?"

"Oscar was." I told her about the necklaces. "It gets worse."

"Let me guess," Barbara said. "Clea hopped into bed with Oscar."

"Bingo. They screwed like bunnies for the rest of the summer. Many shells on the necklace."

"What a perfect way for the abandoned child to get even with the biological mom. So how on earth did they end up sharing a house again?"

"Jeannette moved to Lewis and Karen's house last summer, and Clea went back to Oscar's, though by that time they'd both moved on."

"Jeannette still felt ambivalent, though, I bet," Barbara said. "She must have yearned for the daughter she'd hoped Clea would be, or she wouldn't have come back at all."

She smoothed out the sand adjacent to her towel with a wide sweep of her hand and started drawing patterns in it with one finger.

"You know, Clea's motive for taking up with Oscar might not have been revenge," she said. "She and Oscar were both sexual compulsives."

"Yeah, they wanted another fix," I said. "And to hell with anyone who stood in their way."

Barbara cocked her head.

"Would you care to make an 'I' statement about your feelings?"

"No thanks." My twinge of regret for past behavior wasn't worth sharing. I stood up and shook out my legs.

Barbara held out a hand. I reached down and pulled her to her feet.

"Let's go in," she said. "The water looks great." She tugged at my hand, and we made our way toward the ocean. The jade expanse sent breakers, not big enough to be threatening, ashore at a steady pace. "So what else did she tell you?"

"How hurt she was."

"At the betrayal," Barbara said. "Oscar rejected her sexually, and Clea rejected her too."

"She knew she couldn't expect Clea to love an unknown mother. But she still felt stabbed to the heart."

"Would she have killed her, though?" Barbara splashed into the water up to her knees. She scooped some up and splashed it over her arms.

I inched a few cautious toes past the leading edge of a wave. Long Island beach veterans called August water warm. I found that debatable.

"I don't know. She said Clea was cruel."

"I wonder if she played the weight card," Barbara said. " 'I'm nothing like you, mom, you're fat and I'm thin, so don't try to claim me after throwing me away when I was born.' "

"They had the same eyes," I said.

"Clea had amazing green eyes," she said. "They were part of her beauty."

"Jeannette has green eyes too. They're just like Clea's, but I never noticed."

"Me neither. That's sad."

"Yeah. She said to me and Cindy, 'Who notices a fat woman's eyes?' "

After our swim, we raced each other back to where we'd left our towels. We didn't have a lot of gear. Barbara had parked the car at the Dedhampton lot, but then we'd walked, at her insistence, down to the deserted stretch of beach in front of Oscar's.

"I wonder where the gang at Oscar's is," Barbara said, glancing up at the house.

"I suppose we should call it Corky's now."

The house looked more than ever like a ship, its hull made of weathered cedar, riding high against the burning blue sky. The deck appeared empty, but as we watched, a figurehead appeared on the prow: Corky, topless as a mermaid, emerged from the house. She stood leaning against the wall by the door. In lieu of a scaly tail, she wore a flimsy blue and green wrap around her hips. The sea colored cloth fluttered in the wind.

"I wonder if she's wearing so much as a thong under that pareo," Barbara said. "Should we hail her?"

"Wait," I said.

A man stepped through the dark doorway. He wore a striped towel around his waist. Corky turned and pressed herself against his chest. His arms closed around her waist.

"Who is that?" Barbara shaded her eyes with her hand and squinted. "Oh. It's faithful Dobbin. Love conquers all."

"Shep? I didn't know they were an item," I said. "How did you?"

"I've seen him look at her. I don't know if it's a fling or a thing."

"Want to go up and say hello?"

The stairs down which Oscar had fallen to his death looked innocent. A couple of pots of cheerful red geraniums framed the topmost step. An assortment of flip-flops and beach toys were arranged around the bottom.

"Let's wait and watch them. I wonder if anything actually happened until Oscar died. Look, he's going in."

"So's the sun."

Barbara turned and surveyed the beach to left and right.

"You're right. Where did it go?"

I pointed out to sea.

"Look, a fog is rolling in." The horizon had vanished, and a thick mat of pearly gray blotted out the sun. Five minutes before, the air had sparkled. Now it felt soft and damp.

"So much for sunbathing," Barbara said.

"Let's go say hello to Corky," I suggested.

"She's putting on a T-shirt," Barbara remarked. "No more bare-breasted maiden."

"Good. I'll be marginally less embarrassed when you pry into her love life."

"So let's go," Barbara said. "It's cold and gray. It might even rain. Race you there." She trotted toward the steps, waving and calling, "Yoo-hoo!"

Corky came forward to the deck rail and started waving back.

I picked up my towel and followed.

As we approached, Corky rearranged her pareo so it covered her breasts and knotted it at one shoulder. She did have a thong on underneath.

"How do you like our microclimate?"

"What happened to the sunshine?" Barbara asked.

"It's probably smiling down on your place as we speak."

"Likes to go slumming, huh?"

"Even south of the highway, money can't buy everything," Corky said. "The nearer the ocean, the worse the weather. Stay a while. Have a seat. Would you like some lemonade?"

"No, thanks," I said.

"Yes, please," Barbara said.

As Corky turned to go in and play hostess, a bolt of lightning ripped the rapidly blackening sky out over the ocean. Thunder rumbled as if someone up there was rolling giant boulders around. A couple of fat raindrops hit my face.

"On second thought," Corky said, "why don't you come in? Looks like it's about to pour."

On the heels of her words, the rain came down. I followed Corky into the house. Barbara lingered on the deck to raise her face and arms to the sky and open her mouth wide.

"Barbara!"

"It's okay, I'm still wet anyway."

I held the door until she gave up trying to catch raindrops on her tongue or commune with the thunder gods and scurried in. By that time, the rain was coming down in sheets and rattling the windows. Corky knelt in front of the fireplace, laying kindling for a fire. Barbara crouched down next to her and eyed the sticks with the air of an expert.

"Oh, you make a tepee first—so do I. And then a log cabin around it?"

"Sometimes. This time, I'm going to use driftwood. It doesn't arrange that neatly, but the salts give the flames some amazing colors, blue and green and sometimes violet. You'll see."

"Were you a Girl Scout? I was."

"Yeah. I guess I'd better make this a one-match fire, huh?"

They grinned at each other. Barbara didn't have to make eye contact for me to know she'd just crossed Corky off her suspect list. When I got her alone, I'd remind her how many times she'd told me and Jimmy that Girl Scouts were exceptionally self-reliant. So were murderers.

"Is there any chance that you could lend us some clothes?" Barbara asked.

"Of course! It's like a lost and found here, with so many people coming and going, and Oscar's things are all still in his closet."

Barbara took the box of matches from her hand.

"Go ahead, I'll finish the fire."

"You don't mind?" Corky asked.

"You made her day," I assured her.

"Give me those towels," Corky said, "I'll run them through the washing machine. And I'll find you some underwear. You can throw your suits in too. Stay for dinner. That rain isn't going to stop any time soon."

Half an hour later, we sat curled up nursing hot lemonade and admiring the multicolored flames. Corky set out crackers, nuts, and cheese. Barbara positioned herself close to the Camembert and chipped away at it. Shep joined us as soon as the fire started to take hold, before Barbara got a chance to interrogate Corky about her sex life. We managed to avoid talking about the murders, too. Corky had been coming out here since she was a kid. They'd had a house in Springs before Oscar built this one in Dedhampton. She had a fund of stories about the East End and the locals, including the Bonackers over in East Hampton and the few remaining Montauk Indians. I had a good time. The reprobate in me thought the lemonade would have been better for a shot of whiskey. But you can't have everything.

The rain was no longer torrential but still falling steadily when we heard a knock on the door.

"Who could that be?" Shep asked. "Nobody uses that door, and usually everybody just walks in, anyhow."

"I'll go see," Corky said. She disappeared toward the front of the house. A minute later, we heard her greeting someone warmly.

"Oh, are those for me? That is so sweet of you! Of course we can use them. Come in, come in. Never mind about the water. If you want, you can drop your slicker right on the floor here. No, really, it's fine, we love footprints. Come in and have some lemonade. You must be freezing. We're just sitting around the fire."

The clumping of heavy boots and the patter of Corky's bare feet heralded her return. Right behind her, still wearing his yellow slicker hat, was Mr. Dowling.

"Look what Mr. Dowling brought us!" She held up a large, heavy plastic bag, beaded with droplets of water and oozing slightly. "Bluefish! I was going to nuke some steaks for dinner, but this is much better."

"They're fresh," Dowling said gruffly. "Went out this morning, got more than I needed. I cleaned 'em too. Those are good fillets in there. Corinne here never did like the cleaning part."

"Sounds like you've known each other a long time," Barbara said.

"Ben taught me how to fish," Corky said. "A long time ago."

"Started you on snappers," he agreed, "and worked your way up to thirty-six-inch blues. You used to love coming out in the boat. It's been a while, missy."

"Too long, I know. And lately, with everything happening—I'll come out with you, Ben, I promise." She turned to us.

"Did you know he takes parties out fishing? You should do it before the end of the summer. His rates are better than anyone else's, and he knows everything there is to know about fishing and the waters around here."

"You don't mind clumsy beginners who squeak when they have to bait the hook and might knock their fishing pole into the water?" Barbara asked.

"Not at all," he said. "Everybody starts somewhere." He had an unexpectedly charming smile.

"It sounds great," she said. "Do you have a card or something?"

"Corinne can give you my number, or you can stop by the stand." He chuckled. "We don't go in for cards much around here. If I'm not there, leave a message with my wife, and I'll get back to you."

"You must be so busy on your farm right now," Barbara said. "And all the other work you do—I'm sure we aren't your only customers."

"Ben's the best," Corky said. "And he's definitely in demand. They worship a good handyman around here."

"There's always time for fishin'," Dowling said.

He wouldn't sit down or stay for some lemonade. Corky saw him to the door. Her voice floated back to us.

"I can't thank you enough for the fish. We didn't see much of you last summer, and I missed you."

Corky's effusive thanks and Dowling's self-deprecating replies faded as she stepped outside to wave him off. We heard his truck cough and start.

"You should do it," she said as she came back into the room. "You'll have a great time. He'll tell you wonderful stories about the area. And the fishing itself is fun."

"Gutting and filleting are not the fun part," I said. "I think I can remember that."

"This has been a great evening," Barbara said two hours later. "I'm stuffed."

"It was all delicious," I told Corky. "I like bluefish better than I expected to."

"It's brain food," Barbara said. "Oh, my tummy! It's a good thing I'm wearing Oscar's clothes. Oops. Is it okay to talk about Oscar?"

"It's fine," Corky said. "I think about him all the time." Shep, who was sitting next to her on a squashy loveseat, took her hand and clasped her fingers in his. "I'm almost ready to deal with his ashes."

"You had him cremated?" Barbara asked.

I looked around, as if the ashes might be sitting on top of the mantel or on an end table.

"It's what he wanted," Corky said. "The urn is in his room. I didn't want to leave it there, but I couldn't think what to do with it until this evening."

"What will you do?" Barbara asked.

"I asked Ben to take me out past Montauk to scatter them, and he said he would."

"It sounds perfect," Barbara said.

"Is it legal?" I asked.

"I don't know and I don't care," Corky said. "We'll go out toward Block Island, but we'll stay away from the fishing fleet. Ben doesn't mind."

"Can I come?" Shep asked, playing with her hand.

"No, this is something I have to do by myself."

"With Dowling," Barbara said. "If he's known you since you were a kid, he must have known Oscar a long time too."

"They were friends," Corky said. "Ben is only a few years older than Oscar was."

"I wouldn't have guessed. Mr. Dowling looks so weather-beaten."

"That's the way farmers and baymen look," Corky said.

"Is Mrs. Dowling younger than she looks too?" Barbara asked.

"Younger than Oscar," Corky said. "I've seen her at town functions, and you'd be surprised at how good she looks when she dresses up a little. She's from one of the old families, too, the Dedhams. Everybody knows them. She's got a brother on the town board."

"There's a family named Dedham?" Barbara asked.

"They were the original settlers."

"Jimmy would love to hear this," Barbara said. "He's a history buff."

"Understatement," I said.

"Oscar was very interested in the town's history," Corky said. "He would have loved telling Jimmy all about it."

"Maybe that's why Oscar and Dowling got along," I said.

"They were on different sides, farmer and developer, but Oscar loved history."

"And Mr. Dowling *was* history," Barbara said.

"A lot of farms out here have been in the same family for two hundred years or more," Corky said. "You know, land out here can cost upwards of a million an acre, and a cornfield can be fifty acres or more."

"Awesome when you do the math," I said. "I wouldn't be mad at a friend who offered me that kind of money, even if I didn't want to sell. It's a wonder any of the local farmers stick it out." This spectacular oceanfront property Corky had just inherited was worth a bundle.

"Oscar would bring it up from time to time. Ben always told him to forget it, he'd never sell, but I thought in the last year or so he started to waver."

"Did any other big developers make him an offer?" Barbara asked. "Like Morton Day, the one who's doing the new golf course?"

"He tried," Corky said. "Dowling turned him down flat. If Ben had sold to anyone, it would have been to Oscar."

Chapter Twenty-Five

"How was your day?" Barbara asked, draping herself over Jimmy as he sat at the computer.

"Don't strangle the man," I said.

"My day was fine," Jimmy said. "What on earth are you wearing?"

"Oscar's clothes. Where is everybody?"

"They all went to the movies."

"Did you find anything interesting online?"

"Yep. I read Clea's whole series of articles in the *Deeds* about how the developers are milking the area and what different groups are doing to stop it, or at least slow it down. It ran all last summer. The paper promised more revelations to come. I guess she meant to write more about it this year."

"Don't they publish the paper in the winter?"

"Yes, but not much happens. The Hamptons turn into a pumpkin by November or so. I also found out—"

"Hold that thought," Barbara said. She dashed out of the room, and we heard her rummaging in the kitchen.

"Barbara, what are you doing?"

"Just looking," she called back. "Jimmy, did you eat?"

"We had a huge dinner," I told him.

Barbara reappeared in the doorway.

"There's plenty in there. Leftover baby back ribs, gallons of ice cream."

"I'm fine," Jimmy said. "And the gang said they'd bring me

back pizza and popcorn. Don't you want to hear what I found out?"

"Yes, of course."

"Phil filed for bankruptcy a year ago," Jimmy said. "Chapter Eleven, anyway, which allowed him to reorganize his business as long as his creditors and the court approved his plan to pay off his debts."

"What was the business?" I asked.

"He called it communications consulting, which could mean anything," Jimmy said. "I was more interested in the financing than in what he actually did."

"I bet he didn't tell the court his debt repayment plan consisted of going to Atlantic City and playing blackjack until everything was copacetic," I remarked.

"No, but somehow he got himself back together. There was an influx of money from somewhere."

"You mean the money didn't necessarily come from where he said it did," Barbara said.

"Exactly," Jimmy said. He shut down the computer and shoved back his chair. "I have to do some more digging, but not tonight, peach. I almost dozed off waiting for you. Let's go to bed."

"Me, too." I yawned wide enough to hear the little click the hinge of my jaw makes when I ask too much of it. "Today I got baked and then dipped in brine and then soaked, with a big meal on top of it. I'm very, very sleepy." The second "very" came out on an even bigger yawn. "Night night, guys. See you in the morning."

I checked the bedside clock, but I don't remember hitting the pillow. I slept soundly for three and a half hours and woke up refreshed and wide awake at three in the morning. I don't know how long I lay there, listening to the night sounds: Stewie's heavy breathing in the next bed, a loon on the bay scaring the bejesus out of anybody who didn't know what made that eldritch cry, the tock of the old-fashioned battery clock on the wall as its hands jerked from second to second, minute to minute. A door down the hall opened with a furtive squeal. I heard the rush of running water. The toilet flushed. The electric pump hummed as it replenished the water in the tank.

This group house thing was oddly intimate. I'd lived on my own for a long time. Even during my marriage, we'd both kept our own places. In New York, a rent-controlled apartment like mine and a SoHo loft like Laura's were both too hard come by to give up. Besides, we'd both maintained barriers of alcohol and drugs, not to mention her intermittent off-the-wall mental state. Here, we saw a lot of skin and heard a lot of body noises.

On the other hand, living at such close quarters, people kept a lot of walls up. For example, Cindy and I hadn't gotten very far. Or had the murders derailed our journey toward each other? I could hardly blame her for remaining wary. Maybe it was simply a matter of logistics. Although the house was big and everybody walked around half naked, she shared the loft upstairs with Jeannette and Stephanie, and I slept with Stewie. I couldn't make myself ask if he'd clear out long enough for me to get Cindy into bed.

I knew damn well that wasn't it either. They said sobriety fucked up your drinking. It also played hell with your ability to bullshit yourself. I held back with Cindy because I was afraid I wasn't up to her weight. I didn't know what her mysterious job was, but I was certain she did something focused and responsible. What I did was a joke. How could she take a male pink-collar temp seriously? Everybody said a recovery job was okay for a while. Focus on sobriety, go to meetings, take your time on that bridge back to life. So far, I hadn't a clue as to where I wanted mine to lead.

I lay there thinking and listening to Stewie run a buzz saw

through his tonsils until the groan of a warped board in the floor above my head brought an end to my reverie. I hadn't heard the stairs creak. Most likely, one of my housemates was raiding the refrigerator. It might even be Cindy. On the other hand, I'd look awfully foolish if it turned out that a killer had cut someone's throat or a burglar had stolen Jimmy's iPad, and I'd lain here idly listening as he did it. I'd better go investigate.

I rolled out of bed and pulled on my shorts. I kicked around the stuff I'd dumped on the floor at my bedside—my storage system—looking for a pair of shoes. Then I decided to go barefoot. If I meant to catch someone sneaking around upstairs, I'd be stealthy too. Should I arm myself? The house didn't provide much choice of weapons. I'd seen a can of ammonia-based cleaning spray and one of pesticide under the downstairs bathroom sink. If the intruder was a dirty ant or hornet, I'd be all set. A beach umbrella to use as a lance? A heavy shoe to throw? I could tie a pair together by the laces, whirl them over my head, and let fly with it, like a bolo or mace. Jimmy, with his encyclopedic knowledge of military history, would be better at this. I settled for the sawed-off broom handle someone had left propped up at the foot of the stairs after a half-assed game of stickball in the back yard a couple of days before.

Stick in hand, I crept up the stairs. I kept my back against the wall and my feet at the edge of the steps, where I figured they'd be better supported and therefore less likely to creak. As my head emerged from the stairwell, I saw lights in the kitchen. My precautions were probably unnecessary. An intruder would have left the light off or used a flashlight. I straightened up. The refrigerator door stood open. I was about to toss the stick to one side when I heard a snuffling sound coming from behind the counter, down near the floor. Could a raccoon have gotten in? Squirrels? I inched cautiously forward. Snuffle, chomp, scuffle, and a crackling and rustling of what sounded like cellophane bags. I peered over the counter, prepared for anything.

"Barbara! What the hell are you doing?"

Barbara sat sprawled on the floor, her back against the cabinet under the kitchen sink. She wore a stained, pale blue T-shirt so big it had to be Jimmy's. Her hair was matted, her bare feet thrust carelessly out in front of her. Her face was streaked with tears. In general, she looked as if she'd just crawled out from under a rock. On the floor next to her sat a greasy plate piled with well-gnawed ribs. Two or three had toppled and slid part way under the cabinet. Empty potato chip and pretzel bags had been crumpled and tossed. A giant bag still a quarter filled with popcorn had evidently been propped against the counter but had fallen over, spilling kernels far and wide on the kitchen floor. A cylindrical gallon container of ice cream perched on her lap. I identified the flavor as chocolate from the smears on her shirt and face, along with barbecue sauce and mucus from her runny nose. Caught with a spoon in her mouth and a bulging cheek, she stared at me like an animal at bay.

"What's the matter? Have you gone crazy?"

She whimpered, tears spilling from her glazed eyes.

"Are you drunk?"

"I can't—" She choked, removed the spoon from her mouth, and tried again. I watched in horror as her hand dropped limply. The spoon bounced twice on her lap, splattering more chocolate. Creeping paralysis, I thought. Psychotic break. Invasion of the body snatchers.

"I can't stop eating!" She burst into sobs with terrifying abandon. Chocolate spewed out of her nose. "I don't know what to do!" she wailed.

I rounded the counter, slid onto my knees beside her, and took her in my arms. I felt the ooze of barbecue sauce transferring itself to my chest. My prickling knees informed me I was kneeling on popcorn. She sniveled into my shoulder. Her mouth was so distended by painful sobbing that her teeth sank into my arm. I rocked her back and forth as I kept up a soothing babble.

"Shhh, it's all right, Barbara. It's gonna be okay. Go ahead and cry. It's okay, we'll figure it out. You don't have to do it alone. I'll help you, Jimmy will help, it's all gonna be all right. It's just another fucking addiction. You'll join another twelve-step program. It'll be fine."

The sobs ebbed a bit.

"I'm sorry, I'm sorry. I'm such a mess—I didn't mean to let anybody see me like this. I'm so embarrassed. You must be disgusted."

"Shhh, shhh. It's okay, no problem. What's a little snot between friends?"

At that, she fended me off and tried to pull herself together. Running her arm under her nose smeared things even more. She clawed at her hair, which only spread the chocolate around.

I sat back on my heels.

"Hey, I'm not dressed up either. Come as you are."

"I'm a compulsive overeater," she said, her face like the mask of tragedy.

"Hi, Barbara, keep coming back," I said.

That raised a doleful snuffle. I scootched around and sat next to her. I raised my knees and rested my back against the sink. I used an empty bag to brush bones and popcorn away from my bare feet. "As a terrific counselor I know sometimes says to me, that's the disease talking."

"I don't want to be an addict!" she said. "I'm a codependent."

"As the same counselor said when she told me I needed Al-Anon, we're all probably both on some level." I reached over and picked a puff of popcorn out of her hair.

"You have a right to gloat," she said.

"I won't gloat," I said. "Last time I sat on the kitchen floor with a bag of potato chips, it was just about this time of night, and what I really wanted was a drink. You've got a different jones, that's all."

"Only one bag?"

"See? You haven't even lost your sense of humor."

"It's so humiliating!" she burst out. "Look at me! No, don't! All I'm missing is a custard pie in the face. It's not fair. At least alcoholics are sexy."

"We are?"

"Drinking is cool. Overeating is repulsive, unless you're the one in a million women who can eat like a pig and never gain an ounce. Men love that."

I could see my consciousness was about to get raised.

"You think I'm sexy?"

She threw a fistful of popcorn at me.

"Hey, hey! No food fights," I said.

"I guess now I have to go to OA. Honestly, I knew all along that I belonged there. I didn't want to admit it to myself."

"Hmm, I wonder why that sounds familiar."

She slid down a bit and rubbed her cheek against my shoulder.

"You're nicer than me," she said. "When you hit bottom and landed in detox, I gloated."

"Okay, you owe me one," I said. "Anyhow, your eating never hurt me the way my drinking hurt you and Jimmy. That makes us even. Listen, should I go wake him up?"

"Oh, God, no," she said. "I don't want anybody else to see me like this. I'm so ashamed, and you're being so sweet. I'll tell Jimmy in the morning."

"What else can you do different?" I asked, feeding her back one of the lines she used on me when I first got sober.

"I can ask for support from the other women in the house."

"It's kind of obvious Jeannette and Stephanie have body issues."

"The day I went to the nude beach with them," she said, "they both talked about it."

"Maybe you can help each other. Talk to them tomorrow and see what happens."

"For all I know, Karen and Cindy could be bulimic," Barbara said. "Not every woman with a great body has no trouble with food. In fact—"

"What? You can tell me."

"I tried to stick my finger down my throat tonight. Nothing happened, and I was afraid I'd scratch my vocal cords or something, so I stopped."

"Just as well you couldn't do it," I said.

"I know." Barbara sighed. "I don't want to ruin my teeth or get throat cancer. But I'm so afraid of gaining weight."

"One day at a time," I said. "Come on, I'll help you clean up the kitchen."

Barbara leaned heavily on me as she rose to her feet. She crossed the room and started running water in the sink.

"When did you get so smart?"

"I suspect the process started on the Bowery two Christmases ago."

"Oh, Bruce, you've done great, you really have. Jimmy and I are so proud of you."

"Why, thank you." I sounded pleased because I was. Staying sober and everything that had turned out to go along with it, like being a better person, was often more of a struggle than I liked to show.

"Oh, God, and now I'm a beginner again." She squirted detergent into the sinkful of water and put the bottle on the counter. Resting her elbows on the edge of the sink, she put the palms of her hands over her eyes and clutched at her hair. "Hi,

I'm Barbara, and I'm a fucking *food* addict. As you guys like to say, shoot me now, Jesus."

"I don't think Jesus shoots nice Jewish girls."

"I swear I'll do it myself if I can't get a handle on this thing." She held out her hand, and I handed her the plate piled with rib bones. She emptied it into a big black plastic garbage bag and plunged the greasy plate into the sink.

"Don't be silly," I said. "You're too much of a good girl to off yourself."

She groaned.

"Hi, I'm Barbara, I'm a codependent, and I don't get to have any fun at all."

"Poor bunny."

"It's not fair," she said. "I've hardly ever busted out. If I'm in recovery two times over, I never will."

"Trust me, being a fuckup and an asshole isn't as glamorous as it's cracked up to be."

I swept up the evidence of Barbara's binge and whisked it into the garbage bag. I twisted a tie around the bag and swung it over my shoulder.

"Let me do that," she said. "It's my garbage."

"If you insist." If doing penance made her feel better, I wasn't going to get in her way. I watched as she dragged the bag across the kitchen and heaved it into a can by the door.

"Bruce?"

"What?"

"I have to tell you something else."

"Lay it on me." I thought she was going to confess to another gallon of ice cream or a two-pound box of chocolates.

"The night before Phil died, he caught me sneaking into his room."

"What!"

"I wanted to find the notebook. And I did, but he got it away from me before I could open it. He—he was very angry."

"My God, Barbara, were you out of your mind? And why didn't you tell Jimmy and me?"

"He scared me. I was too humiliated. And then, the next morning—I couldn't tell you once we heard that Phil had been killed. As long as you and Jimmy didn't know, you didn't have a motive."

"You should have told us anyway," I said.

"I know," she said in a small voice. She hung her head. She still had popcorn in her hair. "But I was afraid to tell anyone. It gave me a motive too."

"For God's sake, Barbara, what did he do to you? Did he hit you? I *would* have killed him, and so would Jimmy if he'd known."

"I knew you'd react that way. He shook me and called me some ugly names. He almost socked me at one point, but he never lost it completely. He didn't want anybody else to hear."

"How did it end?"

"He told me to get the hell out of there, and I did. Then he got in his car and drove away."

That meant he'd had the notebook with him when he died. Had the cops found it on his body? If they had new information, I'd expect them to use it as leverage. That hadn't happened.

"We should tell the police." I couldn't believe I'd said that. "If the killer took the notebook from his body, that means it wasn't just a hit and run. They met for a reason, and the reason was in that notebook."

"I know," Barbara said. "But we can't. They'd think I did it. Wouldn't you?"

"You don't have the notebook," I pointed out. "But yeah, they would suspect you. Come here and bend your head down."

I picked the last few pieces of popcorn out of her hair. Then I squeezed out a sponge and ran it over one lock of hair at a time.

"Hold still. I can get most of the chocolate out. Beyond that, I recommend shampoo. And promise me you'll tell Jimmy first thing in the morning."

"About Phil and the notebook?"

"And the binge. 'You're as sick as your secrets,' right?"

"I promise." She sighed. "Don't you hate it when the slogans fit?"

"Yes, but I haven't gotten much sympathy about that."

"I'm sorry," she said. "I probably binged because I was keeping it all inside about what happened with Phil."

"You're the one who always says if you stuff down your feelings, they come out sideways," I said. "Don't fidget. I'm almost done."

"I have something else to make amends for," she said. "I'm sorry I gave you a hard time about the driver's license. I used it as a smoke screen. I figured if I guilt-tripped you, you wouldn't wonder what was going on with me. That was unfair."

"I accept your amends." I dropped a light kiss on the top of her head. Her hair still smelled of chocolate.

"Bruce?"

"What now?"

"Will I have to give up ice cream?"

"I have no idea."

"I know abstinence in OA is not a diet," she said. "I think you work out your own food plan with a sponsor. But suppose I do. Will I ever have any fun again?"

It had been a long night. I started laughing and couldn't stop. I snorted and chuckled until tears welled up in the corners of my eyes.

"That's just what I said about beer."

CHAPTER TWENTY-SIX

I had to hand it to Barbara. By the time she and Jimmy emerged from their room the next morning, she had obviously come clean. After breakfast, she had a quiet talk with Jeannette. Then they announced to the whole gang that they were going to an Overeaters Anonymous meeting.

"From now on," Barbara said, "please don't anybody ask me if I want dessert. The answer is, 'Are you crazy? Of course I do!' "

"That goes for me too," Jeannette said. "I admit I'm powerless and my life couldn't be more unmanageable right now." She looked more relaxed than when she'd told us she was Clea's mother. The program says that taking Step One is liberating, and weird though it sounds, it works. When you surrender, the war is over.

"Good for you both," Stephanie said. "I think I'll go with you. I'm not anorexic for today, but a meeting never hurts."

"I'll come too," Stewie said. "Don't everybody look so astounded. The SCA stuff is the last frontier. Before, I was a pothead and a vomiter. I used to live for the munchies." He flexed a well-defined bicep. "This gorgeous bod is my recovery body. Too bad it was also my cruising bod." He glanced at his watch. "Come on, ladies, let's get there on time."

"Want the car?" Barbara asked Jimmy and me.

"Nope, I'm going back online," Jimmy said.

"I don't drive any more, remember?" I said.

"See you later, then," she said.

A minute later, we heard all four doors of the Toyota slam. Jimmy walked over to the window to watch the car crunch away down the gravel drive.

"She's going to be all right," he said.

"Don't worry, bro," I said. "She will be."

"She said she gave you quite a time last night."

I looked around. The others had already dispersed.

"Better me than you," I said. "You would have been more freaked out than me. I'm only the step-boyfriend. I've got some distance. Also, she didn't mind so much with me."

"She ought to know by now I won't stop loving her, no matter what," he said. "God knows I've got my own dark side."

"I know. I'm on your dark side," I said. "But did you know hers had chocolate in its hair?"

"I guessed." He scratched his head, as if the image made his scalp itch. "I'm okay with you being her confidant."

"This way I get points. I guess we're not allowed to call them brownie points any more, huh?"

"The Phil thing freaks me out more than the food thing," Jimmy said. "I wish she wouldn't act on every harebrained impulse without telling me first."

"Barbara is Barbara," I said. "So we keep the notebook business to ourselves?"

"As long as we can, anyhow," Jimmy said.

The weather had done one of its flip-flops. It was hot and clear. Barbara came back from her meeting in high spirits, and we all spent the afternoon on the beach, Jimmy swathed in drapery like the Sheik of Araby. I did some body surfing. I'd practiced enough all summer to get a few exhilarating rides in exchange for the abrasions on my chest and the sand in my trunks and behind my back teeth. When I'd had enough, I flopped down on a towel next to Barbara and zonked out in the sun. I felt desiccated as a mummy.

"So what did you guys do this morning?" Barbara asked.

"I just hung out," I said.

"He mooched around hoping that Cindy would come back from wherever she disappears to," Jimmy said. "She's a bit of a mystery, isn't she?"

"I'm working on it," I said. "I like her, don't you?"

"Sure," Jimmy said, "the little I know of her."

"She's nice, Bruce," Barbara said. "And she seems to be outside this whole mess."

"I have a dumb question," I said. "Do you think she's a lesbian?"

Barbara and Jimmy looked at each other.

"I don't get that vibe," Barbara said.

"I think she's hot for you," Jimmy said.

"Never mind," I said. Whatever lay between Cindy and me was not going to get resolved by committee. "Let's change the subject."

"You know what Jeannette told me?" Barbara said.

"About what?"

"About Clea and Oscar," she said. "Now that we know she was Clea's mother—"

"I hope you didn't tell her I told you," I said.

"Of course not!" Barbara frowned, looking ruffled but cute, like the Mad Bluebird. "I was subtle. I got her to tell me. Anyhow, Jeannette's family was so awful, they make us look good. She likes us."

"What us?"

"The three of us. The Three Musketeers us."

"We're her role model for a family?"

"She's not that far gone," Barbara said. "We're pretty oddball, especially you two. But her family was sick. They made her have the baby and give it up and then basically told her she was going to hell and washed their hands of her."

"I guess when she found Clea," I said, "she hoped that they could become a family."

"Exactly."

"It didn't turn out that way, though," Jimmy said. "Clea wasn't interested in becoming a family."

"Too narcissistic," Barbara said. "When she wanted to get it on with Oscar, she didn't give a damn that she was cutting her own mother out."

"Jeannette admitted that gave her a motive to kill Clea," I said, "even though she said she'd never have hurt her daughter. We know all this already."

"Wait," Barbara said. "There's more. And it has nothing to do with what she told you, Bruce, so you're off the hook. Remember when I went to the nude beach with the women?"

"How could we forget?"

"I told you what Karen said about how she got pregnant. She didn't want to have the baby, because it couldn't have been Lewis's, and she sure didn't want to settle down with Oscar. She didn't admit it was Oscar, but let's assume it was. He wanted a family too. He had fantasies of raising a kid in sobriety, unlike his alcoholic parents."

"Go on about Jeannette," Jimmy said.

"Jeannette heard Karen tell that story too. But that day she hid the fact that she was Clea's mother. She pretended she didn't know her any better than the rest of them, the ones who'd shared a house with her before."

"Clea was the only one who'd died at that point," Jimmy reminded us.

"But here's the thing," Barbara said. "Today Jeannette told me Oscar pulled the same trick with Clea that he did with Karen. Clea got pregnant, and he wanted her to have the baby too. Karen said she knew Oscar wasn't in love with her, but what if she didn't really believe that? It's hard not to have a soft spot for a guy who's in love with you."

"But he wasn't."

"That's my point," Barbara said. "And I bet he wasn't in love with Clea either."

"He just wanted a baby."

"Right—with both of them, it was his ACOA do-over fantasy. But Clea wasn't interested any more than Karen was. And she was younger than Karen. I'd guess she got an abortion with a lot less soul-searching than poor Karen."

"You could say that gave Jeannette two motives to kill Oscar," Jimmy said. "He dropped her for her daughter, and then he put so much pressure on Clea that she aborted Jeannette's granddaughter to get rid of him."

"That's a motive for Jeannette to kill Clea," I said. "But I don't think she did. She was all broken up the other day, after she talked with the cops."

"Today, too, when she talked about it," Barbara said. "The whole baby-abortion-grandmother family thing—that's what she ate over."

"Jeez, why couldn't she just get drunk?" I said. "Don't throw sand! I was kidding!"

"She could have had the family she wanted," Jimmy pointed out, "if Clea had dumped Oscar, had the baby, and let Jeannette play grandma and share the parenting."

"But Clea didn't want a baby," Barbara said, "and she didn't want the kind of bond with her biological mom that Jeannette had been dreaming of. Jeannette was an adoption social worker. She must have seen that particular bubble get punctured thousands of times. She knew better, but she couldn't help hoping."

Until Clea made that impossible.

Chapter Twenty-Seven

"Maybe we're tackling this from the wrong end," Jimmy said.

It was evening. We were sitting out on the deck so I could smoke. The days had started getting shorter. At just past eight o'clock, it was almost dark. This late in the summer, evenings were mercifully cool, even after the hottest day. Katydids and crickets made a racket in the yard.

"What do you mean?" I asked.

"We've been thinking of these crimes as out here crimes because they happened out here. But overdevelopment is a national issue."

"The embattled environment is a global issue," Barbara added. "Clea could have used the local material to write about the bigger problems."

"I haven't read everything she wrote yet," Jimmy said.

"So keep going," Barbara said. "Maybe we'll dig up something new that'll cast light on what happened to her."

"Have you Googled Oscar?" I asked. "He had a national reputation."

"All this sun has toasted my brain," Jimmy said, "but not quite burnt it to a crisp yet. Thousands of hits, many thousands, but I haven't spotted anything that's relevant to the people we know and that the detectives wouldn't have found out for themselves."

"They may have suspects we don't know about," Barbara said.

"You could ask your friend Jeff Bushwick," I said, "if he's heard anything new."

"I will," she said. "Was she a good writer, Jimmy?"

"I thought so," Jimmy said. "She did her homework."

Her homework might have gotten her killed.

"So go for it, Jimmy!" Barbara said.

Jimmy tucked a wisp of her hair behind her ear and laughed. "You're not usually so eager for me to hit the keyboard, pumpkin. How about tomorrow morning?"

"Oh, Jimmy!" she said. "We're all supposed to go fishing. Lewis set it up with Mr. Dowling for tomorrow."

"What kind of boat?" Jimmy asked warily.

"A fishing boat," she said. "I don't know."

"Does it have a roof?"

"I'm sure it does," she said. She took a quick breath to say more, then stopped short. The struggle between honesty and wanting to get Jimmy on that boat played out like a silent film projected onto her face. Finally, she said, "It must have some kind of sun shade. Oh, Jimmy, please come. You can put on a lot of sun block and wear a big hat. We've never gone fishing, and you've told me so many times how much fun you and Bruce used to have."

Our dads used to take us fishing out of Sheepshead Bay. Great role models. The fun was less in the fishing than in the three cases of beer they brought along. We could hardly wait to grow old enough to go out by ourselves. Jimmy squirmed, obviously reluctant to refuse Barbara.

"There you are." Lewis appeared at the screen door. "Dowling just phoned. Our fishing date is off."

"Saved!" Jimmy burst out. He added, "I'm sorry, peach. I know you wanted to go."

"What happened, Lewis?" Barbara asked.

"Something went wrong with the boat," he said. "Engine

trouble. They have to wait for a part."

"Ohhh, I'm so disappointed." Barbara slumped into a chair.

Karen appeared in the doorway next to Lewis.

"You heard, right? It would be a shame for you to miss it. We've been out with Dowling before, but I meant to ask him to take us over to Gardiner's Island and tell the story of how Gardiner blew the whistle on Captain Kidd."

"There's an island?" Barbara asked. "Can we land on it? I love islands."

"It's private," Karen said. "If you land, the caretaker calls the cops. But even a close look from the boat is interesting."

"If we had a boat," Barbara said.

"He said it would be fixed in a few days," Lewis said.

"In time for Labor Day weekend?"

"Well, yeah, but that doesn't help us. He's taking parties out all three days, and I bet they're paying a premium because it's a holiday weekend."

"And then the season will be over." Barbara drooped. "Doesn't he have another boat?"

"Boats don't grow on trees, pumpkin," Jimmy said.

At the same time, Lewis said, "You know, he might."

"So maybe we could go anyway!" Barbara's whole body perked up.

"But not one that's big enough to take seven people fishing. Eight, if you count Dowling."

"Ohhh. Then we can't do it."

"You could call him and ask if he'd take the three of you," Lewis said. "The rest of us all have a Plan B. Karen and I have errands to do, and everybody else said they'd be happy to spend tomorrow at the beach and let the fishing go."

"So let's call and ask," Barbara said.

"Okay, okay," Jimmy said. "Make the call."

"I'll get you the number," Lewis said.

While we waited, I lit another cigarette and blew smoke rings. Jimmy sighed and closed his eyes.

"I got him!" Barbara bounded out onto the deck. Her eyes shone, and her unruly hair flew about her head as if it were about to take off. "Do you want the good news or the bad news first?"

"Good news," Jimmy said without opening his eyes.

"He's got a smaller boat, and he's still willing to take us out tomorrow."

"And the bad news?" I asked.

"He can only take two passengers," she said. "He said it's just a little runabout. It's not big enough for more, not for fishing."

Jimmy's eyes flew open.

"That's good news."

They both looked at me. Jimmy stretched an arm out and rolled it from side to side. We could all see that even though he'd accumulated a crop of freckles since June, the skin underneath was still red and tender. It looked as if it might blister at any time.

Barbara marched over to me and took hold of my wrist. I let her stretch my bronzed arm out. We all looked from my arm to Jimmy's.

"How come when other guys get a world class tan like mine, all that happens is they get the girls?" I complained.

Jimmy grinned broadly.

"You're getting my girl."

He put both arms behind his head and leaned back, conspicuously relaxing. Barbara leaned closer and dropped a smacking kiss on my temple.

"I know," I said with resignation. "You owe me."

Chapter Twenty-Eight

Dowling had said we had to leave by nine in the morning to catch the ebbing tide. I guess it increased our chances of finding the fish at home. I didn't fancy several hours in a small boat with Barbara and no fish. By 8:30, she was loaded for bear.

"What have you got there, pumpkin?" Jimmy asked. He would drop us at Dead Harbor, where the boat was docked.

"Sun hat, sun block, a towel in case I get wet, a sweatshirt in case I get cold," she said. "Rubber gloves in case I have to touch the fish. An LED flashlight in case we get stuck and have to signal, you know, if a fog rolls in."

"There isn't a cloud between here and Rhode Island," Jimmy said. "I checked the forecast *and* looked out the window."

"I wouldn't be surprised if Dowling has a fog horn on the boat," I said. "And radar and a radio."

"Sounds like it's been a while since you took a boat ride," Lewis said. "Nowadays it's a GPS and a cell phone."

He poured himself a mug of coffee and joined us, shaking his head as Barbara packed a paperback mystery, a plastic bottle of hand sanitizer, a box of Band-Aids, two pairs of socks, and a bathing suit in her backpack.

"You're going fishing, not running away from home," I said.

"He'll have life jackets, won't he, Lewis?" she asked.

"Sure, all the boats carry them. The old timers like Dowling aren't so big on wearing them, but you can if you want."

"It's supposed to go up to the low nineties, petunia."

"It'll be cooler on the water," Barbara said. "I like to be prepared."

"Yes, dear," Jimmy said. "Shouldn't we get going?"

"You know how to get there?" Lewis asked.

"Back toward Amagansett," Jimmy said. "He told me a couple of landmarks to look for when it's time to turn. If we get to Napeague Harbor, we've gone too far."

"We may have gone too far already," I muttered.

Ms. Eagle Ears heard me.

"Cut it out, Bruce," she said. "Forget you're an ACOA today. No martyrdom by fun."

"Okay, okay," I said. "I won't be a party pooper. How about a trade? No whining if you don't catch any fish."

Barbara hoisted the backpack and settled the straps across her shoulders.

"I don't whine! And who says I won't catch any fish? I'll catch more fish than you."

"That's the spirit," Jimmy said. "Can we go now, please?"

Nothing like a lively exchange with Barbara to perk me up in the morning.

Dead Harbor looked deserted in the golden morning light. Two wooden docks ran out into an inlet rimmed with bright green grasses. The still boats lined up along both sides of them were paired with their mirror images in the glassy water. On a sandbar out beyond the channel marked with red and green buoys, a white egret with an S-shaped neck stood on one slim black leg, either meditating or contemplating its breakfast.

"Which boat is Dowling's?" I asked.

"I thought we'd see him," Barbara said. "Now what?"

Before either of us could answer, a pickup truck rattled around a curve in the road and pulled up next to Jimmy's Toyota. The door swung open. Not Dowling, but Mrs. Dowling emerged.

"Good, you're here," she said briskly. "Dowling couldn't make it. Let's go. Don't want to miss the tide. Catch 'em while they're running good."

She made for the farther dock as Barbara whispered, "I don't think we're going to hear any stories about Captain Kidd."

"On the other hand, this is positively chatty for Mrs. Dowling. You're not going to suggest she can't drive a boat and fish as well as Mr. D., are you?"

"Are you kidding? May feminists dance on your grave if you so much as think it!"

"Is it okay if I leave?" Jimmy asked. "Will you be okay?"

"Come on, now!" Mrs. Dowling called over her shoulder from halfway down the dock. "Whichever of you is coming, let's get moving. Fish don't stand still and wait around, you know."

"We'll be fine," Barbara said. She gave Jimmy a quick kiss, and I punched him in the arm in a display of male affection I thought Mrs. Dowling would respect.

"You've got your cell phones, right? Call me if you need me."

"We'll be fine, dude," I told him. "Come on, Barbara. We're going fishing."

Mrs. Dowling was already moving around a small white boat. Barbara trotted down the dock and clambered in. I stopped to take a look before I boarded. There was not much to it.

"What kind of a boat is it?" Barbara asked.

"It's a Pursuit, a twenty-two-foot runabout," Mrs. Dowling said. "Come on, come on," she urged me. "If you want to make yourself useful, you can cast off before you come aboard."

I managed to figure out she wanted me to unloop the rope tethering the boat from a cleat attached to the dock. I climbed over the side into a cockpit maybe fifteen feet long. In the stern was a heavy outboard motor. At the bow, the open part ended in the folded back door to a low cabin, just big enough for padded bunks that curved around three sides in a truncated V or pinched-together U.

"Where can we put our things?" Barbara asked

"In there." Mrs. Dowling indicated the cabin door.

I had nothing to throw, but Barbara tossed her backpack onto a bunk.

Two high padded stools with low backs stood before a dashboard and a clear plastic windscreen. A blue canvas canopy provided shade. I hopped onto the left-hand seat. It swiveled. Just like a barstool. Mrs. Dowling took the right-hand seat. The boat was set up like a British car, with the ignition, wheel, and gearshift on the right. She turned the key, and the engine came to life.

"Where do I sit?" Barbara asked.

"Here." I got up and patted the seat. "I can perch on the side if I need to. For now, I'll look over your shoulder."

"Once we start fishing," Mrs. Dowling said, "you won't need a seat. You won't catch any blues sitting on your duff."

"What are the two little screens?" Barbara asked.

"This one's the GPS."

"What are the dotted lines?"

"That's a trail of breadcrumbs." Mrs. Dowling didn't crack a smile. "They mark the route."

"So you use it to navigate."

"Not really." The engine purred as we moved slowly between the ranks of sleeping boats. "I've got these waters in my head."

"And the other one?"

"Depth recorder," she said.

Barbara peered at the screen.

"It says we're in six feet of water now. How deep will it get out the bay?"

"Twenty-five, more or less." She nudged the stick forward, and the engine hummed louder.

"You use the gear shift to accelerate?" Barbara asked.

"That's right."

"Where are the brakes?" Barbara asked. "How do you stop?"

"Put her in reverse." Mrs. Dowling turned and plucked a fishing rod out of a cylindrical holder behind her at the side of the boat. "Let's get these rods set up, and I'll show you how to cast." The boat continued moving as she unhooked a red and white length of plastic like a bitten-off cigar from a small loop halfway down the rod. No hands on the wheel.

"You don't have to watch the road?" Barbara asked.

"Ha! No road."

I looked around. The only boats in sight were far away: a string of sailboats to the right of a distant headland, a couple of motor boats cutting across the horizon.

"What if a boat or a jet ski comes our way?"

"Damn jet skis. I'll hear it long before it gets near us." She handed a fishing rod to each of us and ducked down into the cabin to get one for herself.

"No live bait, thank God," Barbara whispered.

The rod felt comfortable in my hand. I gripped the cork handle and swished it a couple of times. It was very light and flexible. Barbara unhooked her lure and started waving her rod around.

"Watch out with that," I said. "Those hooks are nasty."

She caught the dangling end and examined the lure.

"Ew, poor fish," she said. "A triple hook at the end and another in the middle, and they've got barbs on them." Holding the freed lure between her thumb and forefinger, she looked around the bare deck. "Where do we put the fish we catch?"

"Compartment under your feet."

Barbara jumped, as if she were stepping on fish rather than just a hatch cover flush with the deck.

"That one's got water in it, keep 'em fresh," Mrs. Dowling said. "The others hold equipment, and one is for live bait, which we aren't using today. Now, hold your rods like this: two fingers above the grip, and hook a bit of line through your finger. Next, you open the bail." She flipped a U-shaped piece of metal from one side of the reel to the other. "That frees your line. Make sure your lure is about a third or halfway down the rod and isn't caught on anything. Now watch what I do."

She tipped the rod back over her shoulder, then flipped it expertly forward. The line, an almost invisible filament, played out and disappeared far out over the water.

"And now we reel it in. You can flip the bail back or just start reeling. Can you see the lure?"

"No," I said.

"Where is it?" Barbara asked.

Mrs. Dowling, reeling rapidly, nodded out in the direction of the cast. "You'll see it skipping over the surface of the water, coming toward us. The bluefish think it's bait because of how it moves."

"There it is!" Barbara crowed.

I saw it flashing for a second, skipping toward the boat. Then it disappeared as the tip of Mrs. Dowling's rod curved forward.

"Ha! Come to Mama, you twisty little thing."

I raised one eyebrow at Barbara. She stifled a giggle.

"You've got to play it," Mrs. Dowling said. "Keep on reeling steadily, but not too fast. Sometimes they slip off the hook. But even if that happens, don't stop reeling. They'll go after it again."

We watched the silvery flashes in the churning water as the fish tried to free itself.

"What do they think it is?" Barbara asked. "I mean, what kinds of fish are bait fish?"

"They'll take all kinds," Mrs. Dowling said, still reeling. "Bunker, or they call 'em menhaden. Snappers, even—baby blues."

"Ew, they eat their own babies?"

"If they need to." A triumphant smile spread across her face. "And here you go!"

She flipped the bluefish onto the deck. It flopped and twisted wildly. "Watch out, it's got sharp teeth and a nasty disposition." She bent to grasp it firmly by the middle and disengage the hook. "Open the trap."

Barbara stepped hastily off the hatch cover, and I flipped it back. Mrs. Dowling tossed it into the compartment, where it wriggled a few times in the shallow water, then lay still.

"Sorry, fish," Barbara said as I lowered the cover back down. "Too bad for you we're higher up the food chain."

Mrs. Dowling made us practice casting for a while. Neither of us caught a fish. I got into an easy rhythm after a couple of tries. Barbara hooked the side of the boat, my fishing rod, the canvas canopy, and her own hair.

"If you can't learn to cast properly," Mrs. Dowling said, "you can troll. Just stick the rod in a holder at the stern and let the boat pull the line along till something bites. But I wouldn't call that fishing."

"I'll learn." Barbara set her jaw and swung the wicked little barbs so close to my chest she snagged a loose thread on my T-shirt.

Finally, Mrs. Dowling was satisfied. She pushed the engine into gear.

"Let's go find some blues."

Mrs. Dowling was a competent guide in a minimalist sort of way. As we plunged farther into the blue bowl of sea and sky, she had us scan the area for birds hovering above the surface. If we saw a flock, that's where we'd find a school of blues feeding on a school of bait fish. We passed the forbidden paradise of Gardiner's Island and sailed in shallow water over the hump called the Rip that lay between the island and the ruined fort on its own small isle. Barbara thought the layered slabs of gray stone and crumbling arches looked romantic. Mrs. Dowling told us it had been used for bombing practice during World War II, when Japanese submarines had lurked off Montauk.

"My husband could have told you more about it," Mrs. Dowling said.

"Maybe he can tell us—" Barbara began.

"Two o'clock!" Mrs. Dowling exclaimed.

We looked at our watches.

"Direction," Mrs. Dowling said, deadpan. "Twelve is straight ahead."

The boat swung slowly two notches to the right and nosed forward. We could see quite a commotion on the water. Black and white terns wheeled and dove, while flashes of silver churning up the water marked the bait fish fleeing and the bluefish feeding. The thrill of the chase and the tussle with the beleaguered fish took hold of us. After a few crossed rods and a couple of Barbara's hooks in my hair, we both got the hang of it. We flipped our rods back and flicked them forward, flung our lines far out over the water, and reeled in the blues. Mrs. Dowling, casting expertly beside us, used a pair of pliers to remove the hooks. Her fingers were deft, her arms thin and ropy. She didn't get those muscles at the gym. They came from real work.

By the time we had a dozen fish sloshing in the compartment under the deck, I wanted a cigarette badly. If Mrs. Dowling smoked, I'd seen no sign of it. I knew that Barbara wouldn't appreciate it if I puffed smoke at her in the close quarters of the cockpit. And even I didn't want to fumigate myself by lighting up in the tiny cabin.

"Okay if I sit up in the bow?" I asked. I waggled the pack to indicate why I wanted to. The roof of the cabin formed a forward deck surrounded by a thin metal rail. It wasn't designed for sitting. But I wouldn't fall off.

"Suit yourself," Mrs. Dowling said. "Crouch low and hold onto the rail. If you go overboard, I can't guarantee you'll be able to get back up."

I hadn't thought of that. I could see what she meant. The boat rode fairly high in the water. And I couldn't see anything like a ladder down the side. I tried to picture Mrs. Dowling and Barbara hauling me back on board, and only succeeded in imagining my arms being wrenched out of their sockets.

"Be careful, okay?" Barbara said.

"I will."

I made my way cautiously around the windscreen and established myself with my back against it, knees up, and elbows on my knees. It wasn't exactly comfortable, but it felt stable. I tapped a cigarette out of the pack and snapped my lighter. I heard shrill cries as a flock of terns whipped up the sky to my right, following the school as it moved on.

Mrs. Dowling kept the engine purring low enough that I felt in no danger of getting jolted off my perch. I heard her say something, and Barbara answered, but the breeze whipped their words away. I closed my eyes and let my head drop back. The midday sun baked my eyelids, cheeks, and forearms. I tossed the smoldering butt of my cigarette into the bay and fell into a meditative state.

That lasted about five minutes. The spiritual awakening they'd promised me in recovery was taking longer than Rip Van Winkle's. I still got restless fast. I remembered my cell phone and pulled it out of my back pocket.

"Yo, Jimmy. How's it going, dude?"

Apart from a few crackling electrons, Jimmy's voice came through clearly.

"Are you having fun yet?"

"Believe it or not, I am. Fishing is kind of addictive. And Barbara is having a blast. I hope you're prepared for fish for dinner. Maybe several dinners. What are you doing?"

That would have been a dumb question if I'd meant "Are you online?" Jimmy was always online.

"I'm reading Clea's articles on the environment and how the developers could kill Long Island. Did you know the Nature Conservancy calls Peconic Bay and Great South Bay one of the Last Great Places?"

"No, Jimmy, I didn't know that," I said in the bright, deliberate tones of a straight man on educational TV. In my own voice, I asked, "Did you find anything personal?"

"Reading between the lines, I'd say I did," Jimmy said. "I'm going back three or four years to when she was just getting started. She was only in her twenties, you know. I think you can plot the course of her affair with Oscar by how she wrote about him in these stories."

"How do you mean?"

"She started mentioning him by name a couple of years ago. They could have met in AA, or maybe she interviewed him for a story."

"Maybe both," I said. "Sparks can fly when two people who are attracted keep running into each other."

"Could be. First she started mentioning his name a lot. Let's call that a sign that romance was brewing. Then she started going out of her way to make him look good."

"How did she do that? The guy was building McMansions."

"With one hand. With the other hand, he was donating money and tradeoff land to outfits like the Nature Conservancy."

"Tradeoff land?"

"They call it real estate donation. You donate your property, not what they call preserve quality land, any property. The organization sells it and uses the proceeds to fund their programs. That made him an enlightened developer."

"You're saying he stayed enlightened as long as she was sleeping with him?"

"Yep. In the more recent articles, he figures as just another bad guy."

"Developers are in it to make money. Bottom line, literally. Did she simply sour on him, or did he stop giving to environmental charities?"

"I'm working on that," he said. "She attacked him in a couple of pieces. It got personal, all right. At least one editor thought it would sell papers. Oscar wasn't only a developer. He was a big party guy around here before he got clean and sober, and he still knew everybody. He struck me as a guy whose reputation mattered to him."

"I agree. Okay, he had a motive to kill Clea."

"He had opportunity. She was killed at his back door. All he had to do was get out of bed, walk down the steps, and shove her in the ocean."

"He could have done it. But why now?"

"Maybe she was planning to expose some dirty business dealing of his. She could have had notes on it in the missing notebook or even in the papers the cops got."

"If he dumped her, she had a motive to kill him. But she died first."

"It's just as likely she dumped him." I could hear Jimmy tapping the keyboard and a ballgame in the background. Always multitasking. "They were both sexual predators. And she wasn't an ecoterrorist. Why kill him when she could skewer him in print?"

"If Oscar killed Clea, then who killed Oscar?"

"Hmmm. Somebody who loved Clea?"

"I don't know who that would be," I said. "Not Phil. Lewis wasn't in love with her either. He told me so."

"Ted?"

"He thought he was," I said. "In a fatal attraction kind of

way. But when he gets past the denial, I bet he'll feel relieved."

"Slept with all, loved by none," Jimmy said. "What an epitaph."

"How about Jeannette? Do you believe she really hit a deer?"

"Hard to imagine her giving that hard a shove," Jimmy said. "He was a big guy. Besides, she had as much reason to hate Clea as to love her. Maybe they canceled each other out."

"She had the same reason to hate Oscar. More. And as far as the cops are concerned, she didn't have an alibi for either him or Phil."

Nobody had loved Phil, I thought. Maybe someone who loved Oscar had killed Phil. Corky. Or Shep, who seemed to be in love with Corky. Or somebody Clea had mentioned in the notebook. Phil's compulsive gambling had left him with a chronic need for money.

"I can see him as a blackmailer," I said. "Anybody could have done it."

"If they had a car," Jimmy said, "and weren't already dead. The three deaths were different, but it's hard to believe there was more than one murderer." He lowered his voice. "How about Dowling?"

I glanced over my shoulder. The wheel was untended, the motor off. Mrs. Dowling and Barbara were fishing off the stern. We rocked gently at a distance I couldn't gauge off what must be the dark side of Gardiner's Island, the side you couldn't see from land. An abundance of green topped pinkish sand cliffs and scallops of deserted beach.

"Motive?"

"One of Clea's articles focused on what she called collaborators: local landowners who sell out. She saw it as collusion with the developers and betrayal of the land. If Dowling was thinking of selling, he might have wanted to shut her up."

"He can't be the only farmer being offered big bucks to sell,"

I said. "But how many farmers did she know?"

"She knew all the big developers," Jimmy said. "She wrote about them."

Like Morton Day, the guy who'd been celebrating his success at the party. He might think it would be a lot easier to outmaneuver Corky than Oscar in his bid to suburbanize the Hamptons. He wouldn't have liked Clea's pro-environmental snooping any more than Oscar did. He might have thought he could cut a better deal with Corky than with Oscar.

Maybe Corky saw Phil push or chase Clea into the water. That whole house had a potential front-row view of Clea's murder. Maybe Corky didn't love Oscar as much as everybody thought she did. Maybe she wanted to inherit all that property. She could have figured since Phil really did kill Clea, it would be easy to pin Oscar's death on him. Maybe Shep had done it for her. Maybe he wanted to marry all that property.

"Are we sure that Corky inherited?" I asked. "She's acting like she did, but what you said about donations makes me wonder. He could have left it all to save the Last Great Places. He couldn't take it with him, so why not?"

"The trouble is the three deaths were all so different," Jimmy said. "The killer had to have a reason to want all three of them dead. On the other hand, the murders were opportunistic. They could even have been accidents."

"Only if the person was bullshitting himself, at least after the first time."

"Read what she wrote about Day again," I said. "And find out what you can about other farmers."

"Will do. Go catch a fish."

I flipped the phone closed and stuffed it back in my pocket. My knees felt stiff, and my lower back throbbed. I'd been sitting in one position for far too long. I stretched first one leg, then the other, out in front of me. I could hear the joints creak.

My left foot had gone to sleep. I waited for the pins and needles to subside, then swiveled around and knelt facing the stern. I held onto the windscreen with both hands. I'd need it to push myself up.

Barbara turned, a squirming silver-blue three-pounder clutched in one hand and a fishing rod, its barbed hooks neatly tucked into their loops, in the other. Her dark curly hair caught the breeze and flew straight up over her head. Her cheeks were flushed.

"This is exhilarating!"

"Glad you're having fun," I said.

"What did you do, fall asleep up there?"

"No, I was talking to Jimmy on my cell."

"What did you talk about?" Barbara always wants to know what Jimmy and I talk about.

I stared pointedly at Mrs. Dowling's back. She was fully engaged in reeling in a lively fish, maybe an exceptionally big one, because her rod was bent almost double.

"I'll tell you later."

I had just taken up my rod again when the fish all decided to swim away. The birds followed them.

"Off to bluer pastures," Barbara said. She secured the hook and slotted her rod neatly into one of the rod holders. "Wow, that was fun!"

"Are you having a good time?" Mrs. Dowling asked gaily. What had happened to American Gothic? She had a febrile energy that sat oddly on her habitual dourness. Maybe fishing pumped her up, and we were seeing the real Mrs. Dowling.

Behind her back, Barbara mouthed the word "manic" at me, holding up a thumb and forefinger half an inch apart, as if she were playing charades. "A little manic."

I shrugged.

"What now? Do we follow the school?" I asked.

"If you want to," Mrs. Dowling said. "But it's getting crowded out here."

I looked around. Three other fishing boats had been drawn to our hot spot. Now they all started their engines up and moved slowly in the direction the wheeling birds had taken. I guess that passed for crowded on the open water.

"I'd love to take another look at the ruined fort," Barbara said. "Maybe we can get in closer. We're as likely to find blues there as anywhere, aren't we?"

"They feed around the Rip," Mrs. Dowling said. "Though wherever you find fish, you'll get company. We can circle the fort and then head out toward Plum Island." She took the wheel, powered up, swung the boat around, and headed away from traffic.

"I've heard about Plum Island," Barbara said. "Doesn't the government do mysterious research there?"

"Not so mysterious," Mrs. Dowling said. "Animal diseases. Homeland Security took it over a few years ago."

"That sounds creepy," Barbara said. "Islands, islands everywhere, and not a place to land. But that's okay. It's beautiful out here. I don't care where we go, as long as I get to catch a few more fish before we go back."

"We've already got a binful down there," I objected. "Who's going to clean them all?"

Barbara didn't answer. That meant not her. Probably me. I remembered that Karen had said Mr. Dowling was usually willing to clean the catch. I noticed Mrs. Dowling didn't volunteer to wield the knife. Barbara slid down onto the deck with her back against the side in much the same position I'd taken on the bow. I sat down next to her. She raised her face to the sun and closed her eyes. I slumped back against the windscreen and did the same.

The ring of a telephone woke me. It sounded weirdly

domestic above the roar of the engine. The source of the ringing seemed to be Barbara's cleavage. She extracted her cell from the bikini top she'd stripped to at some point in the trip. She checked the caller ID and flipped it open as mine started ringing too. I struggled to extract it from my pocket, where it was tightly wedged.

"Hi, baby." Barbara stuck a finger into her other ear. Now that the motor was running, it was hard to hear anything else. "Can you ask Mrs. Dowling to slow down?"

Getting up would free my phone, which still shrilled in my pocket. My foot had gone to sleep again. I held up one finger to tell Barbara she'd have to wait, slid back down, and started to massage the foot. Barbara went on bellowing.

"What?" Barbara screeched. "Dead what? Something about Dedhampton," she said to me. "Dedham, okay, I heard that, what about it? Sirens where? No, I can't hear sirens in the background, I can hardly hear you."

The fizzing in my foot subsided. I tried again to stand. As I hopped on the other foot, Mrs. Dowling cast a quick glance over her shoulder. Then I saw her deliberately push the stick not back, but forward. The motor responded with a burst of speed. We flew through the water. The white foam of our wake stretched out behind us like a bride's train as it would look if the bride was late and sprinting down the aisle.

"Oh, my God!" Barbara said. "She what? Oh, no! Oh, my God! Listen, I'm getting off. I have to tell Bruce. Do something! Call someone! Call the Marine Patrol!"

Chapter Twenty-Nine

"It's her!" Barbara clutched the phone to her chest. "She killed all three of them!"

"What are you talking about?" I leaped to my feet.

"They found her husband over at the farm," Barbara babbled. "He's bleeding to death! She's dangerous! What do we do?" She clutched at me, and the cell phone clattered to the deck.

Mrs. Dowling jerked the gearshift back into reverse and cut the engine. The boat halted so abruptly that spray flew over the side. I braced myself, grabbed Barbara's hand, and pulled her up. Mrs. Dowling whirled to face us, snarling. In her hand, she held a knife with a thin, curved blade. She looked ready to gut and fillet us.

I held out a conciliatory hand.

"Now wait a minute, Mrs. Dowling. Please don't do anything you'll regret. Can we talk about this?"

"Talk!" she spat. "All you city people do is talk!"

She half crouched and shifted the knife in a weaving motion, like a street fighter looking for an opening. I tried to push Barbara behind me without taking a step forward, which Mrs. Dowling might find threatening. Barbara wouldn't go. She gets all feminist at the worst moments. But I admit I found the warmth of her sturdy tanned arm against mine comforting.

"So it's your turn now, and that's okay," Barbara said in her counselor voice. "Go ahead, we're listening." Damned if she didn't cock her head to one side like an inquisitive bird. She'd told me once her own therapist did that to encourage a client to fill the silence.

"Don't you take one step toward me," Mrs. Dowling warned, "or you'll be sorry. I'm getting out, and you can't stop me. I don't want to hurt you, but I will if I have to."

Barbara spread her hands, palms outward, and relaxed her body backward. We were backed up against the side of the boat already. I flattened myself as best I could. The gunwale dug against the backs of my thighs. I hoped we wouldn't go overboard.

"You're a Dedham," Barbara said. "The farm was yours."

"My family settled here in sixteen eighty-three," she said fiercely. "We fished and clammed and made the land so rich, we grew the best corn and potatoes on Long Island. The land means everything to me. What did Ben Dowling care? His father was born in Center Moriches and his grandpa came from New Jersey. New Jersey!" Her voice dripped contempt. "He worked the land with me, but he didn't love it."

"What did you have against Clea?" I asked. I tried to meet her eyes, even though the knife had me mesmerized. "She was against development. She tried to get people interested in keeping the land the way it is."

"That tramp! She bewitched Ben Dowling, that's what she did!"

Oh.

"I know what you think!" Her glance darted from my face to Barbara's and back again. "To you he's nothing but a grim old farmer, the handyman, the funny old bayman who digs your clams and sets the traps for your lobsters. She set a trap for him all right! He was an old fool, but he was my old fool, and that little slut couldn't rest until she'd stolen him out of my bed into hers."

Barbara said with extreme gentleness, "You were angry."

Duh. She pulled that one out of her bag of counseling tricks. Reflection, if I remembered right. I thought it would piss Mrs. Dowling off. It did whenever she tried it on Jimmy and me. But it worked. Mrs. Dowling calmed down some.

"I didn't mean to make her drown. I just wanted her to leave us alone. He went sneaking off to her all last summer. He'd tell me he was going fishing, knowing I'd have to stay and mind the stand. Fishing! But I thought it was over. Then in the spring he started getting shifty again. When I spotted that mop of hair of hers in town, I knew they'd started up again."

"You met her on the beach." I borrowed Barbara's method and didn't make it a question. I wanted to keep her going until I figured out a safe way to jump her and get the knife away. Or maybe once she got to tell her story she'd see reason and take us back to shore. I didn't care what she did after that. Run or surrender, whatever she wanted.

"She had the nerve to come up to me at the stand and ask for a pint of strawberries. Who did she think she was! We knew each other, all right. I'd been a fool too, telling her all about my family and how Dedhampton used to be Dedham, named for us and the town we came from."

So that's what Jimmy meant. Barbara dug a surreptitious elbow into my ribs.

"I told her we needed to talk. She said she'd meet me on the beach. I didn't tell her then that I knew what she was up to. I let her think I'd give her another interview. We made it early because I said I didn't want Dowling to know. I didn't have to say much, because she already knew he was planning to sell the land. The old fool told her. If she was such an environmentalist, she should have kicked him out. She wanted him because she could have him, and for no other reason."

"But if the land belonged to you," Barbara said, "how could he sell it?"

"How could I work it if he left?" she demanded bitterly. "You think I could hire someone to plow and plant and harvest? Nobody wants to be a farmer anymore."

"So you went to meet her on the beach," I prompted.

"I was desperate. All I wanted was for her to leave us alone. She had all the young men she wanted. She didn't need Ben Dowling, who'd been mine since high school. I begged her to let him go, and she laughed at me. I was so mad I went after her with my bare hands. I don't know if I meant to slap or strangle her. I chased her into the water. I stood there with the ocean coming up around my ankles and my shoes sinking into the wet sand, and I screamed at her. She wouldn't stop laughing. I screamed, and she laughed at me, and then she had some sort of fit. Her eyes rolled up in her head, and her body jerked, and she went under. And I stood there and let the ocean take her."

She fell silent. For a minute we all stood there. I had chills up the back of my neck. Barbara clutched my hand tightly. The boat rocked from side to side. The ruined fort lay behind us. As far as I could see, the bay was empty. No birds, no churning waters alive with fish. No other boats to get us out of this.

"I found her little recording doohickey and threw it in after her. I didn't play it. I didn't want to hear her voice again."

"Her things were on the beach, all neatly folded," Barbara said.

"You think that slut left them that way?" She gave a raucous laugh like a crow's caw. "I folded them myself. I wore my gardening gloves. Had 'em right in my pocket."

"Please, Mrs. Dowling, put the knife down," I said. "We're sorry for what happened to you. Please take us back, and then you can do what you like."

"I've made my plans," she said. "I've got a full tank of gas. I can be long gone when they come after me."

I thought we'd heard as much of Mrs. Dowling's story as she would tell us. If she started up again, she might work herself into another rage. She had already killed three people, maybe four, if Dowling was dead too. But Barbara always feels impelled to ask another question.

"Did Oscar Ainsworth see you on the beach that morning? Is that why you had to—to do something about him?"

"Ainsworth!" The ferocity in her voice startled both of us. She hated the developers. But if one went down, two more sprang up in his place. Had building McMansions gotten Oscar killed? She couldn't kill them all.

"He was another of the same kind. A beast—immoral. He killed my daughter."

I had forgotten the photo I'd seen at Oscar's. The luminous laughing girl with the expressive eyes. He'd seduced her, and she'd fallen in love with him. He'd turned her on to drugs, and she'd OD'd. Corky'd said he'd tried to get her into recovery once he got clean himself. Maybe. If I'd been her mother, I wouldn't have been grateful either.

"I'm so sorry about your daughter," Barbara said.

"I'm sorry, too," I said. "I saw her picture. She was a beautiful girl."

"He killed Amelia," she said, "and didn't think twice about it. The only reason I let him live is that I wasn't a killer. But after that girl drowned, I thought, now I am, so what's the difference?"

"How did you come to be there?" Barbara asked.

"I told myself I'd give him one more chance to show some remorse. I went to see him. There was a party. I saw them all prancing around buck naked on the beach. Disgusting!"

Beside me, Barbara tensed.

"I came back later. They were all leaving. I made sure that no one saw me."

"You tried to reason with him," Barbara said.

"He got on his high horse," Mrs. Dowling said. "He said he couldn't take responsibility for another human being. She had choices, he said. He'd given up drugs and offered to help her. Help her! He'd ruined her! My beautiful girl."

A tear ran down her cheek. I watched her knife hand, hoping she'd raise it to wipe the tear away, but she ignored it. My arm would have been aching if I'd been holding up a knife this long. But we already knew how strong she was.

"I just wanted to get him away from me. I couldn't bear standing that close to him for another second. I pushed hard at him with both hands."

I could picture her ramming at his chest in rage and grief, doing a kind of horizontal pushup with those muscular arms.

"I caught him off balance, and he tripped and tumbled down the stairs. He looked surprised."

I bet he did.

"And then Phil tried to blackmail you. We know he had a notebook of Clea's."

"He said he knew I did it. She'd written about Amelia and about my husband's hanky-panky. And she had notes about my family history, things I was stupid enough to tell her three years ago, and Ben Dowling must have told her more. He wanted money. Money! Farmers don't have money. Everything we own is in the land. And our boats, of course. We're baymen too, and cash flow is a bayman's problem as much as it is a farmer's. That's why we're a dying breed. We go into debt, and then there's a bad year, the government makes up one more rule against us, and then we bleed until we die. I'll lose the land anyway now."

So she had figured that out. Whether she ran and got away or ended up in prison, those fields were lost to her. I wondered if she thought she'd run Phil over by accident too. But even Barbara had too much sense to ask that particular question.

"What happened to the notebook?" she asked instead.

"I took it off him as he lay there in the road. And now it lies in twenty-five feet of water around behind Gardiner's Island, where no one ever goes. If you'd been watching, you could have seen it go."

"That's probably the best place for it," Barbara said.

For a moment, we all breathed together in a silence that held an odd kind of communion. Then Mrs. Dowling kind of shook herself and settled the knife more firmly in her grip.

"But now you both know everything that was in the notebook. I can't let you go. I want you to turn around, both of you, with your backs toward me. And stay close together."

A fillet knife is not an Uzi. She realized that if we moved apart, she could only cover one of us.

"You don't have to do this," Barbara said.

I wouldn't have bothered. In the movies, it was what the victims always said right before the murderer killed them anyway.

"I'll be the judge of that," Mrs. Dowling said. "Now turn around!"

I felt Barbara's muscles tighten. If we exposed our backs to that wicked knife, at least one of us was a goner. My shoulder blades turned to water just thinking about it.

Mrs. Dowling reached behind her with her free hand and came up with a spool of fishing line. Damn. She'd thought of tying us up first. If she was smart, she'd have one of us truss up the other.

"No more shilly-shallying," she barked. "Move!"

It was now or never. We moved, but not the way she'd ordered. I lunged toward her. At the same time, Barbara leaped to one side, freeing the trap door we'd been standing on. As I made a flying tackle for Mrs. Dowling's legs, Barbara flipped back the trap, scooped up a bluefish, and flung it straight at Mrs. Dowling's head. It hit her shoulder and bounced off. She stumbled and went down. The spool of line went rolling across the deck. But she held onto the knife.

Barbara threw another bluefish. It hit the back of my neck as I grappled with Mrs. Dowling. In my peripheral vision, I could see her arm starting to come down. I had her pinned with one knee, but that left my back exposed. Not good. I grabbed her knife arm and hung on. We rolled over. The deck pressed into my back. Her arm pushed downward. Mine pushed up to fend her off. My muscles trembled. Hers felt steady as a rock. I had to hold her off. I clawed at her face. She jerked up and away from me without releasing the pressure on my arm. The knife started to sweep downward, overcoming my resistance.

Emitting a howl like a barbarian warrior, Barbara launched herself onto Mrs. Dowling's back. This time she didn't throw the bluefish. She clutched it like a dagger and stabbed it into Mrs. Dowling's neck. Mrs. Dowling yowled with pain as the thrashing fish chomped down on the curve where her neck met her shoulder. Blood sprang up under the onslaught of those rows of little sharp teeth. At the same time, Barbara bared her own teeth and sank them into Mrs. Dowling's forearm.

The knife clattered to the deck. The pressure on my chest released enough for me to throw her off me and grab her other flailing arm. I twisted it behind her back and pulled her around till she lay face down. I dug my knees into the backs of her legs to keep her there. She jerked her chest up backward, trying to butt me with the back of her head. But she couldn't reach me. Barbara and the bluefish still hung onto her by the teeth like a couple of terriers.

"Enough! Barbara, enough!"

She opened her jaws and released Mrs. Dowling's arm. The bluefish fell to the deck and stopped twitching. It had reached its limit for survival out of water. I yanked the woman's other arm higher and ground my knees into the backs of hers. I had to keep her immobilized until we could tie her up.

Barbara looked dazed.

"I went berserk," she said hoarsely.

"Let me go!" Mrs. Dowling said. The commanding tone had degenerated into a whine. "I'll take you back to shore."

"Too late," I said, bearing down harder as she bucked and squirmed under me.

"Barbara, get the knife and the spool of line. We'll have to tie her up."

"Don't hurt her, Bruce," Barbara said as she collected them. Pretty good for someone whose toothmarks were darkening into purple bruises on our captive's arm. She handed me the knife. I held it to the nape of Mrs. Dowling's neck. She stopped struggling. I was careful not to prick her. I didn't know if I could have used it even in the heat of battle. But as a deterrent, it worked fine.

Barbara scooted over to the trap, which was still open. On her knees, she reached in and selected another bluefish. She'd found her weapon of choice.

"If you try anything, this one goes right into your face," she told Mrs. Dowling.

Mrs. Dowling groaned, her cheek against the deck. Barbara tucked the bluefish under her arm like a football and started wrapping fishing line around Mrs. Dowling's ankles.

"I hate bluefish," Mrs. Dowling said. "All the times I worked or sat home alone so he could run after his goddamn blues—it must add up to years. I won't even eat the things anymore."

"You took us out today," Barbara pointed out. "You fished with me."

"I had to be somewhere after I'd taken a knife to Ben Dowling and run him over with his own damn pickup. On the water was as good a place as any."

"You weren't coming back," Barbara said. We all took the point: she'd known all along that she had to get rid of us one way or another.

"It was bad enough losing him to the goddamn blues. That little tramp was the last straw."

We tied her hand and foot and propped her up against the side, sitting on the deck. She had tried halfheartedly to negotiate, saying we needed her cooperation to get home. But she'd already told us how to get home: follow the trail of breadcrumbs on the GPS. Anyhow, we could see where we were. Belatedly, we remembered we had three cell phones on board. But before we could call 911, the Marine Patrol found us. A man with the same weather-beaten look as Dowling stood in the bow of the white police boat with its broad blue stripe on the side. As the boat pulled alongside, he looked from us to Mrs. Dowling and shook his head sadly.

"Oh, Mary," he said. "What have you done?"

Chapter Thirty

Dowling survived. Mrs. Dowling had left him for dead in the farmhouse driveway, where Karen found him when she wandered over there to ask him to fix the leaky showerhead in our outdoor shower. If Mrs. Dowling hadn't been in a hurry to meet us at the boat, she'd have done the job properly. She'd been all ready to run. The fuel tank on the boat held a hundred gallons, and she'd filled it up and stashed money, extra fuel, and everything she needed to take with her on board. If Dowling had set foot on the boat, he'd have known. She'd meant to buy herself some lead time by taking us out, dumping us, and leaving him to wonder why she didn't come back. But he argued. Going out for blues was such a passion that he didn't want to miss a day of it, even with a couple of novices as passengers. So she stopped him the only way she could.

Guess who cleaned the fish we caught with Mrs. Dowling? Amid all the uproar, Barbara insisted we bring them home. She had committed to fish for dinner, so fish it had to be. Lewis instructed, Barbara supervised, Jimmy provided moral support, and I whacked off fish heads and scraped fish from the bone with a knife much like the one Mrs. Dowling had threatened us with. Karen marinated, Lewis grilled, and we all ate it.

"Bluefish is loaded with omega-three," Barbara said. "Don't you want to prevent heart disease, cancer, and rheumatoid arthritis? It'll also improve your memory and your mood."

"Thank you for sharing," I said. "My mood is grumpy, and I

remember I never liked fish."

"Finish your fish," Barbara said. "Think of the starving children. Oh, God, I sound exactly like my mother."

"Okay, okay," I said. "It tastes fine. It's good. I love fresh bluefish."

" 'And when we were wrong, promptly admitted it,' " Jimmy quoted.

If I'd known recovery meant you couldn't even eat your dinner without the Twelve Steps coming into it, I'd never have given up drinking.

"In her mind," Barbara said when we talked it over later, "he'd been unfaithful to her every time he went out fishing. The affair with Clea was the last straw."

"She had a few last straws," Jimmy said. "He wanted to sell the farm, and it was her farm that had been in her family for generations."

"He wanted to do a geographic," Barbara said. "People always think things will be better somewhere else, but it's an illusion."

"Maybe he just didn't want to farm," I said. "A few million bucks would make life a lot easier."

"You've still got to solve your life, though," Barbara said. "What was he going to do if he didn't farm?"

"He could have bought a bigger boat," Jimmy said, "and spent the rest of his life casting for blues."

"You know when that marriage really ended?" Barbara said. "When the daughter died. Lots of families break down over the death of a child."

"Mrs. Dowling blamed Oscar for what happened to Amelia," I said.

"He was a lot older than her," Barbara said. "Her first lover, maybe. He sleeps with her, he turns her on to drugs, and then he drops her. The fact that he got clean and sober and lived happily ever after while she OD'd must have made it worse."

"He didn't live happily ever after," Jimmy said, "thanks to mom."

"She didn't want him to get away with it," I said. "But how come Dowling managed to stay friends with him? Why didn't he hate Oscar too?"

"Maybe Dowling didn't know as much about Amelia as her mother did," Barbara said. "I've told my mother many, many things I would never tell my father."

Gradually, we put a lot of pieces of the puzzle together. It turned out that the Dowlings were not the only ones Phil had targeted for blackmail. He needed money badly, not just to keep on gambling, but to keep the legbreakers at bay. He must have been more scared of them than of the chance one of his victims would turn on him. Another gamble that he'd lost. Jeannette hadn't been as candid with us that day in the car as we'd thought. She had left out her motive for killing Phil. He'd known she was Clea's mother. Clea had told him. That's also how he knew that Lewis had slept with Clea. Lewis admitted that Phil had demanded money not to tell Karen. Lewis had outfoxed him by telling Karen himself and making amends. Once Mrs. Dowling had been arrested, Karen confessed her affair with Oscar too. They forgave each other so thoroughly that they went to bed and didn't come out of their room for two days. As Jimmy pointed out, the ninth step works.

On the Saturday night of Labor Day weekend, Corky and Shep gave a big party at what everybody still called Oscar's house. Oscar's pre-recovery end-of-summer blasts had been legendary. And in recent years, they'd become the clean and sober event of the season. Now that the shadow of death had passed from Dedhampton, everybody talked fast, laughed hard, and danced with abandon.

When the moon rode high in the sky, Corky jumped up on a picnic table and banged a couple of sauce pan lids together to get everybody's attention.

"Listen up, everybody," she shouted. "Shep and I have got an announcement to make!"

"You're engaged!" Barbara blurted.

"Nope." Shep reached up and squeezed Corky's ankle, since she still had a pot cover in each hand. "We're married."

"Have been all summer," Corky confirmed with a grin.

Then there was a lot of squealing and hugging and warm fuzzy stuff that I enjoyed more than I'd admit, especially to Barbara.

"So why didn't you tell anyone?" Barbara asked Corky later. A bunch of us sat on the steps looking out at the moon over the ocean. The ocean was still warm, but nobody suggested skinny dipping. We could hear the faint music of other Labor Day parties up and down the beach and see the red-gold flicker of bonfires.

"Oscar knew," Corky said.

"She was on the run," Shep said.

"I had an abusive ex looking for me," Corky explained. "He knew me as Corinne. And when I married Shep, I took his last name."

"So why was your being Oscar's sister such a big mystery?"

"You couldn't hide Oscar."

"You hid in plain sight," Barbara said.

They couldn't tell anyone else, because the wedding of Oscar Ainsworth's sister would have been news, at least in the Hamptons.

"She looked different, too," Shep said, playing with the spikes of Corky's punk hair.

"Would you believe big blond hair and beige pants suits?" Corky shook her head. "Talk about losing yourself in a bad marriage. But that's over now."

"You aren't still scared about the bad guy catching up with

you?" Barbara asked.

Corky shrugged.

"If he turns up now, I can afford to protect myself. Or buy him off. But that's not it. It was time to let go."

"No point living in fear," Shep said. "All we've got is today."

I thought for the umpteenth time how ridiculous program sayings sound and how much better they can make you feel.

"We went out on Ben's boat this morning," Corky said. "Well, our boat—we bought the Pursuit from him. He wanted to give it to us, but we wouldn't let him. We went way out, maybe halfway to Block Island, and scattered Oscar's ashes."

"How was it?"

"It was peaceful," Corky said. "We saw whales. Not a big show, just a couple of finbacks gliding along. Like Higher Power saying what Shep just did—that all we've got is today."

"Hear that, cowboy?" I felt a light hand on my shoulder and warm breath at my ear. "We've only got today. Come for a walk."

Cindy took my hand and drew me up. We picked our way among the people perched on the steps and kicked off our shoes at the bottom, so we could enjoy the cool feel of the sand.

I put my arm around her.

"Why cowboy?" I asked. "I go back to the city on Monday."

"Me too," she said. "I don't know. I saw you sitting there, and I thought, are we going to let this pony run or not?"

I turned her around to face me without letting go. I ran my hands gently up from her waist to her shoulders, then her neck. Cupping her face between my palms, I drew her toward me. Our lips met. Whoa! Suddenly things weren't gentle any more. We devoured each other's mouths like a couple of bluefish leaping on a school of mackerel. Pressed together from breast to thigh, we completed some kind of circuit, so high voltage I could practically hear the sizzle.

When we drew back, we were both panting. She grinned at me, the moonlight gleaming on those wolfish little incisors of hers.

"So, cowboy? Do we rip each other's clothes off in the dunes and get sand mixed in with all our body fluids, or do we take my car back to the house and do it right?"

We did both, along with an interlude in the car and another in the outdoor shower. Everybody else stayed at the party long enough for us to make all the noise we wanted. It felt great to howl.

Finally, we fell back against the damp pillows. I had never felt better in my life. I didn't even want a cigarette.

"I wish we could just lie here till the full moon," she said. "It's only a few days. I'd like to see if we can howl any louder."

"I knew you were part vampire. We'll have to move soon. I have a roommate."

"And I have two," she said. "Let's grab some clean sheets and move into Phil's room."

"Clea's room?"

"Why not? It's empty."

"You wouldn't mind?" I asked. "Sleeping in two dead people's bed?"

"Not at all," she said. "It'll be like Corky scattering the ashes. Put their spirits at rest. I think we're as life-affirming as a couple of finback whales, don't you? And who said we were going to sleep?"

Half an hour later, snuggled in with her, I felt almost drowsy except that the current was still switched on. My whole body glowed and hummed. We'd left the shade up. Moonlight slanted through. I propped myself up on one elbow so I could watch her face. Her eyes were closed, but she was still glowing and humming too. Her lips curved upward in a smile, the pointy tips of the teeth peeping out on either side. The effect was enigmatic. There was so much I didn't know about her.

I reached out and flicked a damp lock of hair off her forehead. Then I ran my finger along her mouth. The smile widened. Her eyes stayed closed.

"Tell me something," I said.

"What?"

"Anything," I said. "Something I don't know about you."

"Ask me something."

"Okay, what's with you and Detective Butler?"

"We have mutual friends," she said.

"Yeah, you met her in Montauk. I already knew that. Do you mean she's in the program? Are you protecting her anonymity?"

She shook her head. Her smile wavered. She opened her eyes and looked at me, searching my face as if deciding whether to trust me.

"Come on," I said. "It's okay, whatever it is. You can't shock me."

She took a deep, slightly wobbly breath.

She said, "I'm a cop."

ABOUT THE AUTHOR

Elizabeth Zelvin is a New York City psychotherapist whose previous mysteries about recovering alcoholic Bruce Kohler include *Death Will Get You Sober*, *Death Will Help You Leave Him*, and several short stories. Three of her stories have been nominated for the Agatha Award for Best Short Story. Zelvin's short fiction has appeared in *Ellery Queen's Mystery Magazine* as well as various anthologies and e-zines. She blogs with other mystery writers on Poe's Deadly Daughters and SleuthSayers. Zelvin's published work includes two volumes of poetry and a book about gender and addictions. Current projects include a novel about Columbus's second voyage and a CD of her own songs. You can visit Liz on her website at www.elizabethzelvin.com.